HYPATIA

In Her Own Words

By LUKMAN CLARK

Riverside, CA

HYPATIA

In Her Own Words

Disclaimer This is a work of fiction. Names, characters, businesses, places, events, and incidents are either the products of the author's imagination or used in a fictitious manner. Any resemblance to actual persons, living or dead, or actual events is purely coincidental.

ISBN: 978-0-9788752-4-4 (H)

Cover Design by Lukman Clark

Riverside, CA

To My Parents:

This is what I wanted to do when I grew up.

Contents

Translator's Foreword

Several years ago, I dug up five ancient papyrus scrolls buried in a North African cave. My discovery came about through a harrowing session of past life regression uncovering a life as an Arab hydrologist back in the 10th century. While sniffing out parts of the Cyrenaic desert for underground aquifers this man stumbled upon a balsamic-smelling chest buried in a corner of what today is Libya. Finding the box carried a number of thick scrolls, he hid it in a nearby cave, meaning to retrieve it after his geological appraisal was done.

Hypnosis also revealed he—meaning me—did not survive to bring the scrolls to light back then.

The rediscovery of those five scrolls centuries later has turned out to be a tale of international intrigue and spiritual reckoning, which I may one day tell. However, I believe the story of the discoverer is far less compelling than the discovery itself. In this case, because of the woman who authored the scrolls.

As popularly conceived in our day, this woman might well be likened to a wax figure in a Madame Tussauds Museum made over to suit modern tastes for history documentaries. As with other legendary figures, the real woman of the scrolls turns out to be completely different from the romanticized and Europeanized narrative we have been fed. The truth is at once more prosaic and more wonderful.

Of course, things like grammar and other stylistic practices have changed greatly over the centuries; not to mention modern readers have different expectations from those for whom the scrolls were written. While keeping to the spirit of the original I have made editorial adjustments, such as organizing the text according to the various places the writer lived at different times of her life. Thus, my divisions correspond roughly with her growth from girlhood to late middle age.

In making this translation I have held nothing back. There certainly is enough horror, intrigue and magic here to entice general readers as well as keep scholars busy for years to come. Others are free to check my translation against the original scrolls when I make them available. Finally, for the record, the only things in the chest were these scrolls. There were no advanced mathematical treatises or original philosophic expositions. There certainly was no astrolabe.

Brandon Blake, Translator
Los Angeles • New York • Oaxaca • Lago di Varano

Scroll #1: Casting The Net

Setting: HELIOPOLIS

☽ 1 ☾

In my thirty-first year, a monster from my youth contrived to get himself ordained as Bishop of Alexandria. Though I had escaped his deviltry some years previous, a chill shot down my spine upon hearing the news of his ascension. I did not know whether to scream or cry. Inside, I did both.

But my story begins long before his ordination and before I met him. It was the morning I lost my father. Impossible to know at the time that this was the beginning of my whole world crumbling down and putting me in harm's way. I was a young girl, impudent and unmindful in my innocence despite my father's efforts to prepare me for the world. I thought he would be there always to teach, to protect, to make me laugh. After his departure the world became my teacher but the world, I soon discovered, neither protects nor guides. Instead, I was compelled to find guidance elsewhere, not just to survive the violence and treachery of the times but to navigate strange dreams, visions and visitations, as well as trust in the warmth and scents of some few others.

The night before he left my father tucked me into bed with a prayer. He smelled of leather and metal polish. Not yet ready to go to sleep I pestered him about why he prayed when he always was so fond of saying the gods never listen to us anyway. He answered in his usual measured way.

"Daughter, let the gods be. When the water rises, just swim with the current of fate."

"So, Papa, are you saying we should not pray?"

"No, daughter. Pray. Just not to the gods."

These were the last words he said to me before snuffing out the oil lamp. Next morning he was gone. My mother said he was on assignment. Again.

Though it is now long past, my father's words still light the road traveled from that adoring girl to the woman I am today.

☽ 2 ☾

For all his kindness, Papa was a strict teacher. He drilled me in the Roman ways and their language. Though Greek is our common tongue, Latin still gives one a leg up when dealing with the government. This set me and my family apart from most others and, as I was to painfully learn, could also bring trouble.

Papa always taught my sister and me to work with numbers, reminding us such skills might prove more valuable than anything else, especially if one day he could not be with us. I did not, could not, know what he meant by that, but I think he was right. I mean, mostly Papa was right but other things are good to know, too. I'm pretty sure even what is Roman has to be part of something bigger.

Besides numbers, Papa taught me a little how to read. Once I got started I worked out more on my own. People in the marketplace have come to know I am good in this way. They ask for my help with reading and writing, despite my age.

My name is Tuya. My sister's is Tem. Our Momma named us this way because she never wanted us to forget we are Egyptians. That we are Egypt. The land. That's what she told us when we got older, though I'm not sure what she meant by it.

Tem and I were born in the Year 70 A.D., anno Diocletiani. *[354 anno Dominus – BB]*. Diocletian is dead now, along with a couple of other emperors who came after him. So Papa said to us sometime before me and Tem reached eleven just a while ago. I remember he looked at each of us then with sad eyes below his short haircut and, with his voice breaking a little, said the world just changed too fast for his liking. But for me, it seems time moves too slowly and I will never grow up and I will always be in this place where I remember having lived my whole life with my twin sister.

Oh, yes, my sister and I are twins. She came out of our Momma just a short time after me. Momma says Tem almost didn't make it because she didn't cry right away. Tem has that extra finger on her left hand though and the midwife told Momma maybe that's what finally helped her, but she should try to not let people know about it.

As though the midwife herself wouldn't talk. I know she did because people stare and whisper. Even about me. Twins, you know. Or maybe it's something else, but I don't mind.

I'm glad I have my twin sister. Funny, even though we are twins, we are not a lot like each other the way some twins are. My hair is reddish brown. Hers is brownish black. I talk a lot. Tem is the quiet one. Those who know both of us say I am the more practical, too. Then there is Tem's extra finger.

Over a month ago, like I said, we passed our first *decem anni* by one year. Ten years plus one together. Me first. Then Tem. But together.

Many children do not get as far as us, I know. Women are always losing their babies here and it must be the same everywhere. Papa told me how he was the third baby his momma had had. One came out blue and dead; the other came out with too many arms and legs, so both times they paid someone to leave them on a hilltop in the night. That really made Papa the first, like me; the oldest brother, like I'm the older sister. But he had four more after him. Three sisters and one brother. I just have my sister Tem. I love her and am glad no one took her out to a hilltop—but I think she's enough.

Papa says he is more than four tens old. Quadraguinta. This seems a really long time to me, but somehow I can't think of Papa as old. I mean, he doesn't seem old to me at all. I just wonder where he is and when he'll come back.

"Back before your mother and I met, I was not much more than a foot soldier. They came through our village in my father's land of Macedonia—Great Alexander's birthplace—looking for conscripts. You remember where Macedonia is, right?"

"Across the big sea!"

"Yes, Tuya—miau, across the big, big sea. Mare Nostrum. Good girl. Well, then they shipped myself and another hundred or so conscripts off to serve under the Dux Aegypti. Tem—Tem, it's your turn to tell me what that is."

Tem only stared at the floor and didn't say anything, so Papa continued his story. I don't know how many times he had told it to us, but I never tired of hearing it.

"Well, Dux Aegypti is the Egypt Command. So, having never been at sea before, I got terribly ill–"

"And you barfed your guts out over the side but it was ok because it fed the hungry fishes, right?"

"Exactly right. Unfortunately, our sea passage met with worse than sea sickness. Some men fell overboard but the ship's pilot would not go back to save them. Then after the third sunset–"

"You all tried to take the ship and turn it back!"

"Ha! Not quite the way it happened! You know your Papa would never do something like that! Nor would most others. Being a mutineer shows a lack of honor and a lack of understanding about the work of Fate. But the few experienced soldiers on board quickly got matters under control and the rebel leaders were dealt with severely."

"They got dragged behind the ship so the sharks could eat them up! Yeah!"

At this point, Tem usually faked being asleep. She would wake up soon enough and when Papa finished she would jump off his lap and run to the kitchen where Momma would be making preparations for next day's breakfast.

"Things went smoothly after that trouble. No one dared try anything again. Once back on land in the port of Alexandria, I quickly recovered from my sea—sickness. Then, as luck would have it, they marched me off to Heliopolis with a detachment of other soldiers. All now joined with the 5th Macedonian Legion. Along the way, I befriended a barbarian soldier named Cunos, and together we mostly patrolled the city streets and alleyways. Just our being around kept the peace during the day.

"Night patrol was a different story. Drunken men and women brawling and screaming in taverns and in the streets. People killing each other in fetid alleyways and on rooftops. Spouses who normally did not have to face each other by day, quarreled once both at home after dark–too often with evil effects for one or the other, and too often for any children they might have."

In anticipation, I stayed quiet. The best part laid ahead.

"Thieves did what thieves do; especially the bands of roving youth, brigands who as often as not would taunt and attack us soldiers to have something to brag to friends about. During one night's round— up, while dispatching an infamous gang we had cornered in a dead—end alley, it was then I found your mother."

☽ 3 ☾

Because of my smart soldier Papa—now optio, not just munifex, as I like to remind people—that's how I know a lot of what I know. The rest I find out for myself.

I can keep track of how more than ten tens or so kinds of different birds live around our river parts. For each kind though, they number too many to count. I mean, if you could even count them when they all fly up so beautifully together. Their wings glint in the day sky like the stars in the night sky. I think sometimes the way they group or cry must have some hidden meaning. Really, I think they do talk to us in their way. Some people say they are messengers and we just need to learn how to listen or read their signs.

I try.

Other times, too, I think like Tem says maybe there are things not meant to be counted or named.

Then, birds are just birds.

Still, I try to follow what kinds of birds come and go with the seasons, wondering where they go and why they return. Maybe they are like the nomads who seem to wander without aim or maybe they have relatives they left behind. I watch for the long—legged ones like the Great Cormorants, the pink—backed pelicans and cranes that come in winter. Usually they don't lay eggs here, but they come back with young birds, so they must make babies in the other places but find our land better for raising their children.

Some kinds of kingfishers, shrikes and kestrels do all nest with us, staying here all the time.

Maybe birds are like people. So, even those really different from one another can get along, maybe even marry and have babies. Just like Momma and Papa, who could be no more different from each other.

There's one bird, a dusky—shaded brown and green ibis, who flies in to visit its cousin called Pharaoh's Ibis with its striking, black-fringed wings. I like pretending our stay-at-home ibis invites its distant relative in for lotos and beer in exchange for stories of far-away lands.

Like I said, many other birds stay here all the time, just like we do. The benu, egrets and bitterns and the Horus falcons and vultures all seem to like it here well enough. But, like the ibis, they have winged cousins calling on them year-round, while no one ever comes by to see our family. Some day maybe our families from across the sea to the north and the desert to the south will visit us. That would be nice, I think.

Meanwhile, it's helpful I learn so much about birds because along with Papa's salary, birds add to our family livelihood. Me and Tem have been coming out with throw sticks and nets to catch them since we were old enough to sit quietly in boat or blind, first with Papa and later with Momma when Papa started getting called away more and more. Because Momma has other things to do, later just me and Tem went out by ourselves.

Other birders, either singly or in groups, hunt with arrows, slings, and clap-nets. Some use tethered bitterns with their eyelids sewn shut to trick curious others with their pitiful cries. I do well enough without such deceits.

In recent months, Tem has come out less and less. When I ask if she will accompany me in the reed boat Papa made for us to hunt along more of the river bank, she stiffens her back and shoulders, saying she needs to stay home to help Momma. She says seeing I am the one who likes sitting out under the hot sun with the flies, gnats and crocodiles, why don't I just go by myself? Then she turns and walks away. I don't know what has gotten into her, but if all she's going to do is complain and scare the birds off she can stay home sweeping the dust from the floor and washing down the walls with natron.

Speaking of crocodiles, I don't know what Tem is afraid of. They never bother me. It's like they don't even hear or smell me. I am less than a shadow to them, I think. It's like we move in two different worlds. Besides, there are a pair of hawks who always seem to fly low overhead as a kind of warning for me to get off the river and, sure enough, then something you don't want around comes around. One time, a hawk dove right down to the back of my skiff and took off again. It happened fast but when I spun to look all I saw was the hawk flying off with a cobra in its talons.

Another time I thought I heard something coming from the papyrus thickets and though both hawks tried to warn me away, I went in to have a look. Eí! I found dead bodies! Of people! I didn't think animals had killed them, because no animal I know of puts heads on stakes. After this, I always listened to my hawk friends.

Anyway, Momma used to make Tem go out with me, but lately she seems to want to keep my sister close. Maybe that's because I snare more without Tem and bargain better in the market for what I catch. There may be plenty of kinds of birds on the river and in the swamp, but I target the ones people want in the marketplace for eating and to use their feathers for stuffing pillows. Nothing goes to waste.

Well, this is what life was like until I met the one people call "Specul-Anus" and other names even less nice at her place on the market's far side.

She is a strange old woman sitting in a tent—really, a tent within a tent—off to the east from the river's quayside market, past the camel bazaar and nearer to the tall obelisk in the city close to the Tree of Mary. My meeting with this seer-woman came during the full moon in April, after I had reached eleven. Momma—and Tem, too—say I'm making all this up but I'm not.

It started off as a good day, with me bringing a fine catch to market.

☽ 4 ☾

I had been out since before dawn. That's the very best time of day. Gliding downstream in the reed boat along the thick stands of papyrus growing down to the river's edge and into its shallows, the boat is like a second home to me though small and narrow. I feel safe in it. So much so I could and sometimes do nap tied up to the tall reeds in the shade. At such times, I might dream that the river is a path snaking warmly through a shadowy forest like those Papa speaks of. I am very familiar with this path because it feels like my path, as familiar as the river that dreams along with me.

But, as much as I like to daydream, I do have things to do. Things like checking the simple traps I have learned to set, putting up nets and trying to locate nests by the hungry cries of young birds.

Like I said, sunrise is the best of times to be out and about. Life on the river is awakening for the new day. The birds are rousing to sing praises to the sun. They are hungry from their night fast and tend not to pay much attention to a little girl quietly drifting with the current.

So, as the sun stretches its arms out over the eastern desert and the Southern Sea, its hopeful rays warming the air and chasing away the river mists, I unwrap a piece of bread to chew on to quash my belly rumblings. From around a weedy sand bank, a coot family, the mother bird and seven grey, still fuzzy and not fully fledged young, come up to my boat, curious, I think, about my breakfast. I break off a corner of bread and toss it on the water, whereupon the mother bird snatches it up to make sure it is good for her young. I throw several more pieces a little forward of my skiff, while slowly taking hold the handle of my hoop net. By now the chicks have joined the fray for my bread with their mother's permission, which gives me the chance to bring my net quickly over the lot.

I'm not fast enough due to nearly losing my balance. I succeed in catching only four young ones. The mother and the rest of her brood run across the water's surface in a flash, beyond my reach, splashing and squawking noisily along the way. All that commotion puts an end to any sneakiness I may have enjoyed, so I quiet the little birds, stow them and turn about to pole back upriver toward home.

On the way, I think about how coot are not the tastiest of birds, especially the adults, unless prepared the right way like Momma does. The younger birds however you may simply salt, spit and roast. Each makes a nice snack in itself. I shouldn't have any trouble selling the four little ones I caught. It's too bad I didn't get the mother. Besides being plump, her black feathers seemed shiny and healthy. I could sell them to the clothiers to dress up their wares. Or use them myself.

I collect feathers the different birds drop and have used these to make a cap that is formed tightly to my head. By gradually bending the main spine of longer feathers from falcons and the like, I can shape them to my head without breaking the spine. The way I wear the cap is with the notches to the front and the quills in the back. I use the smaller fluffy feathers to fill in and cover the quills like a fringe. Tem wants me to make her one, too, but says she wants one where the feathers stand up, not lying flat like mine.

The day is warming up quickly, so I need to unload my morning's catch, which has grown with the addition of a huge turtle that could take a finger or two if I'm not careful. Also, a clutch of dozens of round, white turtle eggs, and three quail from my set traps. The heat will spoil both birds and turtle eggs, already attracting an army of flies to the basket where I have stored them—the seven birds with their necks wrung. Also, though the turtle hides in its shell when I rap it sharply with my pole, it keeps coming out to try to escape over the side, making it all the more necessary to hurry back.

Quayside at the town market, I climb the embankment and am happy to immediately sell the turtle for its meat and shell to a fish broiler my Papa knows by the name of Felix. As two of his helpers carry the creature from my boat and away to slaughter, he laughs with his hands on his hips, saying,

"You must be a child of Anukis to be able to subdue such a beast without losing all your toes and fingers to its rapacious jaws."

I smile up at him, sweat dripping down along my nose, and reply, "My Momma prays to Dedwen to accompany me at market, so that I may be paid well for my work."

I cock my head a little to one side and give Felix the Eye, just to see if this has any effect on him. With that, his robust guffaw turns neighboring heads as he puts a generous sum into my outstretched palm.

I slip the money unobtrusively into a leather wallet held at my side by a rawhide string across my bare chest, just as Felix scrunches up his nose while looking down at my other hand holding the covered basket with the dead fowl. He raises his eyebrows as though to ask about the odor insinuating itself over that of fish, cooking oil and offal in his sector of the market. With a gleam in my eye, I inform him my luck did not stop with turtles, so I had better move on to where people eat real food. I'm not quick enough to dodge a light slap to the back of my head that knocks my cap askew.

Our market, like most run by the Romans, is laid out in a grid fashion with different numbered sectors, each with its assigned products. Papa had explained this made it easier to control what people sold. Because the prefecture also sets the prices for every type of commodity, it makes it easier to locate and fine cheats, largely because sellers keep their eyes on other sellers in their sector. The aisles crisscrossing and joining the sectors are wide and vendors are supposed to keep them clear of goods. Papa told us this is so soldiers can move with speed through the market when there is any trouble.

As many vendors, not just fishermen, bring their wares by boat, quayside is Sector One. It is from here I then walk east, away from the river, through the vegetable sector. Onions, radishes, leeks, cucumbers, figs, grapes, cabbages, turnips, melons all reach out with their fresh scents to grab at my growling stomach as I pass. I walk quickly to get through to the fowl and poultry sector to finish my business.

Farmers and market workers I have known for years call out greetings to me. Customers haggle, despite the administration's price controls. Small groups of squatting men drink tea, play with their 20-sided dice and natter. Women laugh and scold their children. Drool slips from one corner of my mouth as my stomach rumbles and I wipe it away with the back of my hand. The dank, gamey river smell on my hands puts my hunger down.

Finally, my straw basket is lighter. My purse is heavier. The leavened barley bread smeared with olive oil and broad bean paste with garlic sits well in my belly, as does the draught of old style henqet beer. A small belch serves as a flavorful reminder of this well-deserved meal.

Just as I am heading for a latrine area outside the market perimeter, I hear a commotion in the poultry and fowl sector behind and to my left. Although the spice sector and prepared foods sector are between me and it, I see many shoppers and shopkeepers alike drifting that way and crowding around what is beginning to turn into something more than a scrap. I know this will quickly draw soldiers to keep the order, which means people are going to get hurt.

Later, I found that Timothy the live goose monger had gotten into an argument with a customer over something. The customer at one point pushed Timothy hard, saying Christians like him were just brainless goose shit and ought to be thrown into the river for the crocodiles. Timothy then slashed out with a short-bladed butchering knife, cutting the man's arm, while calling him a pagan son of a temple whore. At this point, others in the crowd began taking sides and egging them on. Christians against pagans. Pagans against Christians. Jews in it just for a good argument, like so many others looking to have something to spice up their dull lives so they might talk big in the taverns.

Papa warned it doesn't pay to stick around to watch brawls like this because you never know how big they will get or how violent.

"Movete! Movete!"

That would be soldiers coming at double-time, telling people to get out of the way. There are just two men, each strong and grim-faced; each carrying his light, round catra shield and short sword, with a pugio on his belt. The crowd will be no match for them and I know this promises to be yet another of what Papa calls "bone-breaker containments". Although necessary, in the end it will give fuel to rabble-rousers to stir up more hatred against the Prefect and his soldiers.

The pair jogs along the aisle where I am, so I jump off to my right side. A baker's apprentice, an older boy I have seen before called Peter, trips me and follows up with a shove while calling me "bird brain." I try to keep to my feet but fall full on my front side, getting mean scrapes on my face, chest, arms and legs.

Blinking rapidly as I regain my feet, I fight back tears, turn to my abuser, and clench my teeth. An animal growl rises in my throat, when a firm hand grasps my shoulder from behind.

"Don't," comes a woman's voice. "There's trouble enough in the market today."

☽ 5 ☾

The stranger takes my hand and pulls me along, bleeding and sucking air. I reach up to make sure my cap is still with me, as we head straight into a vaulted corridor going through a long wall cutting across the market areas I know. This opens onto a mixed grove of fruit trees, date palms and shrubs . On the other side of this orchard, there is a hillock and beyond that another wall with a bowered gate that lets us in to a kind of stadium surrounded by stone walls.

I never have had any reason before to be in the camel bazaar. By the time the woman pulls me into it, I have nearly regained my senses but our entry takes my breath away again and makes me even shakier after my rough tumble.

Camels are everywhere. Most are tethered in some way, but a few amble about with rough harnesses around their heads. The sounds of pissing and shitting are almost as overwhelming and stupefying as the stench. Human voices call out to each other and to the animals, adding to the confusion.

Papa always says if you have no reason to be in a place, don't go there. Yet, here I am, stumbling and gagging while in the tow of a woman I do not know. From behind, I see she wears a simple but clean, blue caftan cut to ankle length. Her hair is swathed in a darker blue veil, an end of which she holds over her face as we zigzag through knots of camels and men crowding the space and jostling each other. The mucky corral floor soils her sandaled feet.

The woman is tall. Taller even than Papa. Maybe five cubits or more. Also, slender and strong. I am no match for her but I need to know if she is abductor or savior.

Abruptly, I pull on the woman's arm and lean back. She is too big for me to stop her completely, so I end up being pulled into a skid; the soggy ground oozing up between my toes and around my ankles.

"Where are you taking me? Who are you and what do you want?"

We stop in front of a line of a dozen or so camels to our left, all in a row standing side by side, each with a left front leg tied up to keep it hobbled. Every beast is chewing cud, and they seem to take turns snuffling, snorting or growling. One nips at its neighbor, bringing forth a mewling complaint. A herder comes over and smacks both biter and bitten on their necks with his reed cane.

Neither animals nor humans seem to notice we two females in their midst. No one bothers us. Everyone carries on with their business.

"First, who I am."

The woman turns to face me. The veil still covers her nose and mouth. Only her eyes and forehead show. Momma had once told me that some women make up their eyes with something called kohl to make them look larger and more beautiful. Momma has the most beautiful eyes and never needs kohl and as my unplanned-for escort looks down at me, it is like looking into Momma's eyes. I can't help but smile up at her.

After a long moment, we both laugh. Speaking through her veil, the woman says,

"My name is Agrippina."

"And my name is—"

"Tuya. Yes, we know you. That should answer one more of your questions. I come because I come for you."

I pause to take this in.

To our right, a passing camel stops, turns its head and looks at us. I have seen camels before, of course, but never this close. The animal must be twice my height! Or more! A shiny, silver bridle winds around its muzzle and ears, with a soft woven cloth beneath it like a hat to prevent chafing. Little blue tassels fringe the patterned cap. Necklaces of beads dangle off the neck and an artistically crafted saddle pad in blues and silver adorns the hump. Instead of tassels, the pad is edged with many small, flat, shiny mirror stones that click together rhythmically with the camel's movements.

Leaning its great head down, the camel snuffles gently as if in recognition of Agrippina and, strangely, of me. It's beautiful, long-lashed eyes glisten and I can feel the warmth of its muzzle close to us. Just then it shows its yellow-brown teeth in what I suppose may be a camel smile, while exhaling an odor like middens outside of residential walls. This sends us both back a step.

Agrippina gives what sounds like a command in a language I do not understand. The creature turns to continue on its way and I see then it is female and that there is a curious and unexpected pattern shaved into the tawny hair on her sides.

I reach out to touch her without thinking, causing her to nod and make a jubilant bray. Agrippina shouts over the market noise,

"Come. We must go or we will be trampled into the filth of this place."

"But, where...?"

"The Seer has seen you in her glass. She sent me to bring you to her. Not a moment too soon, it would seem."

"You mean the one people call…" I cannot make myself say it.

The she-camel already has been let out of a gate on the far side of the corral, as though she is known by the gatekeepers, like someone's visiting aunt. She is soon out of sight. We follow, as those manning the gate avert their eyes.

"Specul-Anus? Yes, the same. But do not call her that. Hurry. We must clean you up and tend to your scrapes first."

No longer being tugged about, I walk alongside Agrippina but still hold her hand. It is soft but strong. As the sting of camel pong clears from my eyes, nose and throat, I become more aware of how much my scrapes smart. It is only now that I see my left nipple is very badly grazed and bleeding, as are my elbows and knees. The thought of getting cleaned up makes me feel a little giddy, but I check myself in order to take note of my surroundings. We pass a milestone, but I can't tell if this is the first due to not paying attention before.

We are not on the road I usually take to and from the river from our house, as we live a little to the southwest central city, close to the garrison. This road, like most, including ours, is lined with tall, slender palm trees all heavy with flowers hanging like golden pennants. On either side are farms with bare-chested workers and oxen bringing in the early grain harvest. The fields are dotted with white-plastered silos and threshing floors.

Snuffling, my nose picks up cattle and pig smells hanging in the air, but not anything as bad as the camel market. Donkeys, some pulling carts, some not, plod both directions on the road with their cargoes.

By and by, we come to a grove of smaller date palms with silvery leafed shrubs and clumps of sharp-bladed grasses surrounding a very large tent. It is the kind that the desert people live in, though this one is more magnificent than others I have seen. Agrippina says that we have arrived to our destination.

The warm air here carries a whiff of fresh thyme like that around our house.

☽ 6 ☾

Agrippina leaves me in the care of two young women, one short and one tall. She gives them instructions in the same tongue she had used to send the she-camel on her way.

Each girl is wearing a long, white linen cloth draped over one shoulder and hanging past her knees. A slim silvery tie around each waist shows off their shapely forms under the garments. Their dusky arms are bare but for metal bands encircling their upper arms, and more delicate bracelets at their wrists. Each wears her hair in braids held up off the neck with a bright blue, cloth headband.

The two lead me to a low, clay brick building with a vaulted roof a short distance from the tent. Here, we have to duck our heads to get through a door, where stairs lead down below ground level and let out beneath an arched ceiling of patterned brickwork. One girl motions me to a little open chamber to one side of the room, where I can see a clean, well-tended latrine. I had been holding myself in for so long, I had forgotten I needed to empty my lower parts before this venture had begun; but now I am grateful for the opportunity to void.

The girls have removed their linen coverings and stand naked except for their head and arm bands. They indicate for me to do the same. As I only have on a much soiled and reeking loincloth, I am happy to let it fall away. But I put my feather cap and my leather pouch with my day's earnings under a bench off to the side. The two eye me, probably trying to guess my age, for compared to them I am built like a boy, still a little puella next to them with their nice breasts, rounded buttocks and trim dark hair masking the place Momma says we should keep to ourselves.

The girls next pour a couple buckets of warm water over me and scrub me with rough cloths. Everywhere. It makes my scratches cry out but feels good elsewhere. At first, I feel shy about being touched by strangers like this, so I try shielding myself with my hands and arms but the two are persistent. Soon, as I feel the dried sweat from my morning on the river, along with the grime and mess from the market and camel souk coming off, I stop thinking about being uncovered and touched by someone other than my Momma.

After this initial scrub down and rinse, with the water running into a grate in the middle of the floor, I am shepherded to another chamber. This room has more light because above and between the arches there are raised areas with window openings. The floor's earth-toned tiles warm my feet. The walls are decorated in colorful mosaic designs; none depicting animals or people like walls I'd gotten a peek at in some homes of Greeks and Jews Papa had taken me to. Pools on either end of the rectangular space each might easily hold a whole family. I sniff the air, for there seems to be a faint scent to it. Moving my head in different directions while taking in short breaths through my nose, I am unable to determine where the pleasant fragrance comes from.

A long, slow exhale brings relief and opens my mind. I want to find out more about this place, so I leave the two girls at the doorway and begin to walk about. I see what I think to be cleaning instruments, along with other things that are a mystery to me. I open jars, some holding aromatic creams and a couple filled with foul-smelling, sticky substances.

The shorter girl picks up a jar of nice smelling stuff and beckons me to come to the pool that has steam coming off it. She steps into the water and smiles, gesturing that I should join her. I touch the water with a hand, because I have never bathed in anything but cold or tepid rain water. It seems much too hot to stand in, much less set my culus in. I shake my head softly and pull my brows together, which makes the girl in the steaming pool laugh. She says something to her companion, who then joins her in the water. After splashing water gently over their bodies, one scoops her fingers into the jar now sitting on the raised edge of the pool, taking up a small amount of yellowish goo. She then rubs this stuff over the other girl, who has shut her eyes and is humming.

The girl who got herself covered with yolky cream that bubbled as she washed, sits in the water and rinses away what

I now take to be a kind of soap, but smelling much nicer than anything Momma has ever used. While she does this, I splash water up my legs and by doing so find I am getting used to it.

I step into the pool. Finally I sit down. Carefully.

The hot water sends a tremor through my body. The scrapes on my front side feel like they want to scream and jump off my body. The rest of me though suddenly relaxes and tears roll down my face.

Before they are done with me, I almost begin to feel like the two girls are my friends. They have thoroughly and very gently washed my whole body, including my hair; although they used a different kind of cream with a reddish tint for that part. I just want to lie back in the water at this point, but they make me get up and practically have to carry me to the other end of the room because I am so relaxed and drowsy. One steps into the bath there and holds out her hand to me. I gladly accept it and let her take me into the water. My eyes pop open and all my muscles tighten. This second pool is frigid compared with the first, as though it came from a deep well. Before I can go back, the girl splashes me with one hand until I am breathless, while the other pushes me to the center, where they both sit down.

By this time, I have figured out this is part of their bathing ritual and I should do as they do. Perhaps because I am now so much more compliant, after a short, brisk soak, we three go back to the steaming bath to enjoy its healing medicine.

I lean my head back on the edge of the pool with my eyes unfocused and half shut. It appears as if the flowing mosaic designs on the opposite wall are slowly moving as if they have their own secret life. In this state, it strikes me for the first time that time itself is moving; not only moving but very gradually accelerating like someone dilly-dallying who suddenly remembers she is out for a purpose but can't quite recall what it may be.

As relaxed as I am, I do not much care. There is something soothing about it though, like when I am floating in my boat.

Sometimes while lying quietly in my boat along the river's edge under a hot sun, not a cloud moving, nor any breeze in the rushes and papyrus, the water itself seeming motionless, a slight current would curve in, dawdling along with my fingers in the water to make a lazy eddy that would little by little quicken until I might spin out into the central flow where the river takes on a more treacherous life; where a fowler might more easily lose her life.

Am I in such a current now? If so, why this blissful exhilaration?

Agrippina comes in giving orders to my companions. With that, the girls help me out from the pool, towel me off with thick cloths with tassels on the ends and before dressing me in robes similar to what they had been wearing, gently rub a soothing emolument onto my cuts and scrapes. With some difficulty, they manage to brush and braid my hair; commenting all the time about I know not what. Finally, one places sandals on my feet, while the other fetches my leather pouch and cap.

I am ready, but for what?

☽ 7 ☾

She is sitting inside a tent within the big tent next to the bath house from which Agrippina has just taken me. A house within a house, it seems; setting her apart from whatever goes on around her and putting two walls between her and the outside.

The main tent is carpeted throughout. Agrippina had directed me upon leaving the bright outdoors to remove the sandals given to me earlier. While adjusting my eyes to the light coming from the many oil lamps set about on small tables, I graze the sole of my right foot in a small circle where I stand, making the foot tingle and the hair on my arms stand up. I wish we could have a floor like this in our house. I think I would sleep on it instead of my pallet. Colorful cushions and pillows that look equally inviting are scattered about the room near the tables.

Judging from its huge size, it seems to me the inside must be divided to make other rooms. The room where I have entered, while still large, probably acts as a vestibule, though enclosed. It would make for a shift from the outside world of streets, markets and nosy neighbors to an unseen inner sanctum. Yet, she still had set up a private tabernacle at the back wall facing the entrance through which I had come.

The bottom part of her tent has six sides I can see, which means there must be six more on the opposite side that rise up to just above my waist. From there, the roof becomes conical, ending in something like a spear point at its center. The covering materials are thick and heavy, like the carpets on the floor.

It must be stifling hot inside, I think.

Biting a fingernail, I quell a rolling sensation in my stomach. I recall that Agrippina had told me—warned me?—not to use the vulgar name common in the city and market for her patroness. If patroness is what she is.

Agrippina always called the woman Seer. That can't be so bad. With such thoughts, I take a step toward the small tent, hitting the back of one heel with the big toe of my other foot. Ouch! I stumble a little.

Papa always said when you have to do something that makes you nervous or anxious, it is best to get it over with or else risk turning into a eunuch. He would say such things when he thought Momma would not hear.

Crossing to the 12-sided tent, I stop at the open door with my arms wrapped around my chest. I see the woman sitting cross-legged toward the back.

"Hello, mother. Agrippina…she brought me here…to see you, so she said."

Silence. Then,

"No need to be afraid, child. I'm certainly not anyone who means you any harm. You may come in."

Her name is Nyla. She says to continue by calling her Mother. Mother Nyla. I have overhead people in the market say she comes in from the Red Desert far to the east. She comes and goes. No one knows when or why.

I think it is going to take me a while to get used to her. From her crinkly skin, it is clear she is an old one, yet her tits remain firm like a woman who never suckled a child. She doesn't guard them like decent women do and that makes me tug my robe in place. She wears a necklace of shiny mirror stones hanging down past her ribs. It is a nice-looking necklace, but does little to cover her mindits, as Momma calls them, or distract from the fact that the nipples are made up to look like a couple of eyes staring out from where you least expect anything to be looking at you. Some kind of animal skin clings around her wrinkled belly and hips, almost like it is still alive. Her rough, knobby feet likely have not seen sandals for a long time.

I keep my eyes down while still keeping an eye on her. She keeps me standing for a little while, all the time polishing the largest mirror stone between a thumb and forefinger as she examines me with one rheumy eye open, the other obscured, half shut.

"Girl, your shifting from one foot to the other is going to make me dizzy and puke. You may sit down. There."

Gladly, I scrunch myself onto a squashy cushion in front of Mother Nyla, but still leaning back a little. I begin twisting a corner of my after-bath wrap under the gaze of her two painted-on eyes, now seeming to smile with sympathy as real eyes will do. Nyla brings a shallow hand basin from one side to place between us. She next unwraps a highly polished, flat, blue stone from a cloth with The Hand embroidered on it. The Hand bears the ancient eye used by olden Egyptians in its palm. She lays the stone in the basin, folds the cloth and puts it aside. From her other side, Mother Nyla takes up a pitcher and tips water into the basin to just cover the blue stone.

All of this she does with deliberation, while reciting something scarcely audible that may have been in the same tongue Agrippina spoke to others. Or not. The wet stone shimmers under the flickering light of two lamps, one on each side of Mother Nyla, making it difficult to concentrate.

"Scoot yourself closer, child, and give me both your hands."

I can't say I trust her at this point, but her voice draws me closer. The long day, with its strange turn of events, its unusual places and experiences, maybe especially the baths, and the great heat in the enclosed space, have drained me. Heavy-eyed, I believe I am falling asleep. That would explain this dream. It begins with a silent popping feeling. The hut grows dark and begins to spin. As it spins faster and faster, blue ambient light from the stone encircles us and we are lifted off the ground, as though Aeolus has picked up the tent and is ferrying us away. The wind spirit sings soothingly in my ears. Along with other voices. Voices long lost to me. Voices from before my birth.

Images of what-could-be flash through my head making me want to run from the tent if I could, yet the voices also incite incredible longing, fixing me in place.

☽ 8 ☾

The ceiling I see is the one I see every night before falling asleep and every morning when I wake up. The bed feels like my own. I'm under my favorite linen coverlet with animal pictures on it. Cooking smells tease my nose and stomach, drawing me from muddled dreams.

Tem's voice—

"Momma! Her eyes are open!"

Then quieter to me.

"You're going to get it now!"

"Daughter! Where have you been? What happened to you? Just look at yourself! Have you been fighting again? How many times must I tell you about wrestling those market boys? Letting them put their hands on you! Just wait until I tell your father!"

"Papa?"

I'm confused.

Momma claims I snuck into the house while she and Tem had gone out to do the laundry. She says I did not wake up all the rest of that day and slept the night through, as well. She found me in my bed and says nothing she did would stir me. Tem says she even sat on me and pinched me, but even then I didn't stir or make a peep.

Because of all the scratches on me, Momma says they show I'd been fighting. I fight when I have to, but most boys know to leave me alone. Otherwise, and they know it, they won't grow to be real men. But I remember I had not fought with anyone, despite having been pushed down. There had been a brawl in the market and I was just getting ready to beat up the boy who had pushed me down...but someone had stopped me.

I try telling this to Momma. Tem is standing behind her and looking around at me like I'm some kind of fool but Momma is having none of it. I tell her about being knocked down and, remembering now, being dragged through the camel bazaar by a tall lady and the baths and Old Nyla but she cuts me off.

"All the time you spend out on that river has cooked your brains. You can lie to me all you want but I am not fooled. So! Get yourself dressed and eat something. Hmmpf. At least you showed some good sense putting your wallet under the big bed. Looks like you had a good day I think from how much money you carried home."

Money always has a way of softening Momma's anger.

She brings me a thick, hot porridge and a handful of berries to eat. I sit on the edge of the bed trying to collect myself, with the bowl in my lap and my feet on the floor. I stir the berries into the porridge and dig in. With the first taste of warm food in what I guess is a couple of days at least, I close my eyes and take a deep breath. Momma sits with me and gently rubs some of her calendula ointment onto my chest. I yelp when she touches my left nipple and looking down it looks like it has been practically scraped off.

I should be fighting mad about this. But instead of thinking of how to get back at Peter, I'm feeling suddenly that life is really good. I tear up and clasp Momma's forearm.

So much to be thankful for!

I think about how Tem and I each have a bed of our own, which is more than most kids we know have. The beds are just plain wood frames with short, squared legs, but they get us off the ground. Leather straps interlace and fasten to the side rails and a double layer of rush mats helps make the beds more comfortable. We use wood blocks with a cushion to pillow our heads.

Momma and Papa have a bigger bed because, of course, they are two. The legs are much heavier and shaped by lathe. Theirs is higher than mine and Tem's, too. It also has a pluteus or headboard with horse heads carved on each corner. Papa loves horses and says these carvings are a reminder he will have his own one day. Their bed has a down-filled mattress and a long down-filled bolster as their shared pillow. It is nice to lie on their bed when they let us.

I think it is safe to change the subject now.

"Momma, is Papa back?"

"No. And the soldiers at the garrison have heard nothing yet. Eat. And don't worry about him. None of that will bring him home any sooner. And Tuya, just in case there is the tiniest speck of truth to your lies, I want you to be careful of that old desert woman you talk of. Tits that see! Really! Just so! You know that must mean she has two extra evil eyes putting who knows what spells on this house. That does it. Momma forbids you ever talking with that old bag witch lady any more. No more business in the market with her or anywhere else. Do you understand me?

"Tem! That goes two times as much for you, so stop with your eye rolling. One day those eyes are going to fall out of your oh so pretty head. They will roll right out the door. Bye-bye!

"You both my sweet desert foxes. I love you so much. Tell Momma you're going to stay clear of the evil witch tits lady."

Momma got up and left me alone on the bed, with Tem following. Just then I looked down and saw part of a leather thong sticking out from under the pillow on my head rest. Lifting the pillow, I see the cord looks to be attached to some kind of amulet. I have never seen this before but pick it up, thinking maybe it is something Tem put there, no doubt to get me into even more trouble. The amulet must be a kind of lunula that many girls wear until they marry, though it is larger and thicker. Perhaps three fingers across and a third as thick. This one is a metal disk with a hole through its center like some coins I have seen in the market. It may be brass, but old and tarnished looking. There is a thin, raised lip around the edge, with lines and strange characters engraved on the face of it. The other side also has symbols that don't mean a thing to me. Closer to the center hole, in an otherwise blank spot, there is what may be a script neatly etched into the surface.

አንበቢው

I can read Roman letters but not this. Thinking maybe it's the owner's name, I tuck it under the wood block for later. It could be that it belongs to one of the girls who cleaned me up at the baths and somehow fell in with my things. No reason for anyone else to see it. Nevertheless, I can't stop thinking about it. For its size I think it felt surprisingly light. A riddle in so many ways.

My mother comes from far up the river, from a place called Kush. I like when she tells me and Tem about where she grew up and how different river life is, including the people, from so far away. She says her family had little, so I'm sure that's why Momma likes the extra coin I can bring in. It helps the family, along with what she makes as a medicine woman, especially when Papa is away on patrol like he has been now for half a season. When he is away like this, we have to wait for what the soldiers call their salary.

Momma first came to Heliopolis when "fourteen floodings old," as she says. Her father brought her along on a trading expedition, supposedly to make his fortune but he took ill with vomiting and diarrhea, dying within just a few days. His partners said nothing when grandfather first complained of fever and tremors. They installed him at a cheap inn and bade Momma stay to put cool compresses on his forehead. A day later, grandfather's cousin and their new leader—for grandfather had been the master on the journey downriver—told Momma they would carry out the trading and once finished come back for her. She never saw them again.

Momma got kicked out from the inn the same day her father died. She had no money and no idea what had happened to her father's body. She would never say much about what she did to get by after that, except learning common Greek and presumably finding work.

Sometime later she met Papa.

I think that's why whenever he is away for long periods, Momma tends to get impatient with me and Tem more. She never says out loud maybe something bad has happened to Papa, but I've noticed she prays more and tends to glance at the doorway often. No reason to upset her any more than she is by showing her this disk—thing.

☽ 9 ☾

It is the third week of May, what some of Momma's friends call Opet. She went out with them to visit and pray by their dead relatives sepulchri. She brought lots of perfumy flowers home.

Later that day Tem's menses came on. Not so very sweet smelling but what I imagine is a well—played tragedy by her.

And I still can't recall everything that happened to me at the Bedouin encampment. Plus, I have not had a chance to check out the amulet. Probably the best thing to do is to take it back to the Bedouin camp.

Ever since I got back from Mother Nyla's tent—something no one believes and probably never will, so I have stopped talking about it—Tem had been complaining that her nipples hurt, too. I thought for sure that she was just looking to take attention from me because of how I had gotten grazed up. Now that she has started bleeding, I notice that she also has a pair of walnuts beginning to pop up on her chest.

I always thought I'd be the first, like I have been in everything else. But, no, Tem is getting hit with the titty stick before me and is really letting me know about it. All she does now is march around the house as though she is leading a procession down the temple avenue, flaunting her newborn womanhood.

The scent of her blood at first made it hard for me to fall asleep at night. That and her moaning from cramps.

Momma gives her a borage tonic for the cramps and has shown her how to make cloth pads for catching the blood. I will make sure I am out on the river on laundry day.

So far, what I remember from when it felt like Mother Nyla's tent flew off into the sky, is different voices all whispering at once. Whoever they were, they seemed to be sharing secrets about me. It was like when I overhear Momma and Papa talking quietly among themselves, or other adults confiding private things to one another they don't think *pupae* should know about or understand.

It strikes me that the brass amulet could belong to someone I heard talking, if there were other people in the big tent at the time. Returning it, I might get a reward. If I'm really lucky, it might be a large one.

As I was pretty sure where the Bedouin camp had been pitched, I tried to retrace the path Agrippina took me on. I got as far as the camel market, but this time they would not let me in, much less pass through. I did get a good glimpse inside though and it looked a lot bigger than I remember. It stank just as bad, maybe worse. Anyway, I had to find my way around it and get back on the road east. After a time, I came to the place where the big tent had been. There was now just a very large stretch of dirt, with weeds already laying claim to it. I knew this had to be the right place because of the bath house. I went to its entrance to ask about the whereabouts of Mother Nyla, Agrippina and the girls who had bathed me.

A bearded man at the entrance told me the desert people had loaded their camels and left. From his description, it sounded like they had pulled up stakes within days of my contact with them. When asked where they might have gone to, he just waved his hand to the west as though to say, "Good riddance." With that, he grabbed me by the shoulder and said I should come into the bath house. Wiggling his eyebrows, he said it looked like I needed a good scrubbing.

I raised one of my own eyebrows in answer, gave him a glassy stare, and swatted his arm away. I will not be going back to that place again. I would mention it to Papa when he comes home, but I'm sure he would not be happy I had ventured there.

On the way back, I found the stall in the market where that boy pushed me down. He was not there, so I ask when he might be returning. I'm told he is just an apprentice who works more in the bakery itself than selling in the market. He may come back but the woman there does not know exactly when.

Eight days after Tem's menstrual blood had stopped flowing, several of Momma's friends come by to visit. Momma explains to Tem that the women want to give a special Moon Ceremony for Tem to help her crossover to being a woman. They say it is a kind of celebration just for young girls like her and that it is very, very secret.

Why hadn't we heard of this before? I mean me and Tem? We know all about cunni and tits and how to stimulate ourselves, and how could we not know about bleeding when every woman around us has had her monthlies while we were growing up. We had watched Momma wash out her rags and put them up to dry, while telling us all about the pestis. So it was like something you never wanted to happen to you, but still you looked forward to it just to know what it felt like and be able to tell your own stories about it.

Poor Tem. Now she knows. But she is getting something special now, too, and I am not going to be a part of it. We've always done everything together, so this is hardly fair. I go back to my bed and when I am sure I am alone, I lift my linen and try to see myself down there and talk to whatever spirit might live there to say it is time for me to join my sister, so we can do this Moon Ceremony thing together.

Instead, I have to watch as the women come for Tem and Momma in the dead of night. It's cold and they have their woolen cloaks drawn tight against a wind that's blowing grit around. Everybody, including Momma and Tem, are painted with strange markings on their faces and everywhere else that I can see. I wish now I had made that feathered hat for my sister. She tries to keep a solemn look on her face, but I can tell she is very excited. I am told I have to stay behind and that I had better not try to follow. My time will come, they say.

After dawn, when Tem returns, she's crying loudly and groaning in pain, while holding her lower abdomen. Maybe this Moon Ceremony is not such a good thing after all.

Momma gives my sister something to drink that puts her to sleep, but she still moans and pumps her legs slowly, like she's trying to get a foothold on to something solid. Meanwhile, Momma busies herself in the kitchen. I go up to her quietly. Tears are running down her cheeks, so I cough a little to let her know I am there. She turns and when she sees me, she opens her arms so we can hug.

Now I'm crying and I ask Momma what happened? What did they do to my sister?

Momma takes a few moments to compose herself, then takes me to a bench where we sit side by side. After a few deep breaths, she finds her words; not looking at me just yet.

"Things started so beautiful! Your sister was excited. Me, too. We all walked for an hour and some more, then we came to a place of trees. It's a secret place where the women already had made the safe circle. This is the circle having special magic. All the directions are marked, each with its own special sign. You know, earth, air, water, fire. Tem was told to stand in the center of this circle, then all of us women stood around holding branches of fire. We sang for gods to bless the girl called Tem, for all of us and for our families and for the world. It was a real celebration just like we said."

"It sounds nice, Momma."

" Yes. It was nice—but soon all that changed. One woman from my old home upriver who goes by the name Saka'aye, after an olden times queen—everyone calls her Saka and has much respect for her because she is able to speak direct with the gods. So. Saka drank her magic water from her Look-Ahead Gourd, then she fell to ground. It was like she could no longer hear or see any of us. We thought Saka must be talking be with spirits and we prayed she would come back, bring some good news and bless our Tem."

Momma is breathing in fast, little breaths by this time, so she stops to get herself together again. I already know things could not have gone well or Tem would not be in the state she is in, still fretful in sleep.

"What did Mother Saka say, Momma?"

"Such bad luck for our Tem! When Saka comes back, she said because of Tem's number six finger on her left hand, she is marked for special work as a kahin–"

"What's that, Momma?"

"Oh, I think it's what some here call a manti. Someone like Saka herself."

"But that doesn't sound so bad. Aren't they healers, too? Like you are with all that you know about herbs and medicines?"

"Yes, dear Tuya, like that. This is not bad news though. Saka went on to say the spirits don't want our Tem to bear children. Ever. So, it's then Saka tells us to hold Tem down and she reached inside with one hand while pushing on Tem's stomach with her other. She broke Tem's womb neck. Bent it so no man's seed can find a hold."

I can't speak. I'm nearly exploding inside. Things are moving too quickly. I want to run away. Instead, I burst out with uncontrollable tears.

☽ 10 ☾

Although her menses had ended before her dedication, Tem bled for many days after her "celebration" but it has stopped now. I have been helping Momma nurse Tem along.

Actually, once she could talk, she yelled hoarsely at Momma and told her to go away. Tem is better today but is still shaky, so I hold her up sitting to give her broth and medicines to drink. I wash her and keep her clean in other ways. She lets me brush her hair and asks me to sing to her, which I do in a soft voice while stroking her head.

I think Tem is going to be all right. Some things are going to take longer to heal though. Momma says she has known of women who had this done to them, but they had asked a midwife to do it after already having a baby or two. Tem did not ask for this but now it's done and that's that. After a while, I'll talk with her to get her to talk to Momma. It sounded to me like Momma could not have done anything to stop what Saka did and I see that she feels really bad about it. Tem's tears have dried up but Momma's haven't.

Because we're well into the month of June, I tell Momma that I need to get back out on the river. Caring for Tem has kept me away from my work and, besides, I need to be by myself to think about all that has happened. I don't remember anything ever being this bad in our family before and don't see how they can get any worse.

Usually we do not see vultures this far north. Papa says they stick to the deserts east and west of Heliopolis, or farther upriver where it is dryer. Still, I have seen them on the ground a couple times before making dinner of dead animals. Mostly crows take care of such things though. That's why I was surprised to see a pair of vultures making wide circles over this area. They stayed pretty high up in the sky, going around and around, shaping an invisible snare over the city. Because they did not come down, they must not have spotted any remains. It was more like they were waiting for something to happen. For something to die.

This is on my mind as I make my way home from the river and the market. I only made a little money today as a result of my mind not paying attention to bird sounds and what they mean. There were some dead birds in my traps, but those had been mostly eaten by other animals so were too far gone to even think of selling. I did reset my traps and I will go out tomorrow to check them.

Coming up to our house, my shoulders slump down and I am feeling tired. I don't feel like seeing anyone, not even Tem or Momma, but there are people standing outside our gate. One holds the bridle of a horse.

Papa always talked about finally being able to buy a horse of his own. He says this would make him an eques, so when he retires in a little while he could become someone important in the city, letting him make more money than his military pension alone will give us.

I wonder. Did Papa finally get a horse when he was on this last patrol? And is he home now?

I go through the gate, with a quick look over my shoulder at the beautiful horse, then through the main entryway. Momma is sitting with a strange man, while two other men stand close by. These two glance my way briefly, but go back to the conversation between Momma and the stranger. He is military and from what Papa has told me about insignia and uniforms, he looks to be high ranking. Probably a centurion. That means the horse belongs to him, not Papa.

Though I have to pee, I hold it in and listen to what the man is saying to Momma.

"...so, you see, you are not really a Roman citizen. The one you call your husband and your two daughters are citizens by birth, but Kush is not in the Imperium. I am sorry to have to be the one to tell you this."

"But I'm telling you, I am married to a citizen. To a soldier like you and your two men here."

"Yes, that is all well and good, but you see the laws say that soldiers cannot officially marry. Of course, we realize that they take up with local women all the time, and in your case, a foreign woman."

One of the standing soldiers smirks and makes a knowing nod to the other at this. I restrain myself from kicking him. The centurion continues,

"That is why I have to tell you that you may no longer live in this house."

"What? What are you saying!"

"What I am saying is that legally this property belongs to the army. We requisitioned the house for use by officers when the 5th Macedonian Legion first came to this province. Our headquarters is in Memphis but we established a garrison here in Heliopolis to better police the populace."

"Wait, wait! I'm shocked to hear you say I'm not married! More shocked again to hear you want to throw my daughters and me out into the bad streets! You said my daughters though are Roman citizens. They have rights don't they, if not me?"

"Definitely. The girls have rights as citizens. However, because they are not yet of age, the fiscus will keep their father's earned pension rights in trust for them. They may make application at such time as they become of legal age."

At this, Momma's face hardened and she shifted her gaze out the window for a moment. Turning finally to the man, she said,

"What you said about my husband earlier. It's not true. Cannot be. So. What is it you want me to do?"

☽ 11 ☾

That was nearly a month ago. Everything has changed since. Papa is missing and the army says if he did not desert, he must be dead. The centurion told Momma he had ordered Papa and a few other soldiers to go to the army fort at Dionysias to oversee equipment distribution as a result of some irregularities. As this fort is at an oasis in the Western Desert, it is known there are bandits and Bedouin in the area. At the time, there also had been rain storms and at least one big dust storm. Only one man from the group Papa led made it to the fort. He reported he thought the others had drowned when water suddenly washed down a wadi to their night encampment. It missed him because he was on night watch at the time, squatting behind a bush, under his cloak due to the rain, and some distance from the others in order to relieve himself. A search was made in and around the area, but no bodies were found.

When word had gotten back to the centurion, he gave the surviving soldier a field promotion, directing him to take Papa's place.

His name is Tiberianus. He is now an officer, *optio*, doing what my Papa should be doing. He and his wife, Valeria, and two children—Tabatheus, a girl about the same age as me and my sister, and Claudius, a boy of around seven years—arrived at our house just a few days after the centurion went back to Memphis. They told us we had to get out right away because they wanted to move in and their goods would arrive by the next day.

I think I will remember these people forever. The man is stupid. His wife haughty. Neither are as good as my Papa and Momma. But the two kids acted like know-it-alls and were very snotty to me and Tem. The boy, in particular, kept playing with a knife he had taken out of its sheath at his side, looking at me and Tem like he meant to do something with it. Later that evening when I went out on our rooftop to think, I discovered our pet hoopoe lying dead in a corner where the retaining walls meet. It had been stabbed several times with a knife. I had brought this bird home last summer after finding it hurt beneath an acacia tree on my way back home from the market.

I dare not tell Tem yet, but those kids are going to be real sorry.

We spent the next several days sleeping in friends' homes, usually on the floor because we had to leave our nice beds behind. When I think about those...those novi sleeping in our beds, it makes me feel hot and broken inside. My only consolation are violent fantasies of their destruction.

We left in an unsettling way, to be sure. The new people just barged in and took over, bossing us around and telling us to get out. As we went out the gate like beggars, Tem twisted around and stared at the house. As though called, the family all came to the front doorway and seemed to be waiting for my sister to say something. And she did have something to say but I have no idea what she said or in what language but it sounded like a curse. More than that, she said it so loudly that passersby made a wide arc around us. A couple of Christians crossed themselves as they did so.

I have a new respect for my sister and told her so. Of course, she knew by this time about the murder of our pet hoopoe bird.

Momma had saved some money, so she found us a small, single room to the north of our old home. She said she did not want to live near our old place for fear that she would burn it down in the night and the army would know who to come looking for. She also said this is just temporary, until she can arrange for us to go upriver back to where she came from. Despite the betrayal by her uncle years ago, she is sure there are cousins who will take us in until we can get back on our feet.

Meanwhile, we are making do here in this tiny room. The man she rents from says she can use the courtyard to cook in, as long as she keeps it clean. Fortunately, he is not around much but there is a woman he keeps who looks in on us every now and again. She seemed sympathetic when Momma told her our story but has not offered any real help.

I keep hoping that Papa will show up and take us away from all of this. It won't matter if he is still in the army or not. I don't give a cockroach's right ass cheek for the army at this point.

What with Papa missing, losing our nice house and Tem's agonies, these are just part of our troubles it turns out. Though Momma has money saved up that she keeps well protected, I still need to help out with supporting the family. The walk to my skiff is now longer, given where we have relocated. All of my traps and snares had been damaged or taken, so I have had to redo them. The worst thing though is when I bring my day's catch to market, people act like they hardly know me. Even Felix.

I always thought the way we joked with each other meant we were good friends. When I saw him for the first time after everything bad started happening, he said he had heard about Papa and felt really sorry. The thing is, he said all this in that low, marketplace Greek. We always spoke before in Latin and he acted proud to do so. Even though Papa was from a part of Greece himself, he encouraged us to use the Roman tongue and learn Roman ways as much as possible. But it's not like I grew up not being able to understand Greek. But now everyone in the market, including Felix, only speaks to me in the local Greek.

Not only that, they don't pay as much as they used to for what I bring in to sell. I'm still trying to figure all this out.

Meanwhile, I speak Greek. Even at the place we now call home.

Momma sighs and shakes her head, but her gaze is hard and determined when she thinks I'm not looking. All in all, I wonder how she can stay as calm as she does. A lot calmer than me, for certain.

Because the river waters have been rising Momma says we must leave for the south soon. Her plan is that we will travel by boat as far as Thebes, from there joining a caravan to Meroe. She says we have to be ready to leave quickly, so we find a cheap inn close to the water where the river people stay, for once a boat has its cargo loaded the craft master does not wait around.

It has been several days since we came to the inn. I go every morning to talk with the boat owners, craft masters and crews because I want to know what the river is like to the south. It is hard to say who is telling the truth and who is stretching it just to either scare me or impress me, but I am getting an idea of what we can expect. It will be different.

Momma comes down to the docks later in the day to check on the progress of a certain boat and its cargo. She has made a small advance to its master, who is very dark like Momma, and has agreed to take on cooking and cleaning chores once underway. He assures her the material he is waiting for won't arrive for a few more days.

Momma says this man's word is good, so I decide to have a last day in the field.

It is the twenty-first of July in the Year 81 anno Diocletiani. [*Translator's note: 365 anno Domini.*] Sirius the Dog Star joins the Sun at dawn during these hottest days. I know this because I have been counting the days since we lost our home. This is going to be my last summer here in Heliopolis.

So, before we go, I feel an urge to visit my old river haunts one last time.

Getting up before dawn I decide, seeing as I still have the amulet with the funny writing on the back, I will wear it for good luck. Something we could use about now! I throw on a tunic and then hike back up to the house where Tem and me were born and lived for most of our lives with Papa and Momma. It is still dark when I reach the place, at least the place where I remembered our house to be. The house, or what is left of it, looks to have burned down to the ground. Seeing it, I jump back a step with a small yelp. Heus! Suddenly, I feel chilled, then realize I've broken out into a cold sweat because if anyone sees me in this place they might remember I used to live here and how we were moved out. This means someone might also remember Tem's curse on the people who took the place over. As her sister, some would say I am as much to blame as Tem for the evil that caught up with the soldier and his hateful family.

Doesn't seem they made any friends while here.

Once I uproot myself from the spot and get my feet to move again, I run towards the market quayside in hopes of finding the old reed boat Papa had made for us. It is there, hidden in the papyrus reeds nearby. I climb in, move out to catch the current and float downriver.

Cradled by the boat, my breath comes easier and I let myself lie back. The eastern sky is just beginning to brighten and a few birds are making their morning songs. This day it seems like they are singing not just to make the sun rise but also for me. I am as much a part of this place as are the birds. They are letting me know that just as they nest here, to greet their blind hatchlings into this river world, that this place has been my nest in a way, too. Though I may be curled inside a shell of my own and my eyes may yet be closed, light slowly penetrates my lids.

Fingering the metallic disk around my neck, I think: It must be time for me to hatch, to learn to fly. As if to welcome me, the blue sky reaches down in an embrace. Things will be different now. They have to be.

And so it was, as something so staggering and fantastic came down upon me at that moment I banished it from memory for many, many years to come.

Scroll #2: Desert Mothers & Fathers

Setting: NITRIA

☽ 1 ☾

As he often did, Elder Theophilus interrupted my chores. Cursing under my breath, I knew I was in for another lesson on rectitude and godliness.

"This friend of yours called Emelia, how often have I advised you not to spend so much time in her company. As you know, I pray often for your eternal soul. My hope for you has been her lamentable influence over you will not compromise and impede your salvation. Be that as it may, the problem will not much longer be with us. That woman shall be sent away before the month is out. There can be no place at our monastery for the likes of her, so I have recommended to the Patriarch she be cast out like the filth she is. She has polluted these grounds much too long and he finally agrees with my proposal.

"You should know, too, starting from today I am to take over as your catechist. Your progress toward baptism under Sister Prisca's tutelage has been crawling along at best. Not surprising, as I well know your spiritual guide indulges in much useless nattering. Under me, however, you will learn the Church is a temple for divine education, not a place for idle women's chatter.

"I see you are displeased. Good. We will peel away your leprous crust like the blind worm you are to better know the

Light. Consider yourself as my pupil from now on and apply yourself to the memorization of Scripture."

Leprous crust? Blind worm? Would this man ever stop?

"Further, after this unclean friend of yours departs, you will accompany me on my next desert retreat. I will help you better focus on your spiritual salvation and teach you to pray properly. Think on this meanwhile: 'How narrow is the gate, and strait is the way that leadeth to Life: and few there are that find it.'"

Elder Theophilus turned and left. Exhaling deliberately, I thanked whatever god spared me any more of his harangue.

I repeat his words here only because they so well show his character. To say the least, I was displeased about having to spend more time in his loathsome presence. As though he might teach me anything. One day I may have to teach him a lesson or two.

Given what I know of him, it is strange to hear him quoting Scripture. He is a homely man, but with other attractions some evidently find seductive. His imprecations however about my dearest friend, Emelia, were not at all welcomed. He should mind his own soul, not mine.

☽ 2 ☾

Emelia first arrived at the monastery in Nitria nearly two years ago, when we were both eighteen years old and she was about five or six months pregnant. It was obvious there was something different about her, aside from the fact of her pregnancy. Where some instinctively drew back from her, I knew from when we first saw the light in each other's eyes we would become fast friends. Or maybe I just needed a friend and hoped Emelia's coming might be the godsend for which I had been waiting to end my feelings of dislocation, isolation and instinctive vigilance. More than anything, I needed someone I could trust and talk to like I used to with my sister so many years ago.

We met in mid-November, still called the ides by some, with both Isis and Diana as its guardians. I prefer these to the Christian martyrs remembered in this month.

The sun had just withdrawn over the horizon, casting its last phobic rays toward the encroachment of another harsh desert night. Though the day had been comfortably warm, the temperature already had dropped sharply and the wind was once again rising, though not yet enough to blow grit to encrust one's eyes. I tightened my scarf about my head and neck in preparation.

The evening service was about to begin. Scores of people, both residents and visitors—tourists would be a better word—were still finding their way to the torch-lit basilica gateway leading into the courtyard, where more torches and fires in braziers illuminated and warmed the area. The more voluble milled about in the center of this corral-like space, speaking to each other absonantly around a three-stepped, stone bema supporting a lectern, each looking to outdo the others in swapping stories about their adventures while crossing the desert and attending lectures or catechismals by this or that desert mother or father. Many obviously had just come from one or another private tavern in the community. The quieter ones retreated from the churning center to the encircling walls. Not that they could really get away from the din. Everybody pulled their cloaks and scarves tighter around themselves to keep their warmth from escaping into the night.

After years of observing this behavior every Sabbath, except during very inclement weather, I paid it little attention as I went about my duties preparing for the Gospel reading.

Most visitors I have learned are merely curious. It shows in the way they hold themselves, the things they talk about and how they dress. I think, too, many established residents also come and recite the Credo mostly from force of habit rather than from any deeply felt piety.

Emelia was different. When she arrived, the outer congregational area already was fairly packed, but she seemed to have easily made her way through the press to the bema. By tradition, this space had become reserved for men; any woman daring to approach would be rudely rebuked and likely molested. Penetrating to the center, people moved aside nevertheless without necessarily having noticed her approach.

I had just set the light blue, glass oil lamp on the bema's lectern with its windbreak and reflector for the Reader. After lighting the wick, I turned to start down the steps when I felt a different spirit in the courtyard, although at first I didn't know what caused the tingling down my spine. Turning back I met Emelia's lustrous eyes. She had reached the bema's edge and was staring at me. I stared back, paralyzed with a sudden sense we knew each other and our futures would be intertwined.

The Reader just then mounted the steps and elbowed me aside. I elbowed him back as I reached for my staff leaning against the lectern.

Opening the parchment codex to the day's portion, he read from 1 Corinthians 11:1.9. I knew this portion backward and forward. It was all about how men need to keep their heads uncovered and women must have their hair veiled. A man's head is "the image and glory of God," but not a woman's head. Women were made for men, but not vice versa, as I understood it. Any woman who didn't like this risked having her head shaved or worse.

I had lost sight of Emelia until the reading was finished and those who were baptized pushed their way into the apse for chanting psalms, to mumble their faith and take holy communion.

I, myself, had not been and have yet to be baptized. As long as I remain such, I may not enter the sanctum sanctorum but am given duties on the grounds and in the kitchen. Or, like this evening, I make things ready for the Reader in the courtyard, including lighting the warmth-giving braziers. I am content with this because it provides me with a sense of being a Fire Bearer; something my own readings beyond Scripture tell me has always been of sacred significance. Since first coming west, I have studied and learned much, having been helped by a few generous scholars and strong spirits who have opened their libraries, their minds and their hearts to me.

As the unsanctified visitors straggled out the gate to find their hostels, I saw that Emelia stayed behind. Her head, unlike mine, was uncovered, showing long, dark, curling hair that framed a lovely, golden-olive pigmented face with a prominent, straight nose and wide-set inquisitive eyes of a honey color. Hers could have been the face of Eve.

Eve who, as far as I or anyone else knew, certainly never had her head shaved, even after the alleged Fall.

Was she waiting for me?

Thinking this was so, I went up to her but before I could speak, she said this to me,

"So, your religion then is like this. It is for the glory of men alone?"

Like I said, Emelia was different. She reminded me in some ways of my old self, though even more outspoken.

In the weeks to come, I explained to Emelia that this desert place with its monasteries is where I grew into a woman. It was here, too, I began to better understand how people's minds are set in fixed patterns, not all of them wholesome or good. This place is where I also learned more ways—some subtle, some not—to protect myself, to survive, to camouflage and keep my core untouched.

After all, in such a cloistered place one hears every fart, cry, orgasm and grunt. On quiet nights one hears sounds from the latrines, every turd falling and piss raining down. It is worse coming out from the latrines oneself, having to face the knowing smirks of some men who seemed to find a thrill in such things. Not to mention the rawness of one's backside from papyrus wipes.

Emelia knew exactly what I was talking about.

She listened attentively as I told her the monastery to which I am attached is among the oldest desert monasteries, some claiming it was built by Abba Ammonius himself. But it seems that every church around Mt. Nitria makes a similar claim; and if not Abba Ammonius then Abba Antonius. I can't see why it matters. From what I have learned and seen here, the one called Christos hardly seems the kind who would give greater prominence to prayers rising through the roof of an edifice conspicuous for its founder. If, indeed, he hears and considers prayers at all.

Apparently not all agree, because the new Bishop in Alexandria has written more places of worship must be built and all existing basilicas are to be rehabilitated according to his new regulations. For instance, the bema here will soon be moved to the apse inside, off to one side of the altar. Even I can see this will necessitate changes to the order of service, which I have listened to from outside. It certainly will mean I no longer will be permitted to prepare things for the readings unless I accept the sacrament, but the new Bishop has explained the faith is transitioning to what the Christos foresaw when he anointed Apostle Peter as the foundation. Also, he says Church properties are at the forefront of making a needed bulwark against Arian and other heretics; the symbolon or communion host seeming no longer enough.

It seems just as I get accustomed to a certain routine, a predictable rhythm to my life, something comes along to make a hodge-podge of it. Despite what some might call my nonconformist beliefs, if they only knew, I have come to think of this place as my home. I have lived here since the community took me in after what everybody calls the Great Horror.

And for this I should be grateful. So Theophilus reminds me almost daily.

☽ 3 ☾

Emelia knew about the Great Horror. She knew this was the catastrophe that killed many thousands of people when a monstrous wave from the sea overran the coast, including the city of Alexandria to the north of here. But what she knew, she knew from hearsay only.

What I knew and how I knew I had not revealed to anyone before because it was too unbelievable. Nevertheless, I began by telling Emelia just a little of my experiences in Heliopolis following the disaster since she entreated me to tell.

I told her it happened when we both were eleven years old. I lived in Heliopolis with my family, while she lived in Carthage with hers.

Both cities were spared from the cataclysmic, crushing wave. Heliopolis due to the Nile delta acting as a long, staggered breakwater, although the river's current did run briefly backward, pushed by the surge of seawater. The aftermath of the coastal inundation, I told her, grew to be nearly as horrific as the original calamity.

Fearing future destruction from the sea, thousands of people fled Alexandria. Some took off for the countryside and the desert, but most took refuge in other cities, including Heliopolis, which was accessible both overland and by canal. At first, residents took in and aided those who came, but before long both resources and patience were stretched to breaking. In addition, the refugees carried a sense of panic and impending doom with them, like a plague defeating all attempts to put it down. Doomsday criers filled the city streets and neighborhoods and, indeed, it did seem like the end of the world threatened.

The small Roman garrison in Heliopolis, the one my father had served with, was unable to contain the lawlessness and violence that became a scourge. In fact, the few soldiers there often turned to brigandry themselves. The larger detachment of soldiers located in Memphis was of no help. They, too, were overwhelmed by the general confusion and dread, at least in the beginning weeks.

Before long actual contagion snaked its way into the community. Disease defiled whosever it touched such that they bloated with stinking, stygian corruption. Often the hands and feet of the afflicted became black and excruciatingly painful. Rat and crow populations swelled, feeding off garbage, waste and dead bodies left in the open.

Packs of wild dogs threatened people in their own homes and attacked the homeless people in their makeshift shelters, such that armed bands needed to hunt the brutes down. In time, the predations of miasmic disease, feral animals and depraved humans did more than the army could to quell the chaos and anarchy.

Then all at once the outsiders rushed back to their old homes, abandoning Heliopolis and other places as quickly as they had come, like locusts departing from decimated fields.

I survived as the whole world changed around me. I lost not just my father but also my mother and twin sister.

My mother had arranged for us to sail up the Nile to return to her home city of Meroe after my father's disappearance while on military assignment. Wanting a last look at familiar places before our departure, I went out before dawn the day the disaster struck; first to our old home, from which we had been evicted. Strangely, it had been destroyed by fire, and it seemed prudent not to hang about, so I went to visit my river haunts. As the sky was turning to daylight, the Great Horror struck.

☽ 4 ☾

I paused in my first telling to Emelia. From past experience, I was apprehensive at this early stage in our friendship about saying how I had actually witnessed those events. I quickly searched for the right words to relate my fantastic experience. To Emelia's credit, she did not interrupt or show surprise as I continued in the following vein, though still withholding crucial information.

"It is beyond me to explain how or why, but I was shown all of this as if from a great height. That is, I saw and heard the seafloor shake near the island of Crete, as everybody now knows. I then was witness to the waters receding from the distant coasts, building themselves up into the great wave that, when released by what god's hand, smashed everything in its path."

I continued, telling her how at first I stammered out my story to any who would listen but they clearly thought I was mad, like so many others who had been frightened by the trembling ground even as far away as Egypt. This was before news of Alexandria's destruction.

People at the time regarded me much as they had when I tried to tell of my earlier experience with Mother Nyla from some months before. Thereafter, I kept my own counsel and strove harder to find my mother and my sister, Tem.

As it happened, following my experience I must have lain unconscious in my skiff for a day and a night. I discovered when I went to the inn where my family had been staying they had left in a hurry. With a dry throat, I sprinted to the docks to find the boat my mother had planned for us to take. It had left earlier that very morning, as had many others. Frantically, I asked a dock worker where everyone had gone and he told me some craft masters took the shaking as an omen, so they immediately set out to the south. Others who may have been less inclined to see it as a portent of worse to come, but perhaps anticipating the hordes pouring from the cities, decided it could not hurt to get farther away.

I hastened to question other workers, dashing from group to group. Did they remember seeing my mother and sister getting on a certain boat? Everyone said they had been too busy working to have noticed.

For days I found it difficult to think. Nowhere did I find myself welcome. Old acquaintances from the markets looked at me like I was a stranger or else told me they had enough troubles of their own. I looked to the Roman garrison for help and fortunately my father's old friend Cunos gave me food and drink for small errands I performed. Other soldiers jeered at him. Those who recognized me because I was, in their eyes, the whelp of a deserter. Those who did not know me because I was just another street urchin making trouble like all the others.

This gave me the idea to join up with other children like myself who for whatever reason had no home. An empty stomach makes for recklessness and I had to do something to improve my situation.

☽ 5 ☾

When the terrible tide struck Alexandria and other cities, Emelia explained she lived in Carthage with her family. As Carthage is situated to the east of Crete, with several large islands and a peninsula between them, the city was spared any damage. Indeed, their harbor waters barely registered a surge. Her family, however, did have relatives and friends who lived in the east, so it was not long before stories reached them about the disaster.

As we were getting to know each other after her parents had packed her off to the monastery, to have her child where it would bring no disgrace upon them, Emelia was eager to know what things had been like for me after the legendary great wave.

"Tell me true, of your time in Heliopolis after the disaster. Tell me, after you realized both mother and sister had left you, what did you do? If it was Fate that brought you to take refuge in the desert—how? I am ready to believe whatever you tell me!"

I answered by saying again how I lived a safe distance from the sea, along the Nile, sheltered by the delta and its many branches, for Emelia only knew second or third hand details about the Trouble. Most people in those days preferred not to hear such stories, as if not speaking of the disaster made it as though it had never happened. Shaking my head and closing my eyes, I continued. Emelia's eagerness to hear me provided the opportunity both to tell her my name had been Tuya, as well as to warn her about some others whom she undoubtedly would encounter here.

"Wait!" interrupted Emelia. "You were called differently then? Tell me!"

"Yes, dear Emelia. The name my mother had given me was Tuya and my twin sister's name was Tem."

"I mean no offense, but such strange sounding names! Not Greek or some dialect thereof. Maybe something from the barbarian tribes to the north we hear about these days?"

"No. Not Greek. Not barbarian in the way you meant. Not Latin either. My mother said they came down from the ancient names of Egypt, Kush and Punt."

"I understand. Then it was not until you came here that you took the name Catherine. Is that right?"

"Well, it wasn't so much I took the name as it was given to me. The Church people did that with everybody they took in and I thought at the time if such was the price of having food and shelter, it would be foolish to argue. Besides, the Great Disruption changed everything else, so why not Tuya? As you see, the name Catherine has stuck with me all these years since."

"Yes, I want to hear of this. First tell me more about what happened to you while still in Heliopolis. We will visit there together some day for you to show where you used to live and walk about each day. From antiquity I have heard it said that city was greatly renowned in the time of pharaohs."

"Yes, it was, in a time that would be long forgotten if it were not for old monuments that have survived with their strange picture writings. But now I tell you, Emelia, it's a dump. A midden with little to attract, much less entertain, such able women as we two! I guarantee you would be bored senseless there. Anyway, where was I? Oh, right, I was telling you about the company I joined up with."

Having explained the challenges in finding enough to eat and avoiding the numerous occasions for coming to harm, I went on to tell Emelia about how a small group of children came to work together for mutual benefit. There were five of us in total. Three girls and two boys.

About a month after the disaster, I was leaving the garrison with a loaf of bread that Cunos had secreted from the soldiers' stores, when I encountered a boy about my age with his younger sister. They were dirty and looked quite hungry. I bade them come with me to a small grove of trees with shrubbery around it, where I would share my food with them out of sight of others who might take it. The boy was quite wary of my offer until I pulled aside my tunic to reveal the loaf I carried. At this, his sister clasped the lunula hanging around her neck and tugged on the boy's tunic, imploring him with her eyes to accept my offer.

My new friends proved to be much hungrier than me, so I had no problem letting them have the greater part of my treasure. After satisfying our bellies as best we could, the boy and I shared our stories with one another. His name was Delios, while his sister was called Latona. They came from a wealthy family in Heliopolis, which I already had surmised from the girl's amulet. It was silver and the chain included pieces of polished agate. After they told me that both parents had been murdered by three marauders who invaded their home, I was surprised these two still lived and the amulet remained in her possession.

Later in the day, we ran into my old antagonist, Peter, the baker's apprentice. At first, he tried his usual bullying, pushing Delios as he demanded of him to hand over any food or valuables he had. I stepped forward to intervene but he told me to shut up or else. This was my time to get even and I rushed at him, hitting him squarely in the chest and knocking him over. Peter picked himself up with tears and surprise in his eyes. His breath came rapidly through his whimpering mouth.

Peter would have turned and run, but Delios reached out his hand in a gesture of peace. He told Peter he could join us if he would change his manners and was so inclined; how four would get on better than three and so on.

The celerity with which Delios, who was smaller than Peter, took command of this situation amazed me. Especially impressive was how he converted Peter from a threat to an ally. I saw I had much to learn in this changed world and felt inwardly grateful for having met up with such as him. Although I knew I could have sent Peter on his way in worse condition than he came, for I already had humiliated him, I would not have been able or inclined to convert him to our cause.

This was summer and evening was late in coming on, while we still searched for a place to hide during the night. Peter timidly suggested that we go to a minor temple dedicated to Mithras on the northern outskirts of town. There was a wall around the grounds that we could easily scale and once on the other side we would find fruit trees. Possibly a priest would feed us, too, but importantly we would be safer from dogs and men in the night.

It was outside this wall where we found Harmonia. She sat with her back to the wall and it was clear she had been badly beaten. One eye was swollen shut, both lips were puffy, dried blood was smeared across her cheeks, bite marks appeared on her shoulders, and her arms were bruised. Her stola was torn but she had gathered the remnants around her breasts and privates. It looked to be stained with blood and other fluids.

Harmonia, who was fifteen years of age, was in no shape to go over the wall come nightfall. She had not only been savagely beaten, but also raped by her attackers. She made no mention of how many there had been, nor did we ask.

We made camp at that spot. The boys did go over the wall in search of food and water, returning with their find to share with our small troop. They took turns at the night watch, while the girls nursed Harmonia's wounds.

We decided early on though we might be able to help other children, it would not be wise to expand our group. Delios explained a larger band would attract attention, thus endangering everybody, as well as making it harder to secure our necessities. We agreed we would share knowledge, food when we could, but not take on others. In this way, we went on to work, beg or steal for food and shelter, until a series of events drove us from Heliopolis to seek refuge elsewhere.

☽ 6 ☾

"Catherine, how amazing your new friend Delios sounds. But you are equally so, in my estimation. As you told me, you lost your father, your home, your mother and sister—circumstances that would drive others to despair; yet, you overcame great adversity by your wits and audacity. I feel shame to have such ease in life compared with you."

"Thank you, Emelia, but as I have told you, others suffered much more than me. Harmonia is just one example and far from the worst, as I am now about to tell you. Besides, being with child and unmarried has brought you a different sort of hardship or so it seems to me."

“Oh, not at all! Even with the travel to here from Carthage, the pregnancy has been easy and I look forward to giving birth soon. When the child is old enough, we will return to our home. If you were to accompany us to stay with my family I would love this greatly and you would be most welcome. Will you consider this?”

“Well, that is still some time off, so let’s talk about it later. You may even decide not to return to Carthage, so many unexpected things can come up!”

“You are right. So, tell me more of your trials and adversities in coming to this place.”

I took a moment to organize my thoughts. Finally, setting my jaw and taking a breath, I gave Emelia some background to make more sense of things.

The world seems always to have been a dangerous place. Heliopolis was no exception. Prior to the disaster, one group or another was always harassing, if not outright attacking, others and this kept the army busy. The wealthy against the poor and vice versa. Jews, pagans and Christians against each other and Christians against other Christians when they did not see eye to eye on slight matters of belief or their own history.

The Great Horror seemed to license running amok, like the venom of certain spiders that inflames their victims with irrationality. By the time the seasons were turning, each day brought new outrages.

One day, our pentad had to dodge through a narrow alley to avoid being caught between two warring mobs. Missiles already were flying through the air between the two sides when we ran. To this day, I don’t know why they were going at each other, just that they were in a great fury over something and it would not be wise to stick around.

A few days later, early in the morning as we started out scavenging, we came upon a most horrible sight in the middle of a square. A man had been nailed to a tree through his wrists together over his head and through both feet along the sides of the tree. He was completely naked, his eyes had been gouged out and a rod had been pushed up his rectum. His manhood also had been cut away. A sign posted over the man's head proclaimed him a godless degenerate.

Shocked though I was, I looked more closely and am pretty sure I recognized Felix, the fish monger with whom I dealt in the marketplace.

"Catherine? Please, I am sorry. You do not have to go on. This must be very difficult for you and I am making you relive such terrible things."

"Just let me catch my breath for a moment. I will be all right, Emelia. It has just been such a long time since I thought about any of this. But I feel safe with you and I think it may be good for me to finally speak to someone about that time. Someone I can trust."

"Come. Let me hold you until you are at ease again. Here, use this to dry your tears. But if you wish to stop until another day we can wait."

"No. Really, I want to finish. Just keep holding me."

Picking up where I left off I related how as we all stared transfixed at this most gruesome crucifixion, the man's weight pulled on the nail and the sound of his flesh being ripped through reached our ears. His body fell forward but as his feet were yet secured, he dropped face down into his own blood and excrement at the tree's base with a stomach-churning thud. Laughter came from inside a nearby house. Shaking and unable to speak, none of us had to wait for Delios to tell us we should not stay where we were.

After this, we happened upon many more such executions, each worse than the ones preceding, if that's possible. Men, women and even children and some animals were tied or nailed up, their bodies broken, often eviscerated; their faces transfigured into ghastly masks with no eyes or ears, noses and lips cut off, cheeks sliced open from mouth to ears. More and more, it was not just a single crucifixion that made its appearance, but groups of people were killed, possibly families. Finally, the bodies were not just hung up for display but fires were built beneath them, leaving charred unidentifiable remains.

Whichever butchers were responsible for the different atrocities, they always left a sign to warn others. Usually it was a single word: Jew, Donatist, Arian, Melitian, heretic—dealing with religious belief; but soon, Catullian epithets such as cocksucker, buttfucker, whore, adulterer and so on appeared. Any reason for killing seemed as good as any other. Dying in the July Deluge seemed a mercy compared with all this.

One night as we huddled together for security as much as for warmth, we decided we should leave this city. Delios said he and Latona had family in Memphis.

In the morning, we set out by foot to hopefully leave these horrors behind.

☽ 7 ☾

Emelia gave birth to a son a few months after arriving at Nitria.

Though not a Christian himself, her father had settled an endowment upon the monastery for the care of his daughter and future grandchild. It is widely known the Christian community will take in those who otherwise might become outcast, especially unmarried pregnant women, if their families paid. The monastery justified this both as charity and the redemption of fallen women.

Her father also had inveighed upon the father of Emelia's lover to shame him into contributing to the endowment. This introduced certain complications to Emelia's situation.

The lover's name was Aurelius, whom she just called Aurel. He resided in the town of Hippo, to the west of Carthage, with his parents. I never figured out what Emelia saw in him, particularly as he appeared to be easily dominated and swayed by his mother. In fact, now that Emelia's son was nearing two years of age and would soon be weaned, word came about Aurel's mother wanting the boy to live in her household. I did not have to tell Emelia what a bad idea this was.

Although Emelia had named the child Orestes, the mother of her lover had sent a letter saying that he would henceforth be called Adeodatus or "Gift of God". When Emelia told me this, all I could think to say was, "What cheek!"

Nevertheless, my friend would have to leave the monastery before long. The endowment would soon reach the end of its period and both she and her son would be fit to travel. However, it looked as if she would not have to immediately return to Carthage. In a recent letter from her father, he explained that she might wish to stop over at the estate of his brother, located west of Lake Mareotis. Emelia's father said her uncle was in need of a new famulus, a chief housemaid, to manage the household there for some weeks or months while he, the master, was away in Alexandria and elsewhere.

This at least would delay any showdown with the woman who acted as if she were Emelia's mother-in-law. In our discussions, we speculated that maybe the woman's actions indeed presaged a future marriage to her son. I noted how I could not see Emelia living for long under the regime of Aurel's "Imperial Mother".

These events contrived to make Theophilus' comments about Emelia being forced from the monastery open to question. If her farewell already was in the offing, what business did he have suggesting it was any of his doing. Nevertheless, it certainly was perfectly in character for such a braying ass to stick his nose in other's business, as well as to take credit for things in which he had no part.

Furthermore, the idea about him taking over as my catechist and taking me on one of his desert retreats was most unsettling, for I had come to learn what a guileful man he could be.

Oddly, as I related to Emelia, it was partly due to Theophilus that I came to live in a Nitrian monastery shortly after my twelfth birthday.

Delios, his sister Latona, Peter, Harmonia, and myself had found sanctuary with his aunt and her husband in Memphis, just as Delios had hoped. These were good and generous people, but my plan was not to stay long, for I wished to be reunited with my mother and sister. However, days dragged into weeks, and weeks into months. By this time, refugees were returning to Alexandria and other coastal cities; nevertheless, the criminal attacks, forcible violations, and plundering only seemed to increase. The more vicious parts of the population in this larger city took license from the deplorable wickedness unleashed by the Great Horror.

Unlawful crucifixions that had become a horrific commonplace in Heliopolis found their way to Memphis, but with a grim twist. Certain victims first were flayed alive before their hanging, such that their whole body was one huge, suppurating wound. Strangely, all these had similar signs posted above them declaring them to be apostates and beasts.

The military finally clamped down hard on the city. Execution was decreed not only for murderers, insurgents, thieves, and so forth, but for those caught outside after curfew. Justice typically was administered by soldiers at the time of apprehension. Despite the curfew, Peter insisted on going out, as he said, to reconnoiter and sometimes would be gone for several nights. When asked where he stayed, he merely replied he had found some safe places where he could lie low.

Martial law curbed the crucifixions because it became harder to conceal during the act. However, while many fewer bodies were found groaning and putrefying on rough crosses, trees or buildings, the flaying continued unabated. Instead of hanging their human sacrifices out for display, the butcher or butchers just dumped the skinned victims in the streets. In doing so, they refrained from posting the usual epithets announcing the supposed crime being punished, making it seem that anyone might be marked for no reason.

It was under such circumstances that Delios' family decided to abandon Memphis, at least temporarily, until such time as things might return to a more civilized normalcy. Their decision was to sail to Athens as soon as possible, so there was no question of Peter, Harmonia and me being able or wanting to accompany them. Delios' uncle, however, had heard the desert monasteries were succoring those orphaned or widowed by the Deluge, and arranged for we three to join a caravan headed west.

A young man named Jason, who was assistant to the caravan driver, took charge of us. He was a querulous sort, always looking to argue about something to prove himself right about whichever side of an argument he took up.

He eventually stayed on in the religious community with us. I suspect much to the joy of his former master. Later, he changed his name to Theophilus.

Exhausted, I laid my head in Emelia's lap as she stroked my hair. Her touch, her voice, her scent soon had me fall into a deep sleep.

☽ 8 ☾

Emelia requested my assistance with the birthing when her time came. As this is considered women's work anyway, the midwife agreed. I had assisted countless others at their term, so was well experienced in birthing matters, as well as in administering to the dying and those already dead. With the seeming endless stream of women passing into and through this community, many of them dying in childbirth, it would be expected.

Some who come are mere children like I was when first I arrived. Others are of diverse ages. Before making his vows and becoming an Elder, Theophilus continued bringing displaced women and children into the community. To the best of my knowledge, few were with child when first they came, unlike Emelia. But unless a woman object strongly and be willing to make a commotion, she is assigned to a male catechist for training, only to find herself burdened by pregnancy before too long.

I would have none of that, declaring I would rather take my chances back in the city or wander the desert. Eventually, I was assigned to Sister Prisca.

My attraction to Emelia had been strong from our first meeting and it only grew stronger during the final months of her pregnancy. In fact, she had invited me, and the abbot approved at her request, to move in with her to the more spacious room she enjoyed to keep her company. If it is possible, I think I may have been just as excited as Emelia at the advent of her child. In fact, the closer she came to her time, the more relaxed and peacefully surrendered she grew; while I was ready to burst. For her sake, however, I maintained an outward calm and did all I could to indulge her.

Prior to Emelia's arrival, desert mothers had imparted much sound knowledge to me since my own coming to Nitria. Some of it to do with Church teachings; much more to do with the content of people's hearts, affections, attractions, and antipathies, as well. Nurturing the love I hold for Emelia and her child, hopefully has helped me regain some shard of pleasure I once took in this shattered world.

The arrival of her son Orestes thus was a great relief for us both. I have delighted in tending to mother and child together from the moment of his birthing, which I remember well. Although I had seen Emelia unclothed before, she seemed to me exceedingly beautiful during her labor, which was both brief and easy. Having assisted midwives before, I nevertheless felt my heartbeat quicken when Emelia parted her legs and, moving my hands closer to her *mouní* to assist the child, I could not resist touching her in that place with an appreciative sigh. I'm sure she was unaware of my little act of weakness.

Later, watching the boy suckle contentedly at her breast always sent a vague tingle through me, which I decided must be some incipient desire for a time when I might have a child of my own. Once he started to talk, he called me amita or auntie. For me, this all the more confirmed the bond of sisterhood I felt between his mother and me.

Helping Emelia with the care of her child was a great pleasure and diversion for me. Often when I was performing my assigned work tending the vegetables in the gardens—another one of my pleasures—I would catch a glimpse of mother and child playing together. Sometimes I would stop work to join them. As he got older, the boy especially delighted in hearing how the plum-colored mother's mark or nevus on his left calf meant he was destined for great things, like Alexander of old.

Times such as these also allowed Emelia and I more opportunity to converse, sometimes seriously, sometimes comically, and sometimes with a ribaldry that surely would earn censure if overheard.

"Catherine, you mentioned how your father taught you to read, to write and to do simple numbers, things to help in the marketplace and around town, but now you are very erudite, uncommon among women. How did this come about, especially in a place such as this?"

"I think, dear Emelia, it is precisely due to being in this place I have been able to broaden and deepen my education. It seems unlikely to me, had I stayed in Heliopolis or traveled south with my family, my education would have taken this road. I have not yet told you about the months I spent in a community of desert mothers south of here, where I was taught with much kindness and patience not only how to read more difficult texts, in both Latin and Greek, but how to think about what lies beneath the words on the page."

"Well, then, now that Orestes has sucked me dry and fallen into deep slumber, this may be the time to tell that story."

With a small smile and a sigh, I began.

"It so happened that one day during my fourteenth year, a certain Amma Talis walked out from the Red Desert to audit—that being her own word—the monasteries in Nitria and Scetis. Already, both settlements were major attractions in the Christian world, drawing visitors not only from Alexandria and

Carthage, but as far away as Palestine, Jordan, Damascus, as well as Rome and Gaul. Rumored to have a foul mouth, she certainly was a force to be reckoned with and the abbas, elders and brothers all trembled before her and the staff she carried with her.

"According to what she later told me, she had intended to stay but a few days but changed her mind after seeing what the monasteries had become. She called the patriarchs nothing but inn keepers, apostles of lies and ass wipes. Her stay lasted about six weeks, as she sought to understand not just what had happened but the direction events would take in the future.

"When she first arrived, the one who had become Theophilus was in Alexandria, where he had been spending more and more time studying oration and the law under the then Bishop. Shortly after his return, Amma Talis announced she would withdraw again to the wilderness. I was to join her.

"Some thought I was being punished because I had been assigned to serve her during her sojourn. In truth, I began a year of great hardship but even greater revelation and understanding."

☽ 9 ☾

"How long will we stop in this place, Amma. Is it just to rest for a while?"

"Why. Are you tired already. We have only walked two and a half days. Has your monastery softened you so? Don't be such a weakling. Unless you find the place of rest within yourself, you will never know what ease is, even if you live in a grand country villa or a rich city apartment. Or that shithole they call a monastery."

"Forgive me, but you know me well enough by now to know I am at my best when I am fully informed. How better to serve you, Amma?"

"What an impertinent little cunt you are! Don't try such tricks on me, or on anyone else for that matter. It fools you into thinking you're on top. People who are far more clever than you see right through such devices. You'll end up at their mercy if you're not careful. You'll find a little humility goes a long way, as does knowing when to keep your goddamned mouth shut.

"To answer your question though, child, we will be staying in this small community for some time. I have so much to teach you and you, my dear little bitchling, have so very much yet to learn."

"Yes, Amma. It is as you say."

"Besides, young Catherine, it has not escaped me your time of month is upon you or nearly so."

Thus began my second education.

For some reason, I thought I would be lucky. Tem had begun her monthlies nearly three years earlier and though my breasts had started in and were getting more rounded, and though I had nice soft hair growing on my mouní, there had not been any signs of bleeding, just some whitish stuff over the past couple of months. Because of what had been done to my sister, I think I had convinced myself I did not need to go through menses to leave behind childhood.

The next week was horrible. My head already had begun to throb and my abdomen cramp after a day out on the road with Amma Talis. It was like the onset of plague that finished so many after the deluge. I did not want to appear weak to Amma, for despite being well into her fifth decade she was extremely hardy. So I pushed on, saying nothing. By the time we reached the more remote community, I was nearly in tears and just wanted to curl up in a dark room somewhere. My smart-mouthed comment to Amma, which I knew to be arrantly discourteous, had been more to cover my distress.

Despite being rudely reprimanded by Amma Talis, she was very caring and sympathetic about my no longer deniable emergence into womanhood.

It was only after the bleeding had nearly stopped I found the courage to ask her whether I would have to go through the New Moon ceremony. Amma tilted her head to one side and looked at me for a long moment before sighing and saying,

"No, Catherine, we do no such ceremonies out here. While most of us understand the reason for such things, it is enough your body does what it does, with or without you wanting it. Besides, the nights are much too cold these days to be gamboling about after dark...and there are things out there you don't want to meet up with, moon or no moon."

"What kinds of things? I've heard only stories."

"Jackals. Vampires. Spirits. It is said the Pharaoh's lost armies yet roam these parts. Although the desert also can give you redemption. I should know. Anyway, just wait until you reach my age and the second change comes looking for you! Now, do you think you are feeling well enough for a little work and to begin your studies?"

Surprisingly, although the community had only about twenty residents, who referred to themselves collectively as the Friends, it was equipped with a library well-stocked with papyri scrolls. Everyone had free access to the room which housed the scrolls and everyone took turns at being their guardian or the one they called the librarian. This duty typically lasted a day, but could be longer if a person was injured or too ill for the daily work routine but not so ill that they were bed-ridden. This meant that every couple of weeks or so, it became my turn to sit in the library.

My first visit to the library felt as if I had stepped through a magic portal. While it held maybe but a few dozen scrolls, I never had seen so many in one place before. I had to brace myself on the door jamb due to feeling vertigo. For a moment, it was like being back in Mother Nyla's tent. Though new to me the place also felt familiar.

As a trainee I had to learn what each scroll generally contained. So, if a Friend came in and requested an Aristotle or a Cicero, I needed to know in which box to look. I made many mistakes in the beginning. Putting them back from where I got them proved to be just as difficult at first, but people tolerated my errors. Usually, as I reached for one box or another, a Friend would say something like,

"Not that one. A little over to the right. No, one more. Now you have it!"

Mostly though, whoever was librarian was by herself or himself, as there were a handful of men in the community, too. This provided me with opportunities to not only memorize the filing system, but to read. As it turned out, I was expected to read on my own, for after each stretch in the library, Amma would ask me what I had read that day. Unlike my catechist at the monastery, she then would ask me what I thought about what I had read. I did better with the Latin texts, figuring out the meanings of words I did not know from their context. Greek proved more difficult. I understood the everyday Greek spoken in the towns and markets, but philosophy, sciences, mathematics and music were a constant challenge, not to mention first having to learn their alphabet and spellings.

When Amma Talis was not with us, for she had told me she serves other communities, someone else telling me that she travels a regular circuit throughout the year – another Friend, always an older woman, would take over this gentle form of instruction. I found I liked the community's method of teaching, for I learned things much quicker under their tutelage. It was very different from how we were taught at the monastery, where asking questions was, if not overtly punished, very much frowned upon. It gave much more respect to the pupil. While there was rote memorization involved, especially of poetry and certain mathematical principles, finding out for myself what a writer's ideas were and the logic behind their presentation made learning into an adventure for me.

Due to our full work schedules when not in the library, there was little chance to read during most days. After the evening meal, everyone gathered in what I suppose would be called the community's church. This was a hexagonal building, just large enough to accommodate us all. Once gathered here and sitting quietly for a while, one or more Friends would start a low humming, which before long became a kind of wordless song, with others joining in; some picking up the main thread of it and others creating their own strands of sound that strayed but in their way wound around, in and out, higher, lower, over and under the main theme. Everyone seemed free to do whatever she wanted, yet knew just what was needed to make the whole into something beautiful.

Eventually, I learned this is what is called harmony and that people are able to achieve it naturally if allowed the freedom. The chanting I had heard at the monastery during their services—well, it seemed they could learn something from the Friends, so as not to sound so forced.

Song was followed by what the Friends called testimony. This was simply the expressing of thoughts or memories and feelings that had come up during the day. Or it could be the sharing of a dream from a previous night. Those who listened might nod or grunt upon hearing a speaker, but rarely commented on what was said, unless asked by the speaker.

When it appeared no one had anything left to say, the group disbanded after a few moments of silence.

That's how things usually went, but one evening during my fourth month with the Friends, a man by the name of Justin announced he had had what he called a true dream. In this dream, a great wind came and blew down the buildings in which we lived and killed many inhabitants. The powerful wind also

lifted the stone—weighted cover from our well, thus opening it to the elements to be filled with sand so there was no water for the survivors. Justin went on to say a man, who he described as looking like Jesus Christ or maybe Abba Antonius, walked into the community after the storm, promising to restore the well if only the Friends would abandon their sinful ways and embrace the teachings written in the codex he carried.

Much discussion followed, which soon shifted into argument over how to interpret such a dream or even to credit it. Such upheaval had never occurred at these gatherings before that night.

Many left as voices were raised and I joined those who left. On my way back to my compartment, a woman by the name of Chenna who carried a carved staff fell in step with me.

☽ 10 ☾

Twenty-six years old Chenna came from a place I had never heard of called Wagadugu, where they have their own ghana or king. This land is far to the southwest, on the great desert's underside, so it has been untouched by either Rome or Carthage.

She was taller than me and lithe, with coarse-looking black hair that was very soft to the touch, as I later discovered. Chenna had a serious and at times caustic demeanor outwardly but I learned that both sun and moon shone brightly on her inside. Not only was she fluent in Latin and Greek, but she knew other tongues beside her native one. She proved to be much quicker than me at putting her observations together and making insightful determinations. As such, Chenna became for me a source of knowledge about many things, including the community of Friends and the people who had settled here.

This is how our conversation went on the evening after the disruption caused by Justin's dream:

"So, Catherine, do you mind if we drop the 'Friend' business. I would prefer us to be friends rather than just call each other that."

"Yes, of course. I have hoped we would be able to do more than exchange formalities and pleasantries during the day, and get to know each other. As you can imagine, I am quite curious about you and thought maybe you came from around where my mother is from."

"I am darker than anyone else in the community, including yourself, so it is natural for you to wonder. But, no, I am not of your mother's people. Amma Talis has told me about you, which is how I know. She also forewarned me to be on the lookout for the kind of break we witnessed earlier tonight—"

"What? You mean Amma has been expecting this? Why?"

"Catherine, do you know why there are so many people in the desert now? Why many seek communities such as we have enjoyed here?"

"What I have been told is in these troubled times—especially since the Great Horror—people are looking for certainties. They are seeking to be closer to God and believe getting away from the distractions and vicissitudes found in the city helps them do this."

"Yes, for some that no doubt is true, but let me tell you something more. Just so you know, what I will tell you comes directly from Amma's own experience and teaching.

"Sixty years ago, your great king Constantine issued the Edict of Milan, by which he decriminalized Christianity. This is history as it is written. Ever since, different men have been arguing and fighting with each other over what exactly Christianity is, including the nature of their prophet or god, if you will. Over this same period, your Roman Imperium had become so large it split in two, with kings in both the east and the west. There is great disarray in this empire, which has allowed ruthless men to use the new religion of Christianity to their advantage. It did not take long before these men, many of whom have taken on the title of bishop, found they could use their new-found authority to advantage. In a short time, they have accumulated wealth to grow their power and this gives them an appetite for even more. As we know, the greatest source of wealth lies in property.

"Are you aware of how the Church has so quickly become the means for persecuting others with whom they do not agree?"

"If by that you mean the conflicts with the Arians, Donatists and others, I know about these only too well from the time right after the deluge."

"What is called the Great Horror quickened the pace of persecutions, but they started much earlier. Amma Talis could tell you much about that."

"She is gone for longer stretches now, so I don't get to speak with her much. Also, when we do talk it is more about the things I am studying and what I am thinking. There is little room for her to tell me stories about herself or confide in me."

"Amma understands. This is why she instructed me to take you aside if during her absence the break we witnessed tonight should occur."

Chenna and I talked long into the night. As an outsider to our world, she knew more of our history than the smattering I had begun to acquire through my readings and discussions. She told me how the officials pushing the burgeoning Church would hound certain wealthy people, primarily pagans and Jews in the beginning, including threatening them with criminal legal actions. Their aim was to drive them away, if not outright kill them, so they might confiscate their properties. They still do this, but have added another stratagem to their campaign, which is to go after women who have inherited property from a father or a husband.

While a woman is grieving or may be too young and naïve to know better, the bishops and their supporters convince her she will find solace and fulfillment with their Jesus Christ. In this way, they connive to have her donate her inheritance to the Church, which then will care for her the rest of her days. This care consists of her taking a vow of poverty and abstinence; taking up residence in a small room, a cell, connected with a bishop's grand house; and leading a life of prayer and fasting, so as not to consume too much. In this way, she joins those called the Virgins of God, even if she has had children already.

Amma Talis, so Chenna related, was just such a woman. That is, after her husband was taken away by illness, the estate he had built through his own efforts was targeted by a suffragan of Bishop Athanasius. She refused to follow their path, so was harassed into abandoning everything to save her own life. She fled to the desert, where she now consoles others and serves as teacher to those strong enough to abide her methods.

The Church is very clear, she said, about what it calls the Christianization of space and this is one way of accomplishing it. Along the way, it has created thousands of desert refugees in a way the deluge could not, because they have become permanently dispossessed and have nowhere to turn. Added to this, the Church has encouraged city people, also by the thousands, to make pilgrimage to the desert monasteries. By doing so, contact is maintained with the retreats and hermitages, the better to assure the religion in the desert will be at one with the conventions promoted by the bishops.

Amma Talis fears this plan is meeting with success, for many who originally fled the reach of the Church now find the pilgrims view them as teachers and spiritual guides, which is turning their heads. Flattery can be a most powerful weapon. As can money, for the steady stream of pilgrims and tourists creates commerce, which the patriarchs, abbots and deacons are loathe to cut off.

This information coming from Chenna was disquieting, to say the least. Had she not said it was Amma Talis herself who had revealed these many things, including from her own experience, I think I would not have put much store in it. Also, as of yet, I did not see how this had anything to do with Justin and what Chenna called the "break."

There was much here to ponder, but Chenna was to give me little time for thinking.

"We have talked much tonight, Catherine, and it is late. I advise you to get a good night's rest, for tomorrow your physical training must begin."

"What are you talking about? What physical training?"

"Undoubtedly, you have noticed both Amma Talis and I carry a strong staff with us everywhere we go."

"Yes. I supposed they are an aid for long journeys on foot."

"Less than you might think. Their real purpose is for self-defense."

"Self-defense? Chenna, I've always been able to take care of myself and—"

"Catherine, there will be times you will encounter those who are much stronger than you. Amma Talis wants you to learn the art of stick fighting from me, just as she has learned."

"You're telling me you taught Amma Talis how to fight using that staff?"

"Yes and from what I have seen of you, you will be a very quick student."

"Is this really a proper thing for a woman to learn?"

"Believe me. Carrying and knowing how to use a staff could mean the difference between life and death for a woman. Where I come from women are not only taught fighting skills but compete with each other. Everyone understands and respects female power this way. If you prove a quick study with the staff, I may also teach you ngolo. This is a beautiful but deadly way of fighting using your feet. When done well it is like a dance."

And so, another part of my education began.

☽ 11 ☾

"The camel should be passing through any day now."

"What do you mean by that, Chenna? In my time out here, I've yet to see any caravan come near our community, much less visit it. Donkey trains, yes, to bring in needed supplies, but never a camel caravan."

"Not a caravan. Not camels, Catherine. Camel. Just one. She is alone, usually arriving here during the night. That's why you have not seen her, because you probably have been asleep."

"So, how do you know about this camel? Now you chastise me for sleeping. Don't you sleep?"

"Calm down. It wasn't meant as a criticism. But have you never wondered why it is we have such a fine library in a community as small as ours. You must have noticed, too, that new scrolls appear from time to time and others disappear. It does not happen just by magic, you know, nor do se'irim, the evil djinn prowling the desert, tote them in and out on their hairy backsides!"

"Forgive my choler. You are right. Now that you mention it, I just assumed visitors from Alexandria, brought them.. It seemed the most sensible explanation to me, Chenna, seeing there is a grand library there."

"Sensible. Mm-mmm. And you are the sensible one, are you not. Be careful of sensible explanations, I tell you. They are limited by what your five senses inform you about the world and there is so much more to this life we cannot see, hear or smell."

Who did she think she was talking to? I protested,

"Well, I think I know something about experiences past the common, everyday variety…"

Cutting me off, Chenna replied,

"Be that as it may, soon you shall know the truth about the library you find so enthralling. I will make sure you are awake when it happens. The camel is coming."

The next two nights I stayed awake longer than usual, partly in wait for the storied camel and partly to spite Chenna. Due to my work for the community and training with Chenna however, sleep overcame me before long. Chenna's mysterious camel did not arrive and I paid for the lack of sleep during the day, adding to my irritation. On the third night however, just when I was about to give up and lie down, I heard a clinking, almost musical sound outside. There was something familiar about it, though I couldn't say what.

A shadowy figure appeared in the doorway to my room. It was Chenna, with a blanket wrapped around her shoulders and her hand gripping her ever-present staff. Whispering, she told me to put on something warm and follow her outside. Like her, I took up my blanket as a wrap but left my training stick behind.

Two Friends already had come out from their rooms and were heading over to the library across from our meeting room. One carried a lamp, the flame of which cast the other Friend's shadow back our way. As the lamp bearer got closer to the library, I made out a large shape on the ground. It was, indeed, a camel laying down with its forelegs folded under.

I looked around for the person who had ridden the camel to our community. Seeing no one, I assumed he had stepped away to either relieve himself or maybe find something to eat.

Edging closer to the camel, I looked from behind the two Friends, both of whom were men, to see the flickering lamp light dancing in the camel's large eyes, which were looking directly at me. Just then, it gave a soft snort and nodded its great head up and down as if in recognition. And at that moment I realized this had to be the same camel I had encountered years ago when Agrippina had towed me through the rank-smelling camel bazaar in Heliopolis. The camel's harness had the same mirror stones decorating it, which accounted for the krotalías-like rhythm when she walked. Though a blanket was draped over her sides, I had no doubt I would find some arcane design shaved onto her sides beneath it.

While Chenna and I watched, the men opened tasseled saddlebags hanging along both sides of the camel's hump. From this, one withdrew half a dozen or so scrolls and some other items; while the second carefully replaced these with scrolls which presumably came from our community library. The first man took the new scrolls with him to the library, while the other then held out a saboos feed ball for the camel in the palm of his hand.

To my surprise, when the camel had finished eating, it pushed up to a standing position, shook the dust from itself, and on its own started to walk away. As the mirror stones resumed their soft cadence, I looked around for the rider. Seeing no one, I asked Chenna where he might have gone.

"Oh," she said, "There is no rider. Our camel friend knows her way quite well. From here, she goes to other communities before returning to the city."

The riddle raised by the library's scrolls solved itself for me that night, but I was dumbfounded by the return of Mother Nyla's she-camel—for it must have been hers—into my life after so much had happened.

Following these events, which brought me closer to Chenna despite what I felt to be her abrasiveness, I realized I had fallen into unmindfulness. After the upheavals, ordeals and confusion of earlier years, the desert communities had given me a reposeful sanctuary. They had been like the great Ark of legend about which I had read, saving me after the deluge. Since then, I had settled into a regular, everyday rhythm, not always easy but definitely predictable. Plus, I was learning many new things thanks to the library. As unsettling as Chenna could be, for her intelligence, knowledge and physical discipline, as well as her sometimes condescending attitude, I realized she was right. As long as my basic needs were taken care of, I was too accepting of and comfortable with things as they appeared.

So, here was another person from whom I could learn much, if only I could get past my difficulties with her. My biggest obstacle, I must admit, was she was much more in Amma Talis' confidence and therefore privy to special reports and instruction than I could ever hope to be.

At least, this is what I told myself. Amma Talis' next visit to the community of Friends soon nullified this conclusion. Not only did she pour out her concerns and fears to me, but she showed me something so utterly disturbing I will never forget it.

☽ 12 ☾

"We three have more in common than you may know. Chenna and Catherine, you have both encountered my old friend and dearest sister, Mother Nyla. In fact, like me, in a sense you were chosen by her; although she would deny it, preferring to say she was told to reach out to you. To us."

"Yes," said Chenna. "She told me she had seen in her magic stone how I would cross the great desert, eventually to live near the far-reaching river that runs through Egypt; though I have yet to see that river."

"And Agrippina told me I, too, had been found by Mother Nyla's seeing stone. Unfortunately, I have no memory of what her stone showed her when I was invited to her tent…"

Chenna and I were excited by the mention of Mother Nyla, each of us wanting to tell the details of our encounters. Amma Talis interrupted us, telling us to be still, as she had news from Mother Nyla.

The first piece of news was Mother Nyla was dead.

Our excitement melted to grief. With tears flowing down our cheeks, we looked to Amma through blurry eyes for explanation.

On her way back to our community, she explained, she had been intercepted by Agrippina, who is Mother Nyla's granddaughter. Agrippina took Amma by swift camel, the very she-camel I had encountered in the marketplace in Heliopolis, to an encampment where Mother Nyla laid ill. The old woman had prepared messages for Amma to deliver and bade her do so following her death. She also admonished everyone not to grieve for her, as she would be joining the Great Mothers, some of whom she told Amma were already in the tent waiting for her release.

Amma Talis said she had been aware of a pure vibration surrounding Mother Nyla and, indeed, filling the large tent like soothing but, to her ears, barely audible music; so had no doubt what Mother Nyla was telling her was true.

Shortly thereafter, Mother Nyla closed her eyes, smiled, and reached an arm out as though to take someone's hand. As she breathed her last, her arm remained suspended in the air for a long moment, then fell to the bed.

Several women, directed by Agrippina, came in to tend to the body. Agrippina though took Amma Talis with her to another chamber in the big tent, where a hot, calming drink was waiting for them. After a respectful time, Agrippina told Amma that her grandmother had entrusted her scrying stone to her care several weeks previous. It was then she informed Amma about the visions given her by the stone.

In this way, Agrippina confirmed what Amma Talis already suspected of Justin and the future break in the harmony of our community before her return. Agrippina revealed that Justin was an agent for the Bishop of Alexandria and had fabricated the dream solely to sow doubt and dissension in the community. As most Friends were women, the purpose also was to put a man in charge over the community's governance and trading relations with others. Such a change already was underway, as Justin declared a second dream had been given in which the holy man with the codex had declared he should be a deacon, the better to lead the Friends to the true religion.

Though few took him seriously, he announced he would travel to Alexandria to confer with the ecclesiastical authorities about the veracity of his dreams. He had no doubt he would return with a written authorization to guide the remote flock of Friends.

Immediately prior to his departure, disaster struck the community in the middle of the night. The library was burned to the ground with all of its precious contents. Though most considered it an accident, a few who believed Justin's declaration saw it was a further sign from the heavens. I knew otherwise.

That night I had fallen asleep in the library while reading past normal hours. I was awakened by the sounds of flames which already had engulfed the door, barring my exit. Fear for my life brought me fully conscious and alert. In a panic my first thought was to grab as many scrolls as I could to save them from the flames. The roof above me already was ablaze however and, realizing I had but seconds to act I pushed the reading table hard at the fiery door with an unnatural strength, smashing it and continuing through what seemed a wall of flame, singeing my hair and catching my robe on fire, forcing me to roll on the ground to prevent my being burned.

Smoke coming from my clothes and the stench of burned hair in my nostrils, I stood up to scream for help. At that moment I saw a man standing in the shadow of another building. He watched me in silence for a moment, then turned and left without raising the alarm.

With such news from me, Amma Talis said this confirmed both I am under some spiritual protection and also that the takeover by the Bishop was as good as done. When Justin returned, he would have a written order over the Bishop's seal. Thus, it was time to act.

For Amma, that action was to go east after delivering the messages entrusted to her, to the town of Antinopolis on the banks along the Upper Nile. The last two messages she had left for delivery in the west were for Chenna and me. Reaching into her bag, she removed a palm-sized, double-leaved diptych made of wood and handed it to Chenna.

We had, of course, seen such things before. It was a tabula cerata or writing board. When opened up it revealed a wax tablet written upon by a stylus. A message inscribed on this inside surface said Chenna was to accompany Amma Talis and assist her in establishing a monastery for women.

Upon hearing Amma would be leaving, likely never to return here, my jaw fell open and my eyes widened. Then after learning that Chenna would be going with her, I felt my body temperature rise and I let out a loud breath.

"Huh?"

"Don't worry, my impatient Catherine. Mother Nyla has not forgotten you."

Amma took from her bag a small box, which she then handed to me.

Taking the box, I tried putting a smile on my face but could feel it waver. Despite a sinking feeling in my stomach, I opened the box.

Inside was a disk. Running through the diameter of the disk was a groove, wider in the middle while narrowing to points at both edges. Embedded about a knuckle joint's distance from what could be the top edge was a rounded blue gemstone the size of a country chickpea. Around and about the furrow I saw markings inscribed on the disk similar to those on the medallion I had received years earlier. Then my eyes lost their focus.

No one said a word as I sat staring into the box, shoulders humped, chin down and a frown on my face. My eyes began to water again but before tears would come, I got hold of myself. Hitching my shoulders up, I made a slight smile and said in a small voice,

"It's nice. I mean, it's very nice. And thoughtfully given, I'm sure."

The others remained quiet. I could not quite look at Chenna, but forced myself to say,

"I'm really happy for you, Chenna. You know, you finally get to go to the Nile, just like Mother Nyla saw."

My heart had shrunk to about the size of a dried-out lentil. Hearing Amma Talis would be traveling to the Upper Nile had given me a ray of hope for eventually being reunited with my mother and sister. That ray had been just as quickly extinguished.

Just as I was about to excuse myself and maybe do something stupid, like run out into the desert and never come back, Amma gently put a hand upon my arm.

"Child, of course you are disappointed. I am, too. I want you to come with me on my mission, along with Chenna. But that is not to be. No use spilling useless tears over it. So, let me tell you about this gift, as Agrippina has explained it to me. Perhaps this will help to cheer you. If not, at least you will know you have a mission of your own and, from what little I can understand, one much greater than what I am tasked to do. This is something that Agrippina says she wishes to discuss with you the next time you are together."

☽ 13 ☾

We made preparations to leave the community of Friends and return to Nitria, my old home. We wanted to go before Justin's grand entry. The plan was for Amma and Chenna to stay in Nitria a few days, then go on to Alexandria where they would catch a canal boat to the delta and a branch off the great river to go south. I would stay behind.

Amma took me aside one afternoon before her departure to tell me to get ready for a brief expedition in the coming night. It would be only the two of us, for there was something I needed to see for myself or I would never believe it otherwise. She advised me to make no mention of our leaving to anyone, not even Chenna.

Feeling now I was getting something special, I ducked out after dinner to join Amma Talis before the nightly gathering. There was little risk we would be missed because since Justin's initial big scene, a kind of anarchy had descended upon those meetings. Not only were the discussions more unruly, but the singing lacked its previous easy harmonies. As a result, many residents chose to return to quarters after the evening meal.

Our course took us upon a little traveled path out from the community's western edge, as though we were chasing after the already downed sun. We had only stars to light our way, as the moon would not show itself for hours yet. After about two hours, Amma veered left from the path, heading south into a mountain ravine. Before long I lost track of time so could not guess how long we climbed. But the rocks and boulders over and around which we ascended had lost the heat from the day and grown cold before we reached our destination.

Amma stopped by a group of boulders appearing to have a narrow passage winding between them. Instead of taking that passage, she looked around as if to see if anyone might have followed or be waiting for us. Then she veered off the path to the left, picking her way around a thicket of desiccated bushes to a hidden cleft in the side of the ravine. Here, she stopped again and in a low voice asked a seemingly nonsensical question.

"Do you wonder why the stinking bishops and their people commit their holy books to skins and not to papyrus?"

Confused, I shook my head. Now that we had stopped, I was shivering, too.

"Catherine, what you are about to see—well, I know you had seen many terrible things following the Great Horror, but please prepare yourself. Your earlier experiences were the result mostly of people's anger and fear. What you are about to see now will take you into the heart of a very dark magic used by evil men whose only goal is power.

"I would not have brought you to this shithole if I had a choice, but both Mother Nyla and Agrippina insisted this is necessary for what is coming for you."

The cleft was about four times our height and went for about five or six body lengths, after which it opened up into a kind of natural amphitheater. Scattered boulders had been arranged like seats on a down-sloping ramp of earth that stopped before a great stone ledge like a stage for actors or a large bema. A crooked path or aisle ran from our entrance to the ledge, but was only dimly seen through a cold mist slithering along the ground and among the boulders.

By this time, the moon had risen to shine a bleak, funereal light into the dark socket of this sunken space. Amma took me by the hand and led me down towards the front ledge.

As my eyes adjusted to the interplay of light and shadow, I discerned several human-like figures sitting hunched over on rocks near our path and froze. Amma looked at me, nodded, and then continued to pull me forward. I could not help but look back, in dread that those figures might rise up and follow us. Their faces were clearer from this angle, so I could see not only were these the remains, the wreckage, of the dead but that most had been dead for some time. The ruined hollows of their eyeholes sucked at our living flesh for trespassing their fearful, fetid grave.

Turning back to Amma, I stepped on something like a dried stick that made a cracking sound under my foot. Looking down, I made out a skeletal human arm ending in a hand with fingers bent in supplication. I had broken the bones making up a forearm, which made me shriek such that Amma had to quickly and firmly shush me.

The worst was yet to come. Once we reached the great ledge, which was about waist high by me, Amma turned to face what might be called the auditorium, nudging me to do the same.

In the front-most row of stone benches, bodies of men and women had been posed. Some seated with tree branches for support; others kneeling behind their bench in silent prayer, if the unheard screams from their leaning heads might be considered a form of worship. These bodies were less rotted than the ones we had passed in the back. Under the merciless moonlight, it was clear that each had been skinned.

Memories of Memphis flooded my brain. I fainted.

I regained consciousness with Amma gently slapping my cheeks and whispering my name.

"Catherine. Catherine. Wake up. I fear there is more for you to see before we can go."

What worse horror could there be than what I already had seen. Breathing shallowly, I got back on my feet, shaking. Amma had me lean over the stone ledge until I had calmed down sufficiently. With difficulty, I tried to blot from my mind the abominable scene at my back.

"Take a couple of deep breaths. That's it. Now, breath more slowly. Good. Now, one last thing. Look up from where we stand to the East Wall of this place. Yes, look up. Tell me what you see."

At first, I could not put together in my mind what it was I was seeing. The moon shone upon it fully, making it look like a chaotic patchwork of shadows on a bright field of stone. Gradually, an image took shape, but it was too unbelievable to be real.

If this had been an actual theater, the stone ledge would have been the proscenium, while the wall behind it would be called the scaenae frons or the backdrop presiding over the performance.

Seemingly carved into this backdrop was a massive head of a great beast in profile. Like something from a nightmare, its open jaws were lined with sharp teeth as large as my hand. The place where the enormous eyes would be were but cavernous holes. The same for the nostrils. I realized then this was a skull, sepulchral and lording over the dead humans in its immensity. I had no doubt such a dire maw might swallow me whole.

Trailing from the head and likewise embedded in the rock was a bone-like structure, something like a spine or tail disappearing into the rock only to reappear farther down from the head. A protuberance like a prodigious clawed foot near the bottom of the rock face had nearly battered its way out, seeking a foothold in the world of the living.

All Amma and I could hear at this time was the beating of our own hearts, which pounded out the same message:

Escape!

We went back to the entrance as quickly as the rubble—strewn aisle with its human detritus would permit. Before entering the great crevasse, I swung around for a last look. Stammering, I appealed to Amma,

"But, who? Why?"

Amma yanked hard on my arm, but not before I saw or imagined I saw someone moving among the shadows. Once we had descended the ravine and regained the trail eastward, Amma said in a voice like I had never heard from her before,

"Catherine, you ask who would do such things? This is some devil's notion of a church. Yes, someone's idea of a church, where a monster is worshipped and the books are written in blood on the hides of we poor mortals.

"Be wary, Catherine. You can be sure if you have not encountered this demon yet, you will. You will, for so it is prophesized."

☽ 14 ☾

"Your tale is most ominous, dear Catherine. Nightmares must torture you while you sleep."

"Oh, Emelia, if you only knew. You can imagine once Amma Talis and Chenna left, I felt very scared and lonely. After Amma's warning, I didn't know who to trust and kept very much to myself until you came. Even now however, as you have discovered, I wake trembling with cold sweats in the night."

"I am so sorry for you. Sorry for you to bear this burden. But do you have any opinion as to the one your Amma warned of? It was several years ago you were taken to that nether world."

"At first, I suspected everyone. I watched to see who went into the desert south and west of here, whether openly or by stealth. Many tourists are taken to my old community of Friends to meet with their new deacon, the same Justin I told you about, who now fancies himself an enlightened teacher; but where they go from there, if they go, I cannot say. There are just too many people to keep track of and all of this was causing me great headaches. So, I just do my work and bide my time.

"One thing that has helped me is before she left Amma Talis gifted me with her fighting staff. Like a talisman, I keep it near, though I have never yet had to put it nor my new skills to the test.

"Besides, now I have you and Orestes to make me happy!"

"As you make we two happy, so let us not stay on such a somber subject. Now I know why you keep that staff in our quarters. It is good to know Orestes and I are so well protected. But you have yet to tell me about the disk that you were gifted. I would hear about this."

I pulled the medallion up from my bosom, holding it out in my palm for inspection. The disk Mother Nyla had sent to me fit perfectly into the original amulet I had found in my bed after my first encounter with her. Also, the blue stone fit perfectly over the hole in the first disk. Thus, I have no doubts about its source.

Agrippina had instructed Amma Talis to tell me about the necklace. First, I was to understand there may yet be other pieces to this thing. I only have two at this time; any remaining ones will come in their own time. I also am to understand this is not a lunula or amulet as such, although I may find that it protects me some time in the future when it is complete. So, if not a good—luck piece or a bit of decoration, what then. Apparently, it is a device of some kind. According to Agrippina, it could be something like an astrolabe or possibly a lens but one with a special purpose. A purpose I would have to discover for myself. Amma could tell me no more.

Both front and backside of the new disk have a dense network of crisscrossing lines, symbols and characters. I explained I remained in the dark about what the significance of any of this might be, despite having searched in the libraries in both Nitria and the community of Friends. I might have asked someone else about their meaning, but frankly did not feel secure in doing so.

What if the device proved to be something that should not be in the possession of someone like myself? What if it is in some way connected with the baneful person behind the depraved church in the mountains?

The device continued to baffle me, though the addition of the piece with the blue gemstone seemed to give it greater artistry and status.

☽ 15 ☾

A few days before the start of Lent, a driver showed up to take Emelia and Orestes away from the monastery. As her father had suggested, his daughter and grandson would travel as far as the west bank of Lake Mareotis, where Emelia would temporarily assume the duties of famulus to her uncle, the scholar Theon. Their transport was a two-wheeled, covered wagon called a carpentum drawn by two mules.

Our eyes were red and both of us were sniffling, wiping at our noses—already missing each other. My chest ached and I'm sure Emelia's did, too. As usual when feeling a strong emotion, I clutched at my medallion to help me focus.

We had passed the whole night in reminiscence and tears. Little Orestes, of course, slept right through the night and was busy talking to the driver and the mules. Several workers stopped to stare at the carriage and then at Emelia, for not everyone could afford such transportation.

Holding hands, we continued our conversation from the night.

"Catherine, as I love you, I ask you again to join me at my uncle's estate. I know you do not wish to leave immediately. Yet, as we spoke often, nothing is in this place for you any longer. You have squeezed out every bit of what it offers and by staying you might come to harm."

There was nothing I could say, as we had been over and over this ground many times. While I agreed with Emelia, the prospect of another move just took my strength away. I tried to respond but my voice was bound and chained in my throat. Not getting a reply from me, Emelia went on,

"As I have told you, I agree with your Amma Talis. This place is not what it pretends to be. Much goes on here out of sight. I feel it. I must tell you now that some time ago, I listened to that man Theophilus sermonize.

"I know you like to belittle him, Catherine, but you also explain away his faults too easily. You call him a wrong—headed philosopher, a Sophist. He is nothing of the sort. He is a lawyer. His aim is to confuse whoever listens to him. This he does by picking things from Jew and Christian writings. Books few others understand, much less read. He jumps from prophet to prophet taking things out of context and working them into new arguments. So I think.

"This man cares nothing for truth, but looks to put his own thoughts in the minds of others. For power over them. To control them. Winning is everything for him. He is a lawyer. A reptile. Never believe a word from his mouth, Catherine."

As Emelia spoke, I nodded. Although I had no proof, I discerned much of this and would not defend Theophilus to her, especially at this sad time of parting.

With a final hug, we said goodbye. I kissed Orestes on the cheek, while he continued to chatter with the driver. His mother pinched him and looked to me, so that he said,

"Goodbye, Auntie Catherine. I love you."

As the driver commanded the mules to begin their journey, Emelia looked back to me and said,

"Maybe your camel will come to bring you to me!"

At my next religious instruction, Theophilus went on about "the ship of the Church," and how it is "laden with the good merchandise of salvation." When he was not declaiming about demon wiles, this was his next favorite subject. He like to point out how the basilicas themselves were fashioned after ships and our need to build a great classis or fleet of churches.

I thought to myself how what had been the Ark of my physical salvation from anarchy and mayhem was now to become a flotilla to create further mayhem in the world.

True to form, Theophilus' line of thought led to pronouncements on the allegorical meanings hidden in the stories of Noah or Jonah, sayings from the Psalmist or Isaiah, which all would lead to Jesus Christ calming the waters of Galilee, and so forth.

Eventually, he would emphasize the vital importance of Catholic doctrine and avoiding the errors and vices of madmen like Origen. Those he called heretics he attacked with vitriol and damning aspersions; something easily done when the one's under attack were not present to defend themselves. This is what Emelia, in her mordant wisdom, called a theological dumb show—except Theophilus was incapable of carrying out the dumb part.

Since taking over as my catechist, Theophilus had mandated twice-weekly tutorials in religious instruction. My new spiritual director unabashedly informed me each session though I could never aspire to his level of gnosis, I could at least make it to the baptismal fount to partake of holy communion, thereby joining him in the body and blood of Christ. In this way, he declaimed, I would grow a new spiritual skin.

He enjoyed displaying his bound codices for my eyes, opening the pages to read some random passage in his best preaching voice. This evening, he chose a passage from Leviticus 13:9-11.

"'When anyone has a defiling skin disease, they must be brought to the priest. The priest is to examine them, and if there is a white swelling in the skin that has turned the hair white and if there is raw flesh in the swelling, it is a chronic skin disease and the priest shall pronounce them unclean.'"

It was at this time Theophilus reminded me of his upcoming desert retreat. Lent, he said, would be the perfect time, as it corresponded to Christ's forty days in the wilderness contending with Satan and his demons. He pontificated on the aptness of the Leviticus passage, explaining the hidden meaning behind skin disease and uncleanliness. That is to say, skin disease symbolizes spiritual filth to be washed away if not too deep. Otherwise cut away.

Our desert retreat, he expected, surely would be a spiritually cleansing experience for the two of us.

While he talked, I found myself gazing at the leather binding on the codex from which he read. It was slightly different from others I had seen, having a subtle greenish tinge to it, as well as a kind of stippling overall. This could be the result of a different tanning method, but as I knew nothing of leatherworking processes, it remained a disquieting curiosity in the back of my mind. Nevertheless, as he paused a moment to take a breath I asked him,

"Brother Theophilus, how is it this book from which you now read is so different looking from the others on your shelf. Does this perhaps have some special significance?"

Behind his expressionless face and watchful eyes, I sensed his mind hunting for the words to answer my question. After what felt like a long silence, he said,

"It was a gift. A gift from a seeker. Why do your thoughts wander among inconsequential appearances? Rather than paying attention to outer wrappings, you should hearken to the rich teachings inside. I had hoped you would be farther along than this prior to our retreat. As it is, I see we have much work ahead of us."

By the time the lesson was over, my scalp and extremities prickled, yet I told myself nothing was wrong. Theophilus was just being his usual aggravating self. Upon returning to my room, I fell into a deep sleep upon the bed I would no longer share with Emelia.

Toward midnight I awakened with a start, for things had crystallized in my mind.

☽ 16 ☾

The she-camel came that very night.

Scroll #3: Synthesis

Setting: MAREOTIS

☽ 1 ☾

I first began to write after leaving the monastery.

I informed my beloved friend Emelia, whom I had joined at her uncle's house, of my desire to write. For this I would need the proper implements. Paper. Stylus. Ink.

Saying only that it was "about time," she took me to a room in the house that I had not been in previously, thinking it to be a private andron, reserved for men, and unseemly for a female guest to trespass. Emelia laughed away at such a notion, assuring me the master of the house, her uncle, yet away on business, would not take it as an intrusion and even if he did, what did it matter as he was not there. So, my friend led me to the room her uncle calls his study.

Besides there being a large store of scrolls in the room, more than held by the library at the Community of Friends where I lived for a year, the room had a great many scraps of paper in baskets or just lying about. These scraps had all been previously written upon but treated to remove their ink, or most of it. While the result was not pure as freshly made paper, it suited my practice. As I discovered later, paper was not in short supply at Master Theon's estate, which included a paper-making factory.

It did not take me long to fill a great many scraps to their limit. After completing the story of my childhood river exploits I stopped writing about myself for many years. It was like I had come against a wall. There was something I could not yet put into words, even in my own mind. This thing, this occurrence, marked a changeover or conversion from childhood to something else. I felt I needed to understand this before going on.

Until I might find this understanding, I would confine myself to correspondence with friends, and maybe to some few modest, scholarly works of my own. Nevertheless, with so many resources at hand, it is no wonder writing for me gradually grew into a life-long conspiracy with paper and ink. How else account for this very memory book!

After about four months by the lake, Emelia was called back to Carthage with her son. It was feared her father might be close to death, whether from illness or incident was not explained, but he would see his grandson and daughter, perhaps his only chance.

With Emelia's departure, I took over the little correspondence she had undertaken for the conduct of business on behalf of the estate. I also began writing letters to her. And poetry.

O Emelia! My Emelia!

What is Catherine to do

Without your constant companionship?

Gone, the white-petaled narcissus

In the hollows;

Blue-flagged iris in rank and file,

Gone, too.

Thick bunches of asphodel,

Reedy, that everywhere grew,

Now like everything

Brown-curled, bent and dried.

Sand clouds worry the horizons.

Only Prickly Caterpillar blossoms

Tiny and yellow

To remind me

Of flower times with you.

So cries the pen of Catherine

At the departure of

Her beloved, Emelia.

My days following Emelia's departure were spent largely filling in for her in the care of Theon's estate and in waiting for his return. For a time, this helped me from feeling I was once again alone. Thankfully, before she left, my dear friend had explained to the house slaves and field hands I would serve in her place. She assured them they would find me more competent than she, as I had managed a whole monastery.

If anyone saw me blush at this exaggeration, they never said a thing about it. Every person from cook to vineyard tender to olive husbandman was most kind, out of loyalty to their master rather than in deference to myself, of this I am sure.

As a result, after a few weeks, there really was little for me to tend to, for the estate practically ran itself. So when I was not reading from the manuscripts in the scholar's study, which Emelia urged me to do without second thought, saying the scholar himself would want it so, I meandered about the estate.

One of my favorite pastimes was strolling along the shores of the lake, where the papyrus and other bushes did not block the path. Following so many dry, dusty years in the desert and, ironically, among so many other people, being once again close to water was having a liberating effect upon my soul.

Especially because I was able to walk alone, without interruption, nor did I have to give thought to reporting on my day to a spiritual director or concern myself with catechistic responses.

One evening, after the sun had set and darkness had settled its cooler hand upon we lakeside dwellers, I took a walk along a sandy strand to help with digestion and to knit together the diverse ideas encountered during my education to that point. I believed then and now that this education is never-ending, just as I suspect the star-filled sky itself to be infinite and not the ceiling of some vast basilica, as many say.

So saying, one may imagine that on my evening strolls I spent much time in veritable reverie gazing into the deeps of the sky. I had read that those same stars we see at night, or others like them, shine during the day but are overpowered by the brightness of the sun. Questions not yet fully formed about myself and all that had befallen me roiled beneath my consciousness at such thoughts, as deep within as the stars are distant without.

In this frame of mind, I sat on the lake shore for a very long time. A mist had formed a short distance out from the land when, after a while, I saw lights slowly drifting over the water. Surely, it had to be fisher folk out late looking to catch some aquatic creature or another, using their lanterns to attract it. Or it might have been a group of party-goers sailing home after their revelries, though all was quiet when I saw the lights.

Quite suddenly, three airborne lights materialized over both the mist and the waterborne lights. They hovered in place, much as the hummingbird does, and I even heard—no, more like I felt in my body—a kind of thrumming. Then, all the lights both in air and on water appeared to fly away at great speed.

Truly, there must be some natural explanation for this, though I could find nothing in the library. Perhaps the scholar would know of such things. I made a mental note to ask him upon his return.

For now, I just record the event as I witnessed it.

☽ 2 ☾

The scholar Theon, Emelia's uncle, eventually returned. It was one of those very bright, hot days when the cicada chorus ushers the land into hypnopompic stupor. Any manner of strange things might happen. And so they did.

Theon came back to his estate via Carthage, rather than sailing across the Maruit as he normally might have done. Having heard of his brother's unfortunate accident, he changed his plans and took the long way around. Thus, I know from him Emelia's father was mending well. Emelia ensures he does not push himself beyond measure and he is able to delight in his grandson, who helps him tolerate my friend's assiduities, though not without complaint.

About Theon. I must say I was not prepared for the man who drove his own carriage up to the gate and then strode into the atrium giving orders to all his staff, both free and slave. As for these, they seemed so much in awe of him any one of them would step into a fresh pile of dung at a mere nod from him.

It may be because Emelia had not seen him in so long that little of what she told me about him was adequate to portray the person who now presented himself. So many things about this man are different. Might I say bizarre.

With his back to me, he directed slaves to care for the carriage animals and his baggage. All the while, I was standing at the rear of the atrium in the shade of the covered gallery. Even from that spot, I could tell Theon is much shorter than I am. I am no colossus but I now stand taller than most women. Nevertheless, he looked quite stocky, with a mass I estimated at probably well over 200 librae.

When he turned and stepped out of the strong sunlight, he lowered the cowl that had protected his head from the sun. What a sight! His eyes were covered with strange disk—shaped things, smoky grey in color, such that he looked neither human nor like any animal I know. I have seen strange things before, but I found this quite terrifying and glanced at others to see what they thought of it. No one else acted like this was in any way out of the ordinary, but I did move closer to one of the gallery's supporting columns. Fortunately, he removed those devices forthwith.

If this was not startling enough, there is the fact that he was completely bald. Not only was his scalp alopecic, but so was his whole face. Without the eye-coverings, Theon's lack of eyebrows and eyelashes became a new fascination. As he also had no shadow of facial hair, I concluded this was no affectation of fashion achieved through shaving or depilation.

Shaking off his travel robe, which was taken away by a slave, his bare arms and calves confirmed a likely alopecia universalis.

This was when he turned his attention to me.

To tell the truth, until I saw his sparkling, malachite green eyes, I might have thought him possibly one of those unfortunate albino people who appear from time to time, like the monk I knew of in Nitria who never left his cell during the daytime but poked around throughout the night, often venturing west into the desert. Though I strive to be nonjudgmental about others, I stayed clear of this monk due to his night-loving expeditions. The memory makes me shudder still.

"You must be Catherine. No need to hide in the shadows. Come out here where I can get a good look at my niece's friend. She has told me all about you and speaks quite highly of your educational accomplishments. Of course, Emelia can be a twitter—bird at times, so is easily impressed by anyone showing more intellect than her. Anyway, we shall see just how capable you are and if I think you are up to it, you may prove to be just the person I need for my work."

One may well imagine I was too dumbstruck at the time to understand, much less react to, anything Theon said to me at this moment. However, I had never thought of Emelia as a twitter—bird, so I took his comment more as an avuncular endearment.

After this greeting, he noticed I was quite distracted by the eye—cover apparatus he still held in one hand. Holding it up for me to inspect, he informed me the freakish thing was an experiment. He was contriving to ease the strain upon human eyes from the glaring sun with a pair of lenses made from quartz. He called the device a heliopticon. Giving credit where it was due, he let it be known his aim was to improve on something the Emperor Nero had once devised.

I soon discovered this was just one of his many innovations and one more thing to set him apart from other mortals!

Despite my having lived in his domus for over six months, Theon took me on a tour of the house and adjacent lands. I think he did this to contrast his domain with those of other gentry in the area; to give me greater appreciation for where Fate had delivered me.

To begin, he explained how his two-story house contained neither gynaeceum nor andron; that is, separate gathering spaces for women and men. Because he often entertained both male and female guests together, seeking the best of what both may have to offer, his gatherings were held in a communal symposium adjacent to an expanded kitchen. Also, unlike other villas, Theon's had a well in the middle of the atrium, something which was evidence of great forethought, as well as a great convenience both for food preparation and bathing.

His lands encompassed vineyards, from which he produced several wines both for his own consumption and for export to coastal cities on both sides of the Middle Sea. Also, olive groves, which provided revenue from both fruit and oil. Grape and olive presses on the estate were rented out to surrounding landowners at a small fee when not in service for Theon.

Apiaries were scattered here and there about the estate. These ensured the pollination of crops and also provided a rich source of honey.

Lakeside, there was, of course, the wooden dock Emelia and I used to sit on while dangling our feet in the water. Kitchen slaves would come out here, too, to select from the daily catch that fishermen brought. The choicest fish and mollusks were put aside for consumption by Theon's household; the remainder was sold off to inlanders without access to the lake shore.

Standing at the end of this dock provided a vantage point for Theon to show me the extent of his papyrus cultivation.

The plants stretched northward along the coast and to some distance up the Pi Drakon Canal to the south. Theon seemed to glory in the fact, as he said, that his lands were a major source of paper for the Great Library in Alexandria.

Perhaps this is why he took this opportunity to announce to me he had had a private audience with Prefect Publius in Alexandria, who conferred upon him the title and responsibilities of Chief Librarian. It was with this new work he had in mind for me to help him.

☽ 3 ☾

'As you will discover, Catherine, I am a student of all sciences.'

So saying, Theon directed me, several weeks after his return, to follow him to his study on the second floor. This is the warm, sunny room facing south, as you know, and having the small balcony upon which one may stand or sit in contemplation of whatever is on one's mind or of nothing in particular. As you also know, the room is home to thousands of scrolls, which I have no hope of ever making my way through.

Once in this study, the Master—though he has enjoined me not to call him so. He prefers instead either Theon or, seeing Emelia and I call ourselves sisters, I should call him Uncle. This will take some getting used to for me.

Upon entering his study he shooed the large, beat-up looking, orange-striped tomcat that has been hanging about recently from off a work table, where it had stretched itself out atop dozens of scrolls.

"Well, let us get started. First, I need to make you aware of one of the few rules I have. There is to be no sexual contact between you and any of the house slaves. Do you understand?"

"I think so, but I don't—"

"Good. Such activity upsets the balance in the house. They begin to take advantage."

"I see."

"Furthermore, it creates disharmony. Jealousies fester, making for disruptive competitions. It took me over a week to set things straight since my niece left, if you get my drift. That said, do you know what these are, Catherine?"

His laying down this unnecessary house rule flustered me. Truly, I had not noticed any upset after Emelia's departure and as his heliopticon device was sitting at one corner of the table, I asked him if he was looking to improve upon his invention by some information hidden in the scrolls at hand. He moved the heliopticon to a shelf, mumbling about the lenses so distorting vision they made driving difficult, if not hazardous, and how they had given him a great headache. Maybe sometime in the future, he declared, he might fashion some lenses out of glass, if he could find a glassmaker who knew something about light refraction.

By his tone of voice, I surmised he had lost interest in heliopticons and now was about to launch into a new pursuit; one for which he sees some role for me.

Returning to the table, Theon swept an arm through the air over the assembled scrolls, saying,

"What you see here, Catherine, are the complete works of Heron of Alexandria. Over three hundred years ago, he taught and wrote at the Library which recently has been given over to my care. He possessed one of the most fertile and practical engineering minds the world has ever seen or at least since the Great Pyramids were built. Heron demonstrated how man can harness the powers in fire, air and water to perform work more efficiently than humans.

"These papers before you deal with the geometry of planes and solids, pneumatics, mechanics, optics, light, Earth measurement, war machines, and much more.

"So, what do you think we should do with all of these?"

I am sure Theon thinks I am quite dense because too often I have no idea how to respond to sudden questions he will put to me. But as I am getting more accustomed to his ways, based on what he had just said I blurted out,

"Certainly, you would want to preserve treasures such as these…"

"Exactly," came his immediate reply before I might say anything further and possibly make a fool of myself.

"And now," he continued, "It is time I told you why Publius agreed to install me at the head of the Great Library, along with why you surely will find a lifetime of work for yourself in this."

Theon suggested we walk down to the lake shore to talk, away from prying ears. Once there, he explained to me the nature of the discussion between himself and Prefect Publius.

Both men are of the firm opinion the civilized world is on the cusp of great change. The Prefect even citing mankind's movement from the Age of Aries to that of Pisces. Theon elaborated by explaining how the two ends of the Empire are being pressured by outsiders, barbarians as we like to call them. Goths, Visigoths, Gauls, Huns and others all test the weaknesses of our emperors and their armies, east and west. These same Imperial leaders, one after the other, debase our coinage, driving up prices and eroding confidence. The old internal structures of government have been crumbling for some time. Justice is no longer blind if you have enough money, and lawyers multiply like rabbits in a rich man's vegetable garden with no one to catch them.

I listened patiently as Theon continued. What else could I do?

If this was not enough, Nature provided a catalyst in the guise of the Friki that inundated coasts and cities over a decade ago. He referred here, of course, to the Great Horror that killed thousands and inexorably changed so many other lives, including my own.

In fact, he said, some are saying it is because of that natural catastrophe the upstart religion of Christianity has taken such a strong hold on populations everywhere. The bishops would have us think it is because of their god, but it really is because everyone is afraid. They are afraid of the barbarian outsiders and the corrupt insiders. They are afraid of food shortages, of the lack of sound money, of the weather, of the unknowns tomorrow may bring. And now they are told by this new religion to be afraid of where they might go after they die, for most assuredly everyone's body dies.

My years with Emelia among the Christians at the monastery and elsewhere validate what Theon says. She and I, maybe more than others, are aware of the shadows lurking behind the bright promises proffered by their doctrine. We two also know how the deacons and priests use fear to impose their rules and beliefs upon people, to control them for their own benefit.

Because of the circumstances under which I left the monastery, often I feel I am being watched and am suspicious of strangers passing through. Nevertheless, Theon's words and perspective help me to see all this more clearly; helping, too, to dispel my recurring sense of dread.

More and more my nights are free of terrible dreams of destruction.

What, then, is it Theon expects of me?

As a result of the growing strength of the Christian religion, and that its leaders increasingly are infiltrating and taking over civil institutions, Theon and Publius deduce it is but a matter of time before these internal barbarians, as he calls them, attack the Library. Just as they destroy rational debate and argument in their councils and sermons, they will attack all knowledge not issuing from their books.

Thus, the works of those like Heron of Alexandria are in danger; as are all of the works held by Alexandria's several libraries and those abiding in other cities, too.

To preserve this wealth of knowledge Theon, the Librarian, has been tasked with removing it from Alexandria to a safe place. Or to many safe places, as the case may be.

While this must remain secret, he believes I may be of use in the endeavor.

☽ 4 ☾

One night I dreamed of a flock of crows. The birds ignored me, all but one who strutted forth to greet me with a series of grating coos, rattles, and clicks. This went on for some minutes, the bird cocking its head to peer at me all the while. Perhaps there is some divinatory meaning here I do not see. However, my dream made me inquisitive about the actual birds, so I began feeding scraps to and talking with a certain crow loitering near the house. Coincidentally, it did show up not long after its oneiric cousin came to me.

Theon overheard one of these corvine conversations, so knew I was in secret converse with the blackbird. He first spied us together in the olive grove where I fed it morsels from the kitchen. Many would think this not only odd but unbalanced or, worse, that I was in league with some sort of demon who had seduced my reason. Not so Theon. In fact, knowing I had been a fowler in my childhood, he took the opportunity to expound upon the science of ornithomancy for my benefit.

Because everything is related to everything else in some way, he said, it stands to reason the relationship between birds and men at times will take on special import. As an example, he cited the story about Alexander's expeditionary force losing its way in the Libyan desert, where they surely would have died. Two crows, so the tale goes, visited the soldiers and led them out of the desert to the safety of the Siwa Oasis.

The result of this discussion was Theon proposing he and I collaborate on a study dealing with the signs and observations of birds, including the sounds of crows and ravens. I was flattered, of course, to be considered good enough to collaborate with him. However, I remembered what Amma Talis had once told me about showing a little humility. So, I just nodded my head and replied I would be honored.

Living as a member of Theon's household, I get to hear news coming in from different parts of the Empire. For example, though it had been a few months past when Emperor Valens had been killed in a battle near Adrianopolis, it was recent news for us. We learned shortly thereafter that a new emperor, Theodosius, had taken his place in Constantinople.

Such news is delivered by the many visitors Theon receives from every part of the civilized world and beyond. They come because of the Library, but also because of what his estate produces. In addition to guests, Theon maintains a steady correspondence with men and even a few women from all over, through which he encourages their visiting.

In this respect, one of my tasks became ensuring Theon had a steady supply of the finest paper for his epistolary and Library activities, as well as scientific and philosophic journaling. It was amazing how much writing and computation were needed to support these diverse enterprises. Before long I became an expert in the raising of papyrus and the making of various grades of paper, which resulted in me being given charge of the estate's paper—making facilities. In this capacity I not only learned how to keep track of work flow but also picked up accounting methods helpful to refine inventory record keeping.

When papyrus was ready to harvest, I hired crews to bring in the reeds to a warehouse for processing not far from the water. There the stems were cut into smaller pieces, soaked and compressed according to the paper sizes preferred by Theon and needed by the Library. Overall, my oversight helped to reduce the level of wastage accepted by the workers. I admit by having charge of paper manufacture, I finally felt I was coming into my own. Not since I handled fowling as a girl on the Nile, using my innate skills, intelligence and strength, had I felt like my way might be opening again toward something practical. All else since then had been following paths Fate and others had put before me. Making the best of things, doing and studying mostly what others directed and often having my thoughts and opinions discounted, if not dismissed. Though not by everybody.

For this, I had Theon to thank. In many ways, he reminded me of and has been like what I remember of my own father, lost so many years ago. Both men encouraged others to explore the world beyond what tradition may dictate, whether one wore a male or female body; offering praise and encouragement along the way. And all in good humor which, for someone like me who has grown to take things overly serious often times, has helped me keep an even keel.

Gnawing at the back of my mind though was the fear one day I might lose Theon, like I had lost so much else. Tangled with such fear were revenant visions both appalling and fascinating of the crimes committed in Heliopolis and Nitria following the Great Horror. To my mind, these all massed together as a Great Wrong. It was like the stone monster from the desert mountains was tracking my scent across the years, devouring everyone and everything I loved before cornering me to force a confession of unremembered atrocities as sins of my own.

Although I did not take part in those horrors I am unable to join in other people's fun and make friends. If they really knew me—

☽ 5 ☾

Dearest Emelia, from your adoring friend Catherine:

While at breakfast this morning, I was toying carelessly with my medallion when Theon walked into the kitchen. Before this I always had been careful to keep it hidden. I'm not sure why exactly. You would think after the several years I have spent here, having earned his trust, as he has mine, that I would have shown it to him; maybe even asked him about it. After all, as a student—as he likes to remind—of all sciences, he must know something about things of this nature.

But this object has been special to me in ways I cannot describe. Thus, when Theon spied it, he startled me when he cried out,

"Hen's milk, Catherine! Is that what I think it is? It looks very much like part of an astrolabe to my eyes!"

My concealment penetrated, there was no way now I could deny I guarded some secret thing. Theon asked to hold it to better inspect it. So, I removed the thong from around my neck and held out the medallion for him.

"Amazing. How did you come by this? Do you know what its use is?"

Admitting I did not know its exact use, if use it had, I said it nevertheless was quite dear to me.

Theon said some time he would like to hear from me why this was so, but maybe because I could not meet his inquisitive, green eyes, he kindly added I might do so when I felt comfortable telling him. With that he sighed and suggested he could tell me a few things he knew about astrolabes which might help my own understanding of what I carried around my neck.

He handed back my medallion and I nodded to indicate I would like to hear him.

Theon began, as he often does, by telling a story or a legend before getting into the hard facts. I suspect you may never have heard this fable, so I will repeat it here.

It is said that one day Claudius Ptolemy, the great mathematician and astronomer who lived two hundred or so years ago in our own Alexandria, was out and about riding his camel. It so happened he carried in his hand at the time a celestial globe he had fashioned and, as Fate or clumsiness would have it, he dropped it in the sand. The camel, focused upon getting to its next feeding and the company of its own kind, stepped on the globe. This had the effect of flattening it. Seeing what now was a disc rather than a globe, Ptolemy was inspired with the idea that he could project his three-dimensional, celestial sphere onto a two-dimensional disc or plane. He realized this could offer him certain advantages in manipulation of the geometric measures inscribed on the device, for it is easier to work with angles and other figures when in planar aspect.

The story, he pointed out, while amusing, also serves to illustrate how scientific discovery often comes about by accident; in this case by a distracted mathematician and a preoccupied camel working together toward an unexpected end.

Actually, Theon explained, it was neither Ptolemy nor his camel who came up with the original idea for the astrolabe. A similar device was first proposed by Hipparchus of Nicaea, perhaps three hundred years earlier, when he described how a three-dimensional object might be projected on to a flat surface. The object he had in mind apparently was a type of sun dial or clock, but one incorporating a network of stars overlaid upon it.

If I wished, Theon offered to bring the scrolls from the Library so I might study them for myself.

But, let me continue, Emelia, with Theon's account to give you the complete picture.

Despite the work of earlier men, Ptolemy may indeed, with some special dromedary assistance, have created the first working device or prototype.

Unfortunately, and as is so often the case, his discovery has not survived beyond a written treatise. What we have then is something purely theoretical. But, in his treatise, he describes an instrument that resembles an astrolabe, including both a star network and the projection of a coordinate system.

Naturally, Theon said he had studied what Ptolemy described and found it to be incomplete, in that it does not seem to have a necessary apparatus for making direct observations. Such an addition, he said, would enable one to measure the altitude of the sun or stars, such that it might be used as both a navigation and a horoscopic instrument. A more complete device should prove to be an extremely versatile instrument, offering solutions to problems relating to navigation, constructing horoscopes, and for surveying.

I became most intrigued by his mention that students of Ptolemy's often made allusions to certain occult or mystical attributes of such a device, borrowing from Pythagoras and others, though none was sure what those might be.

To the best of Theon's knowledge, until this morning, there were no astrolabes in existence. They remained a theoretical possibility, a dream of mathematicians, astronomers, and philosophers, including himself. This is why he was so astounded by the serendipity of my medallion appearing, despite its not being pieced together wholly, as it was on his mind while making his morning ablutions before coming down for breakfast.

While he believes the medallion might possibly be an unfinished astrolabe, the inscription on the reverse does raise some doubts. If you will recall, it was in an unfamiliar script. He asked to have one more look at the piece, giving special attention to this rubric. After a moment, he scratched his chin and said,

"Odd. If I'm not mistaken this is in an alphabet used by people of the desert to the east of here. I think it means 'Read' or some injunction of the sort. What could that mean? Read what?"

So saying he returned the disk to me and, dear sister, you see there is hardly ever a dull moment here with our Uncle Theon!

I look forward to your next letter, as I am eager to know what new plans Orestes' father and his grandmother Monica have for your son, my nephew, now nearly eight years old. If there is anything I can do to help you in any way, do not hesitate to solicit whatever you require. I am certain Uncle Theon also will want to do what he can to help.

I miss you fiercely. You know how much I love you.

☽ 6 ☾

Fear had prevented me in the past from fully admitting how I felt my medallion made connection to some strange, enigmatic world apart from our everyday world; a world in which I could feel other forces, other beings, moving, like in

Mother Nyla's tent. My fear was both for what other people might think of my mental state and for what else this thing might conjure into my life. Theon's comment about possible occult qualities attached to the medallion and his ostensible translation of the foreign word helped to prompt my thinking. It seemed I knew more than just glimpses of this other world, but as yet had no real comprehension concerning it. Despite doubts, I had to accept the fact something beyond our five senses exists.

How else understand the occasional emissaries like my dream Crow or the blue light in Mother Nyla's tent or the tent spinning and flying through the air? Even the way I reacted in the library fire had a kind of supernatural power behind it. Such things signaled some new apprehension to challenge both mind and heart, and perhaps it was time I paid attention to them.

Certainly, Mother Nyla, the Seer, had been intimate with this other world, as her visions could have their source nowhere else. And then Agrippina, who serves in her place.

Agrippina.

She came again into my life, bringing with her a strange retinue and even stranger experiences and alien feelings. What should have been a joyful reunion instead brought disappointments and discontent.

My bedroom is located on the upper southwest corner of the house. Though the light of the rising sun does not slip into my room directly, I generally am up and about just before or at dawn. Looking out my west facing window, I will see the last stars clinging to night's curtain over the horizon as the silhouettes of farmers, herders and their animals head out to the fields and orchards or to market. It is a time for me to gently come from out of sleep, to remember lingering dreams, and to begin thinking about the day's work ahead.

One morning a very different sight greeted me. A huge tent—one I recognized immediately—had been set up during the night upon a plateau over a low rise a bit to the southwest of the estate. At one end, a knot of camels were tethered together, though not hobbled as I had seen in the souk. A small, lone figure holding a staff stood watch nearby, probably a boy. Other, larger figures stood by low-burning watch fires spaced around the encampment and I had no doubt that they were armed to defend their stations.

Hurriedly, I threw on a robe and ran downstairs to the courtyard. The cold flagstones chilled the soles of my bare feet, but I hardly cared because standing by the well was Agrippina. She was in quiet conversation with Theon. Though she towered over him, they held each other closely in the dim, predawn light.

My abrupt intrusion caused the two to stand straight and step apart. For a brief moment, they still clasped each other's hands before letting go. At this sight, I was overcome with unexpected emotions.

Checking my pell-mell run, I held back, my lips pressed together. Agrippina turned to face me and held out her arms, to which I continued, a little less happily, until I was in her embrace. Theon spoke meanwhile.

"Catherine, our mistress is weary from her travels and making encampment during the night. I have offered our hospitality to her, so she might rest and be refreshed for a special event she tells me she has planned for us in the days ahead. For now, she will retire to the room next to my own. You may take your leave therefore, as you will have plenty of time to catch up with our friend later."

Returning to my room upstairs, I muttered to myself. Our friend. Why doesn't she just move into Theon's room with him?

Later this same day, after having wrestled with negative thoughts about Agrippina since morning, I had another surprise in the form of one of my past companions from the atrocious times in Heliopolis and Memphis, as well as on the escape to the Nitrian religious communities. It was Peter Panifex, the bread maker's apprentice. As he told me, he had been swept up several weeks ago by Agrippina's caravan while on some religious retreat in the desert, along with others whom I would soon be meeting. His summons had been delivered by two armed brigands, rough men who told him a determination had been made concerning his fate and he dare not turn from it. As his life was unsettled and troubled, he decided it best to go with the men, but dubious of the seeming threat of some kind of reckoning. They delivered him to the caravan where, he said, he had been very well treated along the way.

I asked Peter why his life seemed so purposeless and why he had been on a retreat. My memory was he could not get away from Nitria soon enough. What he told me was after I had disappeared into the monastery—his words—he and Harmonia stayed together to look out for each other. Before long, the protective alliance they had formed turned to a deeper caring and love, so they married and settled in Marea along the lower coast of the long, west-extending finger of Lake Mareotis. In this place, he found a patron and set up his own bakery with Harmonia's help and had two children with her along the way.

Rubbing the heel of his palm against his chest, he related with a catch to his voice how not very long ago a plague swept through the area to take away both children. Shortly thereafter, he discovered Harmonia in their home with her throat cut and her body badly mutilated. Due to the desecration of her body, there was no question she had been the victim of some foul butcher rather than having taken her own life out of grief for her children. Peter had been questioned by the authorities but released with sympathy and condolences.

He went on to say how these events drove him nearly mad, causing him to seek out holy men and monks. Finally, he arrived at a sense these things were happening to him because of a sinful and corrupt nature, making it necessary to beg for mercy and exculpation; neither of which, he lamented, had he yet found.

I wished I could comfort him. He looked at me so sadly. I could not find words with which to console; so, with tears welling up in my eyes, I stepped forward and hugged him. An action I later would come to regret.

Agrippina and Theon were caught up in a flurry of preparation and what I secretly assumed to be their shared private passion. I found myself excluded and irritable. This, along with hearing Peter's story, made me feel less than companionable. Instead, when I was not carrying on with my papyrus production work, I wandered by the lake or through this or that grove, reliving in my mind all that had happened over the years. Peter's story haunted me. I could not banish it from my thoughts.

Poor Harmonia! After all she had been through in Heliopolis, to seemingly find happiness, then to have it brutally taken from her once again.

Heliopolis! City of the Sun, indeed.

On the afternoon of the fifth day following Agrippina's arrival, I was sitting on the edge of my bed with my knees pulled up to my chest and my arms wrapped about my legs, staring at nothing in particular. Suddenly overcome with weariness, I fell over sideways onto the bed and went into a deep, dream-filled sleep.

In a sweat and with heart palpitations I awoke in the dark suddenly from a dream. In the dream I was adrift in the middle of the Nile, asking myself why my parents had put me in the skiff and pushed me into the deep current. There it was. Another grieving memory, albeit in a dream, wanting to claim me.

Rubbing my eyes, familiar objects became recognizable again. A pair of eyes at the foot of the bed looked at me. The big tomcat had joined me during my dozing and dreaming.

Swinging my legs over the side, I reached the bottoms of my feet for the floor. It was there. With gratitude, I let relief sink in; taking slow, deep breaths as I did so.

Sounds of many people were coming from downstairs. I went to my bedroom doorway, with the cat following. The two of us then stepped on to the open corridor overlooking the courtyard and the east wing of the house. Everything was bathed in a bluish, beryl light. A large bonfire also blazed a safe distance from the front entrance.

"Catherine! You're up! Come down and join us! We're celebrating Hallowmas!"

☽ 7 ☾

The manufactured papyrus roll, as I had learned, typically contains no more than twenty sheets and most often fewer glued together seamlessly. The book roll, on the other hand, may be considerably longer. For instance, it might contain as much as a single book of Thucydides' history. The usual way of reading is to unroll the scroll with one's right hand, while winding the portion that has been read back up with one's left. To give the roll stiffness and to prevent bending, it is wound around a wooden or ivory rod, forming a cylinder that can be handled by projecting knobs on the ends.

There are times when it feels my life is written out on a book roll. Hour by hour, day by day, it rolls out from a bottom cylinder cloaked in darkness, while simultaneously being taken up by yet another unseen cylinder. The only visible portion of this private scroll is what is before my consciousness at any given moment.

Occasionally, to my consternation, the thread of the narrative seems to lurch into some totally unpredicated direction, as has happened to me in the past, and now seemed to be happening again.

Maybe these breaks are like starts to new books, new histories? Then why do certain things seem to repeat themselves?

The nameless cat and I went downstairs to see what the commotion was about, as well as to find what exactly this festival was to which I was being invited. The house was filled with unfamiliar people nodding at me as though they knew me. I smiled and nodded back, soon feeling overheated due to the press of bodies and their overwhelming odor in the enclosed space.

What we discovered when I found Agrippina, for a had picked up the cat to allay my mounting disorientation, was Hallowmas is some obscure holiday made up by the Celts of Hibernia to honor the souls of their recent dead. Agrippina had first heard of this in the far west from traders out of Britannia. She carried the idea with her for some time, finally thinking to have a festival to honor her dead and those of her friends, particularly Mother Nyla. One of the appeals of this festival for her was the making of lanterns or lights to represent the dead.

This explained the blue lanterns everywhere. A confusion of souls. The fixtures themselves had been fabricated from dyed papyrus and given a flame-resistant treatment. Beneath their glow it seemed my feet barely touched the ground. Floating among them, the lantern flames flickered at me like tongues, speaking in languages of light and shadow beyond my comprehension; their silent chorus seeming to engulf the house and all its celebrants.

Not surprisingly, the whole idea of such a festival had charmed Theon. Not in the least because it had come from Agrippina. And now the atmosphere they had created began to work its queer magic on me.

Having found my way outside, the spell deepened at the resounding thunder of a gong struck from somewhere. Its reverberations undulated throughout the house and the estate for an unnaturally long time. The tomcat squirmed in my arms, jumped down and ran into the night. People around me gradually stopped their gabbling, standing stock-still as though time had suspended. From around the corner there came a hypnotic, bell-like ringing and clicking of finger cymbals made by a troupe of dancers at the head of what developed into a long and unusual procession.

The dancers' bodies flowed in continuous, sinuous movement in time with the cymbal rhythm. Slow travelling steps, turns and spins steadily quickened to the music of a double—flute player joining in. The flute's trills drove the dancers to shimmy and accentuate their hip movements erotically. Backbends and head tosses heightened the frenzy, along with the pulse of every viewer, mine included.

Following this crew came teams of actors and acrobats, as if out of nowhere. The actors wore outlandish costumes and masks. One group dressed as soldiers recited lines from the Iliad, while others portrayed various mythical characters, and yet others put on absurd farces, occasionally pulling in an onlooker to be the butt of crude jokes or pranks.

In the wake of the parade of dancers, musicians, thespians, clowns, torchbearers and others came food-bearing slaves wearing nothing but loincloths or nothing at all. This whole retinue snaked its way to the nearest grove, where tables and benches awaited the trays of food and those who would stuff themselves with their delicacies.

Like the house, the trees in the grove were adorned with hanging blue lanterns. The dead followed us everywhere this night.

Toward the middle of the night the haunting sound of the gong came from across the field where Agrippina's tent city stood. Among the feasting guests several could be heard saying, "She comes! She comes!" and "Athena be praised!" and like kinds of things which I found puzzling. By this time, too, I may have become a bit befuddled from the free-flowing wines and beers produced on Theon's estate. Nevertheless, I asked a well-dressed woman sitting next to me,

"Who comes? What is this about?"

"Nyla comes! Mother Nyla is joining us!"

Choking on a piece of roasted lamb, I could not ask what the woman meant by such an absurdity. Yet, people were leaving the tables to congregate at the grove's edge as if awaiting something. I joined them just as a second torchlight procession started from the tent city in our direction. While the first procession had much about it I thought was silly, this new column portended something more hair-raising. At its head was a camel-sized automaton of a crow or raven lurching our way. The broad black wings of the contraption flapped slowly up and down, while the eyes rolled luridly, all synched somehow with the turning of the wheels. Naked youths pranced around it, crowing raucously to urge it along.

Behind this nightmarish apparition came stilt-walkers staggering and reeling, seeming ready to fall but never falling. The stilts were outfitted to look like birds legs and the acrobats atop were dressed as dreadful avian chimeras.

The wine, the food, and the crowd of mostly strangers was having its effect on me. The stink of fermentation, burning meat, sweat and miasma from temporary latrines made me nauseous and dizzy. What is more, my breast bone beneath my medallion ached tremendously and as more of the macabre caravan came into view I found it difficult to breathe.

In the midst of the snaking line came a palanquin adorned with jingling mirror-stones and tassels, carried by bare-chested men and women. Enthroned upon it was something the shape of a human body, sitting upright and wrapped all about in strips of cloth like the ancient desiccated bodies turned up in the desert. Theon and Agrippina sat cross-legged on either side of these swaddled remains, if such they were. Tethered to the aft-end of the palanquin was Mother Nyla's camel. The very one I had seen years earlier but now old and weary. A platoon of old men shuffled behind, pounding on drums hung from sashes to beat out a tribal drum dirge. Finally, cart loads of logs, faggots and branches completed the line.

The caravan halted before the crowd at the grove. From where there had been awed silence, there now issued a unified shout, followed by frenzied ululating and hooting. Many shouted out the names of Nyla, Theon and Agrippina, stamping their feet as they did so. Those whom I could see around me all showed their teeth in wide grins. Teeth and eyes gleamed in the torchlight. With the appearance of my two protectors I began to feel a camaraderie with the others, for I now grasped what this festival for the dead meant.

Bouncing from foot to foot and clapping my hands along with others, I joined in the celebration.

Standing atop the palanquin, Theon raised his arms to signal the crowd to be silent. What had been a rushing cascade of voices became a babbling brook, became a murmuring streamlet, became still waters. Theon spoke.

"Welcome to my home and thank you all for coming. I am moved deeply so many have come. I know many of you have traveled far to be here tonight and you have been away from your homes for many weeks or months in some cases, so you will be eager to return. So, again, thank you for your sacrifices.

"I also wish to thank our dear sister, Agrippina. For without her, this gathering would not have been possible. Not only did she conceive the idea for a festival to honor the souls of those whom we knew when they ate, drank, laughed and cried among us; but it is she who sent her caravans and ships out to bring you in from the farthest reaches of this once great empire. Just as important as paying our respects to those who have gone, is coming together in companionship with those who remain and are able to work for a better world.

"And now Agrippina will take us to the heart of our ceremony. The reason we are all here."

Agrippina rose. Someone put a chalice in Theon's hands while he settled on the ground. Drinking deeply, he watched Agrippina over the brim of the chalice with the light of Eros in his eyes.

Agrippina briefly thanked Theon for his hospitality, then spoke at length about Mother Nyla. Her eulogy confirmed what I had suspected, which is Theon not only knew the old seer but likely had her to thank for his current position in the world. As Agrippina described him, he was 'Friend to Thoth and to Hermes, as well as Scientist and Master of the House of Scrolls.' Agrippina several times referred to a mysterious Association to which everyone present belonged.

Most everyone, that is, for I certainly was not a member of their Association but I assumed was allowed to participate for having been shown some favor from Mother Nyla. This was confirmed by Agrippina in her speech. However, in addition, myself and two other individuals—Peter Panifex and a young man by the name of Synesius—were to be inducted that very night into their Association.

People turned to look at me. Taken by surprise by this announcement, I could not make eye contact with anyone. My only thought was wishing this would all be over soon.

Thankfully, Agrippina moved on to the true main event of the night. While she had been speaking, the wood carried in the carts at the end of the procession had been unloaded and stacked into a tall, flat-topped heap. At a signal from her, the enshrouded figure from the palanquin was gently taken down by a team of ustoris and laid out atop the wood.

How many years had it been? Amma Talis had reported Nyla's death not long before I departed Nitria in the middle of the night. She had made no mention of the old woman's body being preserved, but preserved it seems to have been. That is, if what had just been placed on the pyre was in fact Mother Nyla and not a doll-like, token offering.

Before setting fire to the bier, the hundred or so guests were enjoined to drink a ladle of brew from several cortinae on tripods scattered through our dining area. I learned later what its contents were. The main ingredient was the floral gem called the Bride of the Nile or lotus, which delighted my eyes with its brilliant blue even as a child on the river. The concoction also contained Artemis' Spike and other herbs I recalled my mother from time to time used to make infusions in her trade, but I had no idea what they did.

As it happened, when combined they enrapture those who imbibe the mixture. The concoction deepened the effects of both the lantern lights and my medallion, which now hummed lightly upon my chest. Everything looked both ordinary and remarkable at the same time. And so it was that as the flames twisted and roared through and around the pyre with its sacred offering, not to any god but to our living memories, our minds whirled upwards with them in rapture.

☽ 8 ☾

Prior to the torches being set to the pyre, I ran into Peter standing near one of the cauldrons with a scowl on his face and shifting about uncomfortably. I turned to him and he glared at me with his arms folded across his chest. Muttering to himself, it was obvious he was not at all into the spirit of the gathering. Annoyed with his behavior, I finally said,

"Don't be such a coward. If you've got something to say, just say it!"

"You're not going to drink this poison are you? This is wrong. It's wrong and you know it as well as me."

Others nearby who already had partaken of the drink were smiling and nodding to one another, as though they had a shared secret. I was not about to let Peter's distemper affect my mood.

"Of course I am. I'd advise you to have some, too. It probably will help your sour attitude."

Peter grabbed my wrist as I reached for a ladle. Never one to brook such interference, especially from Peter, I wrested away from him. Looking him in the eyes, I gulped down a full measure of the infusion, burning my mouth as I did so but making my point. I left him steaming more than the simmering pot.

Walking back to the bier, I picked up a fragment of a conversation between Theon and a well-known female doctor, Leoparda, who had served the Emperor Gratian himself.

"—as was my daughter. Sooner or later, good Doctor, just as you began your studies in medicine at Alexandria, I know we will have to go there to learn what more we can. The city is the fulcrum of the Empire and if the Koinotis, our special society, is to have any influence in the coming few decades, it will be from Alexandria. This may be something for us to discuss later."

I began to feel wonderfully clear-headed and elevated, despite my altercation with Peter. A sense of relaxation and belonging was settling over me, but I wondered whatever did Theon mean about moving to Alexandria? And he mentioned something about his daughter? Yes, he said so himself but I have not seen anyone who might be his daughter. Or maybe I have. Yes, it's possible. And what is Peter doing now?

No sooner had my mind turned to Peter than he came from behind me and grabbed my upper arm. Apparently unable to contain himself any longer, Peter shook his free fist at the crowd and through tight jaws indignantly denounced the proceedings as 'frivolous, heretical and worst of all indecent.' So saying, he angrily tried to drag me away from the gathering. For the second time I had to extract myself from his grip. People nearby who had heard his denunciation seemed amused at what they may have thought was a performance and just another part of the evening.

Peter ran off, disappearing into the night just as the fire starters came forward with their torches to commence the cremation ceremony.

Before putting their flames to the bier however, the seer's camel presented herself to the congregation. Kneeling in front of the pile, she arched her neck far back and gave out a single, powerful bray to call forth a sfagéfs holding a sharp blade. Usually when an animal is slaughtered it is necessary to securely tether and hobble it. Mother Nyla's old friend offered herself up with composed sensibility.

A veiled maiden splashed a bowl of the camel's blood over the swathed corpse on the bier. As she stepped away fire was put to the wood and the first cracklings of kindling caught and broke the silence.

I have been told it happens sometimes the force of the heat in a funeral pyre grows to such intensity the remains are propelled through the air like a fiery comet. Something like this happened with Nyla's body.

The wood must have been very dry because as the fire grew everybody was forced back by its fury, as much by the air being sucked from our lungs as by the heat. The gauze wrapping the body smoldered but did not burn immediately. When it did ignite, the whole of it became an incandescent blue. Stranger still, the body sat up with arms uplifted, as if reaching for the stars above.

While unexpected, all of the foregoing likely has a natural explanation. What happened next does not.

The body suddenly collapsed into itself with a hollow, concussive sound. Just as quickly it burst out into a blue sphere like ball lightning, giving off a sweet, pungent smell. The sphere hovered above the flames for some moments, during which Agrippina sprang from the stunned crowd, falling to her knees by the dead camel to shout,

"I'm here! Mother, I'm here!"

The ball seethed and sizzled, spiraling out horizontally, finally moving slowly inside the circle of we onlookers. Agrippina petitioned the orb once again,

"O, Great Mothers! I am here! I have waited patiently and I am ready"

As if ignoring her, the blue ball stopped in front of me.

☽ 9 ☾

I had read many works on philosophy and the sciences in the years before this congress of Theon's friends, thanks in large part to Theon's work with the Library in Alexandria. In particular, his decision to empty the Library over time to protect the knowledge carried by its scrolls meant most often he brought them first to his Mareotis estate where I pounced upon them. With Theon as my preceptor, the education I began at the monastery continued through our frequent dialogues. He had employed me as copyist, too, as my proficiency with writing grew. There was no better way to learn so much material than by writing it out myself.

This changed after the night in the grove.

When the charged sphere stopped in front of me it compressed in diameter to about one pes. My skin tingled from head to feet and my hair stood out in a dark halo. Smiling, I leaned slightly forward and closed my eyes. The next thing I knew I was moving through a winding tunnel. Slowly, at first. Then, faster than imaginable. At the same time, shadowy figures moved along with me in the periphery of my vision.

Much happened on this fabulous journey, though I only can find fragments of it in my memory. I recall the figures accompanying me felt benign, with a kind of detached love for my well—being. These ushered me into a great hall wherein sat a Council of Elders upon raised benches in a semicircle. There was much discussion among the Councilors about things I either could not understand or cannot remember. Periodically the one in the center of the group, who seemed to be the Director, questioned me. I could not help but answer wholly and truthfully. Though clothed I felt fully exposed. Many of the questions in retrospect I find confusing, as they dealt with my apparent past lives. Though closed to me now, I saw them all clearly in the light of my current life.

After what felt to be several hours I was returned to the circle around Mother Nyla's pyre, where only a few moments had passed. The blue sphere was gone. Agrippina knelt in the dust with a look of horror and desolation on her face. The stone in my medallion blazed brightly. I now knew its function.

Two things have stayed with me from this incident. The most important, which gives me a sense of peace, is I realize I am immortal. Not this body, my corporeal self to carry out this lifetime, but my psyche, my anima mea. The second thing is the meaning of the word etched on my medallion. I was told it translates not as "Read!" but "The Reader." I also was told it connects to a Universal Library, from which we have every book ever written and from which all future books shall come.

Before being sent back, one of the initial guides to the Chamber of Elders came directly in front of me, looking into my eyes, calling out my name indistinctly. The name was not Catherine, the name I knew, but my name nonetheless. Chillingly, I could not deny this other being and I indeed know each other from another time. We are connected in some way.

☽ 10 ☾

With the sudden disappearance of the apparition, my normal life resumed with a rush of sounds, odors, tastes and other physical sensations. The look I had caught on Agrippina's face had been fleeting. She composed her face in an instant, but I saw a smoldering hatred linger in her eyes. Getting up from the ground and dusting off, she once more took charge of the proceedings.

"I think we have passed the zenith of our celebration for this meet. Our minds would take us into a hundred different directions after what we have seen tonight. Such might serve only to confuse and lead to arguments that would undermine our Association, the *Koinotis,* through schisms, the same as we see with the Christians."

As she spoke, her eyes scanned all the faces around her. All but mine, for she would not look me in the eye. Wanting not to be the center of attention any longer, she handed off to Theon.

"I say we ought to call it a night, but we must first hear from Master Theon about further business."

And these were Theon's words,

"Again, I thank you all for giving up so much in order to be here. Beyond that I also wish to thank everybody for their unflagging assistance in helping to relocate the Library. By now, Catherine and I have catalogued most of the items and I would say nearly three—quarters of the materials have been distributed to what hopefully will prove to be safer repositories. As we agreed at a previous meeting, you are free to keep books for your private libraries, pass them along to others, trade them, copy them. As you will.

"Fortunately, a great many books had been relocated to the Serapeum before the great deluge. Some which remained in the Mouseion and the Library proper survived the water due to having been in sealed rooms and subterranean crypts. Those, too, have been moved since the edifices where they were housed had become unsafe and there has been no public will to restore the buildings to their former glory.

"This has been a great and worthy project. It has been largely successful and one for which posterity may thank us.

"Now, however, I wish to bring up a new project for the *Koinotis*: the reconstruction and rehabilitation of the Serapeum itself.

"Why is this needed, you ask?

"It is no secret the bishops have been building a great many basilicas in a campaign, as they call it, to Christianize space. At the same time, the temples of the older religions have fallen into disuse and disrepair, while the bishops and their political allies have either closed down or converted many of them to their own use.

"In Alexandria, the Serapeum remains as a beacon. Nevertheless, over the years many practices have been introduced to pervert the original idea for such a temple. In addition, the New Age we have entered provides us an opportunity to take a new direction; to move away from intermediary priesthoods towards practices more supportive of individual development via direct experience of the divine or even what may be higher dimensions.

"In the coming months, I will finalize plans for how the Serapeum might be at the vanguard of a new, transformative spiritual movement. These I will get out to you for comment and discussion. Once we are in agreement on our direction, we must begin gathering the resources for what will be undoubtedly a huge undertaking."

Agrippina thanked Theon, saying everyone looked forward to hearing more about his plan and seeing his advance drawings for the proposed refurbishment. To close the gathering, she said there was one more piece of business to attend to; that was the induction of new members into Koinotis Fotos. This must come close to being the most difficult thing Agrippina has ever done.

Scroll #4: Gate of the Moon

Setting: ALEXANDRIA

☽ 1 ☾

About a dozen years passed since my baptism into the Koinotis Fotos, the Association of Illumination. Baptism, indeed, for that long night of the Hallowmas ritual, when everything began changing, and the days that followed brought a full immersion into the life behind the lives of people I loved and those I thought I loved.

Agrippina with her scrying stone was the catalyst, but she depended on Theon to orchestrate the event. After the event Agrippina retreated into herself. Whenever in my presence she forced herself to smile but leaned away from me. I wanted to talk with her about what had happened to me, but she always shrugged and changed the subject.

I never knew the whole story, yet it was not difficult to divine. In my mind's eye, I could see Agrippina bent over the glowing, blue stone immersed in its pan of water. Images slowly take vague shape and then vanish like evanescent dreams. Finally, one holds its form and reaches out to her like a bewitching flower to a gardener. Unable to resist, she embraces the vision, realizing she must nurture it into fruition, no matter what it takes. What the complete vision was, she never revealed but I know the stone assuredly pointed a wizardly finger at me.

One thing is clear to me. The Hallowmas celebration itself was a subterfuge, a slight of hand for testing me and for Agrippina to assume her grandmother's mantle. The observance was magical, opening strange new ideas, new perceptions and new worlds for me and, perhaps, closing them off to Agrippina.

Many times over the years, I have asked myself whether Agrippina saw through her stone's agency all the difficulties, letdowns, and misfortunes lying in wait for us? I think not. While some things may have greater certainty than others, I think her scrying stone revealed possibilities more than anything. Otherwise, she would have seen her own catastrophic end.

That Hallowmas marked the last time Agrippina and I would meet, at least in this lifetime. Every few months or so, I might see a large Bedouin encampment and think maybe she was near. Memories would take me over then, as I tried mentally to relive past events. Not more than three years passed however when we heard of Agrippina's death, her murder. Afterwards I wondered again if she had scryed her end in that rock, but finally decided it could not be so. Perhaps we are blind to auguries and warnings concerning ourselves.

The report we received described a full-out assault by a squad of trained assassins, led by a black-robed villain, upon her camp outside the port of Klysma in the Siná region. Who these killers were has never been ascertained. Survivors said they bore neither identifying insignias upon their clothing nor tattoo markings upon their skin.

Given the security she imposed in and around her camp, Agrippina assuredly had been betrayed from within. It was said she had been taken alive, though wounded, along with a handful of slaves. These latter were let go after being made to watch their mistress' execution.

While still living she was flayed by her assailant. Her torture was carried out by a man dressed in the black robe of a monk, who appeared to take a singular delight in and was very skillful at his work. When he finished, he rolled her wet skin up to carry off; signaling to his henchmen to dispatch his victim, writhing and moaning in the dirt. Mercifully, they immediately beheaded Agrippina, but also separated her limbs from her body. Head, arms, legs and torso later were affixed in heinous array upon the points of a wooden pentangle contained by a wheel along the road between Klysma and Heliopolis.

She would not have been identifiable, except for the sign attached to her torso in the center with her name, Agrippina, followed by the words: Sorceress. Harlot.

Despite the breach between us, for a long time after Agrippina's slaying I had difficulty eating and sleeping. It seemed I had a constant headache and a roaring in my ears. I would fantasize about finding the demon monk behind this barbarous act and all the ways I might humiliate him. Unto death.

His. Mine. Everyone's.

I came to realize the crimes I'd witnessed in my youth would forever be with this world. My view of humanity, of men, of women, plunged me back to the despondent distrust I experienced in the early years at the monastery.

In this dark mood, bordering upon misanthropy, I was fairly unreachable. Without Theon, I believe I either would have died from grief or committed some reckless act leading to my getting killed. Either would have suited me.

Theon.

Always prominent in the Koinotis, he took the place of leadership after the butchery of Agrippina; just as she had assumed that role when Mother Nyla passed on. He had no use for the scrying stone, his way of divination and gnosis being through science and numbers. The stone did find its way to him eventually and he asked me to help him bury it among the roots of an old olive tree in our grove. To honor Agrippina.

I think it was with this act I slowly began to regain my sanity. I also realized it was high time for me take leave of my despondency. Theon reminded me of my former high—spirited and at times fearless outlook. He helped me to see again how Agrippina and the others whom I had met at Hallowmas were all people who acted to influence these times according to their degree and capacity. They were agents for change, who sacrificed much for each other.

They were the Association of Illumination. Now I was one of them.

This helped me to see I had been little more than a clever, somewhat educated girl who always seemed to land on her feet. Given much, but giving little back. Who could doubt, I had been extremely lucky over the years. I enjoyed special advantages others did not. To my mind it seemed this had little to do with any native talent or disciplined effort of my own. Things happened around me and to me. I conformed myself to these.

It was at this time I realized I had not understood Theon's reasons for giving me what has proved to be perhaps his greatest gift of all. Nor had I properly thanked him for it.

Immediately subsequent to the funeral services for Mother Nyla, years before Agrippina's death, she announced the accession of two new members to the Association; a scholar named Synesius and myself. Both of us were to have private induction ceremonies, during which we would be questioned and given personalized direction.

I was first. Synesius left the immediate area, waiting to be called in his turn. I wished I could have gone later, as my bladder was full from drinking throughout the night. But I held myself in check, hoping the ceremony, whatever it turned out to be, would be short.

As she had since the incident around the pyre, Agrippina dropped matters into Theon's lap. Not one to be easily flustered, Theon took charge and addressed the group. His speech caught me totally unaware.

"All of you here tonight remember the devastation of Alexandria by the terrible wave. It was not the first time natural disaster had struck the city and I daresay it will not be the last. Many people were lost with each calamity. With this last one, many of those were friends. Or more than friends. Family.

"As you know, I lost my daughter in the Great Horror. She had been visiting with friends in the Bruchium, adjacent to the larger of the two harbors. Besides passing time in the old royal gardens and parks, they attended the theater, played ball games and did other things young people enjoy. It was her ill fortune to be in this area when the cataclysm struck. As her body never was found, we assumed she had been swept out to sea with the retreating waters.

"My grief was terrible. I considered joining the anchorites in the deep desert to spend the rest of my life in solitude, fasting and sorrow. I was ready to abandon the work I had agreed to take on with Koinotis, along with my own scientific pursuits.

"Thanks to Mother Nyla, that was not to be. She administered soothing tonics and anodynes that kept me for a time in a numbed state. Gradually, she brought me back to life. In doing so, she made me a promise. That promise was that I would be given a new daughter to help with our work at some future time.

"That time has come. Tonight, if she agrees, I say before you all that it is my wish to adopt Catherine of the Desert, Tuya of Ta-Mehu, as my daughter."

At this, I passed out to the floor.

☽ 2 ☾

Several hours passed before I came to consciousness again. It was perhaps early afternoon when I opened my eyes. I found I was lying on a divan in another downstairs room opposite the courtyard from the symposium room. I could hear slaves preparing food in the kitchen; another sweeping the corridors; and someone else at the well, singing some simple melody. The big tomcat was stretched out along my side and once he saw my eyes open, he slowly blinked and began to purr loudly.

Sitting up, I brushed my hair out of my face. I was still wearing the clothes I had on from the night before but I wanted to wash my face and clear my nose. I headed out of the room toward the stairs; about halfway up, Agrippina called to me. She looked up at me with narrowed eyes and her arms folded across her chest as she spoke.

"I'm glad you're up. These meetings are always so draining, aren't they? Even I am not entirely used to how exhausting they can be but you obviously found it overwhelming. After you have refreshed yourself, Theon and I would like you to join us in the olive grove. There are things for you to consider yet, so please don't dally."

Under the shade of the oldest trees in the grove, Agrippina and Theon were sitting together upon one of three arced benches arranged in an open circle. While still at a distance, Theon saw me and acknowledged my approach with a smile and a nod, while continuing in quiet discussion with Agrippina. As I neared them, I made out they were talking about the project Theon had announced about revamping the Serapeum. I would have expected them to be deep into engineering and construction details, which are Theon's forte; however, they seemed to be more absorbed by how to best maneuver through Alexandrian politics.

I took a place on one of the other benches, letting my attention wander. Sunlight filtered through the branches and pale green leaves to encourage the abundant fruit which were mainly in their green season. Due to the artfully pruned branches, fruit ran along their whole length. Some of the olives would be harvested soon, to be processed into strong-flavored oil; while the majority would be allowed to ripen further until their skins turned black or purple, according to their variety. Lighter, more delicate oil would be pressed from those not brined for the table.

I could almost feel the peppery pungency of aromatic, delicious oil at the back of my throat, making me suppress a cough.

Finally, Theon leaned over to take my hand, saying while he did, "Catherine. You look lost in a reverie. Are you all right?"

"What? Oh, yes. I was just enjoying the day and the dappling sunlight on the ground. And I was thinking ahead about the olive harvest and how beautiful it is here. So much so I think I never want to leave…and…"

I began to drift off again, but Agrippina broke in.

"Yes, child, we understand. Regretfully, we all must move on. I myself must leave immediately to take up my travels. There clearly is no rest however for the likes of me, that much is certain."

Despite her changed attitude toward me, I blurted,

"Oh, don't go! I want you to stay here with me. With us, I mean. I know you have people whom you visit and do things with, but couldn't you just write letters? I would help you if you can't—Oh, forgive me! I'm sorry! I did not mean to imply…"

Agrippina snorted, deepening the lines at the corners of her eyes. With a heavily sarcastic tone she said,

"You had better be careful or I just might steal you away from Theon to put you to some real work. But, no. I will go. You must stay."

Theon interjected, "In fact, that is why we asked you out here today. We all need to be clear about your future status and what responsibilities you are best suited to take on. You have decisions to make."

Agrippina remained silent as Theon carried on our colloquy. He asked me what the last thing was I recalled from the previous evening. It took me some moments to recollect, as it felt like there was some vast undertaking there to be dealt with, which would mean removing myself from my dreamy detachment and thoughts of the olive harvest. I resisted for a while, then it came to me with a start. My head jerked back and I looked at Theon with incredulity. I'm afraid what I did next was very embarrassing. I let out a loud bark of a laugh, taking all three of us by surprise.

How can I explain this?

It was a kind of breakthrough. It was like a divine wind—an expiration rather than an inspiration—bursting from out of a subterranean chamber deep within myself. Every preconception I had ever had shattered, freeing my body, my mind, my spirit. I felt clean like never before.

Suddenly, it seemed absurd to me how just a few moments before I had wanted nothing more than to stay where I was. I realized I had been clinging to a false reality where nothing changed; where neither fathers nor mothers nor sisters nor teachers nor friends disappeared; where people did not kill or torture other people; where dry books provided solace and comfort.

In an instant, that dream vanished. The reality of the olive grove upon my senses was stark. These trees lived, bore fruit and died. They might live longer than me, but one day they, too, would be gone. Maybe cut down or burned or withered from pests and disease, but these would pass as surely as would everything and everyone. I knew, too, even the sun, the moon and the stars in the sky all have their lives and one day their songs would grow feeble and die.

There is no security in life. There is no one and no thing to rely upon. Life is so utterly beautiful.

At this breathless moment of awakening in Theon's olive grove, I saw the man who said he wanted me as his daughter flush a deep red over a pained frown. Agrippina raised her eyebrows and tilted her chin back. She gripped Theon's thigh and her eyes seemed to say "I told you so."

I think this is when I truly understood the depth of Agrippina's resentment and disappointment. She could not know the seemingly crass explosion I had made was nothing more than me coming into myself; it was not at all a negative reaction to Theon's proposal.

Softening my gaze, I composed myself and looked steadily at Theon. "Yes. My answer is yes. It would be my great honor to be your daughter."

His look brightened and Agrippina stiffened as she loosened her grip upon him.

"Besides, I would much rather call you Father than Uncle or Master."

Theon's laughter, I am sure, was heard clear back to the house. Composing himself, Theon went on to say,

"Well, now that's settled there is still a bit more *Koinotis* business to get out of the way before Agrippina goes.

"First, there is something you need to know about your first father, the man who with your mother brought you over the bridge into this world. Officially, the army recorded him as lost. Some thought he died during a flash flood; others that he deserted. The truth, which Agrippina tells me was revealed by the seeing stone, is he was felled by an assassin while on his last assignment. You need to understand he, too, was a member of our Association and that membership comes with dangers which should not be taken lightly."

To my torrent of questions Agrippina was adamant she had no other information than what the stone had shown her and I should be glad for what was given. Because my father was in the military, it was possible that Marcellinus, a former general who also had attended the celebration for the dead, would know more about his involvement and I might inquire of him. However, she advised I wait until I met him again rather than write to him, for letters have a way of falling into the wrong hands.

Calming myself with a few deep breaths, I asked what other business we needed to cover.

Theon explained to me, upon coming into the Association, a new member—or really any member at any time—had the opportunity to take a new name. The reasons for doing so, if one wished, might be for healing or for recognizing something new about oneself after having undergone the rite of passage into the group. It just as often could be a way to nurture a previously hidden or ignored aspect of oneself. In this way, taking a new name generally was a step toward greater authenticity. As if anticipating my questions, he went on to say the chosen name could be used publicly, in private, or only within group meetings or in correspondences. That, too, would be my choice.

Whatever name I felt to take, whether it came from myself or if I requested it from Agrippina as leader of the Association, he told me I should be aware it would bring power and, if he could use the word, magic to my life. Others would begin to see me in a different light. They would treat me differently and this is something I needed to be prepared for. Theon finished by saying there was no rush to take a name. This might be something I would want to sit on for months or even years.

I asked if Synesius had taken a new name. He had not yet done so, as was his privilege. I then asked both of them if either had changed their names. They looked at each other, then at me. Theon took Agrippina's hand and nodded in the affirmative.

Later, if anyone had asked me, I could not say where it came from other than it all seemed of a piece with my crossing to the Council of Elders when Nyla's light stopped before me. I felt a happy warmth upon my chest, as if my medallion was glowing under my tunic. Then, in a veritable sing—song voice I announced:

"My name is Hypatia!"

☽ 3 ☾

The enthusiasm and buoyancy I felt in the aftermath of the Hallowmas wore off soon enough. Aside from needing to take care of papyrus production and order fulfillment, daily business and personal correspondence, along with household activities, there was the matter of getting used to my new name.

Theon was right. People treated Hypatia differently from Catherine. Some of this was just a matter of getting accustomed to using the new name. It is not as if people changing their names was a completely alien concept, especially those days as more people turned to the Christian god and his church. But for those who had known me for many years, Hypatia initially raised some eyebrows.

I wondered myself if taking this name was not too imperious or haughty. After all, hypatos was a title normally applied to those in high consular offices. As Agrippina also remonstrated, maybe this is something I needed to grow into, though I couldn't imagine how that might come about. Then again, it was not like I had a choice in the way the name just erupted into being.

Theon took to the name immediately. Given the meaning of his own name, this was not really so surprising and I don't know of anyone who thinks he is arrogant because of it. So, for this reason and my joy at becoming his adopted daughter, I persevered in making Hypatia completely mine.

Also, after telling Emelia by letter about it, she replied that she found Hypatia an absolutely delightful and fitting name for me. To use her words,

"Such news! In some way, I've always known. Catherine just reeks of that dry, stale monastery. All smelly monks and suffocating religion. Good riddance, I say. Let Catherine be one of their martyrs and die. Long live Hypatia!"

She always did have her own way with words.

In addition to the tasks already mentioned, another loomed large at the estate. The first fruits of the olive groves needed to be brought in for curing and fermentation.

Shortly after Agrippina and her company pulled up stakes and headed westward, taking Synesius with them, Theon called his field foremen together to plan the harvest. A call would be put out for migrant workers, although some already had begun showing up in anticipation of being needed, just as in previous years. Theon oversaw every aspect of this work, beginning with the inspection of the men and women looking to be pickers, picklers or packers. He and one of his foremen called Juba, a Berber originally from Libya, scrutinized each applicant as though they were buying horses or camels, looking for hidden weaknesses. The two grunted and grumbled at each other, as if in a shared, secret language.

There was much stroking of their chins, cocking of their heads, and supposedly meaningful hand signs. I never saw them reject anyone. In fact, it seemed obvious that everyone involved enjoyed the ritual, with some of the returning applicants pleading their cases with melodramatic stories of sick children or elderly parents at home to convince the patron of their need for paying work and their readiness to do whatever was asked of them. Newer, younger seekers bragged about how their strength and stamina would ensure a bigger, more profitable harvest if they were taken on.

After a few days of this carrying on, a feast was laid out for everyone the evening before work was to begin. Next morning, people were divided into teams and sent out into different parts of the groves to work. Some were equipped with short—handled rakes for combing olives from lower branches; while others had long—handled rakes to reach the higher branches. Special teams took ladders with them to get to the topmost fruit. As these had received more sun exposure, they ripened quicker and needed to be picked before they spoiled. These pickers carried baskets around their necks because their work always was done by hand, so as not to bruise the fruit. The ground crews sometimes raked olives into similar baskets or else they let them fall into nets spread out beneath the trees.

As the days wore on, children served as water bearers to minister to thirst under the hot sun. For long periods, the only sounds one heard were bees and other insects buzzing while olives gently plop—plopped onto the ground nets.

About this time, papyrus work had slowed down and even though I had not shown interest in the olive harvest in previous years, I felt it was time for me to pitch in and be useful. I asked Theon if I might be assigned to one of the teams of pickers. He thought this a good idea, particularly as he was eager to try out a new invention. This was a long, double-headed rake that opened and closed like a bivalve shell, operated by a kind of rope and pulley system at the base of the handle. He wanted me to test it for him.

I found this device to be extremely clumsy to work with. Maybe with much practice a seasoned picker might get proficient with it, but not me. After about an hour of fooling with the device and listening to people joke and laugh about it, I set it aside. I decided that I wanted to be one of the hand-pickers working the treetops. So, I found a basket and looked around for an unused ladder. All of the single-framed, leaning ladders were in use, but a young man about my age called Tabat, who was the youngest son of a family of horse breeders west of Carthage, pointed me to a pyramidal thing with a set of ladder rungs going up one side and plain legs for support on the other. Cracking an engaging smile, he said this was one of Master Theon's contraptions and the pickers were wary about trying it out. This proved to be just another kind of ladder that was quite stable and suited me fine.

Tabat invited me to join him so he could show me how to be a good olive picker. By the end of my first day, I was quite tired, sweaty and itchy. Insect bites and scratches from branches and twigs crusted my face, hands and arms; as well as my lower legs from having hiked my tunic up, the better to climb. Nevertheless, I felt happy, as much from the work as from having made a new friend. Unusual for me, I readily took to Tabat as though we had known each other for many years and now were together again. Perhaps this had to do with now being Hypatia, for Hypatia found Tabat very stimulating.

Although the picking crews dumped their takings from the smaller baskets they carried into larger ones on the ground which were then taken away suspended on two poles borne on the shoulders of carriers, I decided to bring in my last, full basket to the curing station myself. There, much to my surprise, I happened upon Peter. He looked no better than me, which gave us a subject for light banter and an excuse not to go into his discourteous departure from the funeral. As though nothing had happened, Peter told me he had decided to stay on, with Theon's permission, because he really had nothing better to do or anyplace he needed to be. Besides, he said, he found the hard work cleared his head and kept him from dwelling on the past.

Neither of us brought up Hallowmas or the *Koinotis*. Nor was I inclined to speak to him of my induction ceremony or events thereafter, other than my taking the new name. After sharing water, Peter suggested that maybe we could get assigned to the same work crew, the better to see more of each other. This was something Tabat and I already had discussed between ourselves. It seemed we already constituted something more than a crew of our own. I said to Peter I would think about it but it might be best to leave things as they were. We said goodbye and each went to our respective home or encampment.

In the following weeks of work, I became closer to Tabat. We formed our own work crew, talking and singing as we picked. We made much of the fact that together we climbed closer to the sun, there to reap the richest and tastiest fruit. I got to ask him many questions about raising horses; telling him, too, how my father had wanted a horse and maybe one day I would have one of my own. He said where he came from women did own horses, so perhaps I one day would visit his family's estate to see for myself.

In truth it was not uncommon for two pickers to work the same tree together; nor was there anything exceptional about couples stealing away to the bushes, as we did when opportunity arose.

Being the subject of local gossip also was perfectly natural and should not have been unexpected. Of course, Peter had heard the gossip and glared at me whenever we happened to pass each other.

☽ 4 ☾

After regaining a sense of equilibrium following what I increasingly regarded as the Night of Magic, I confided to Theon the details of my marvelous journey through the blue ball of lightning. Eventually, we focused on what I had learned of my medallion.

We agreed it could not be an astrolabe as Theon initially had thought. He questioned me over and over again but I could tell him nothing beyond the translation of the inscription and it being tied somehow to a great library. He wondered aloud if perhaps this meant I would find the medallion helpful with the work we had undertaken regarding Alexandria's great library. Neither of us could make out any obvious connections between the two, as even the Library of Alexandria seemed too limited in range from what I had been told. Finally, we decided while the purpose of the device had been revealed, the means of using it had not.

We had in our hands the what but knew not the how to work it. As the medallion already had been in my possession for a very long time before knowing what it might be, it looked like I would have to wait longer in hopes of learning its instrumentality. For the time being my medallion continued to be a mysterious ornament.

It would not be so for very long, but meanwhile events in my life drew my attention away from such matters.

Word had gotten to Theon about Tabat and Peter, probably through Juba. Tabat because of our carrying on and Peter because he allegedly had threatened the one, I now understood, he saw as a competitor for my affections. Both Tabat and Peter were paid and thanked for their work with the olive harvest, but told their services would no longer be needed for things would soon be winding down.

Master Theon, Juba informed them, wished both well in finding their way and contributing their best to the world but neither should ever again seek employment or benefit at the estate.

Before going both Peter and Tabat separately visited the house under cover of darkness.

First Peter. Standing beneath my bedroom window, he called for me. I had been sitting at the window with my elbows on the sill and with my chin resting on my folded hands. The big cat was curled on my lap. I saw a dark figure approach the side of the house and was a little startled to see it was a man wearing what appeared to be the kind of robe worn by desert monks. When the figure whispered up to me that he had to see me one more time, I recognized Peter's voice. Easing the cat down, I stole quietly downstairs and went to the side of the house.

"Catherine, I have been told I must leave."

"Peter, my name is Hypatia, as you well know. And, yes, I know of your going away."

"But you always will be Catherine to me. That is how I have always known you and who you always will be to me."

"That's not true. You have forgotten that you knew me before as Tuya."

"Yes, you're right. But that was before I really knew you and before we became close through the grace of the True God. You know what this means though, don't you. We belong together. I need you, Catherine, and I want you to come away with me."

"What are you talking about? Where would you take me?"

"I'm sure I could start another bakery somewhere. Maybe in Heliopolis, a place you know well and would feel most comfortable. You could help me with it. We would find a house, have children and be happy together. What do you say? I once had a good life and it could be once again if I have you at my side."

"Peter, you say you know me but you really don't. I can no more be a baker's wife than you can go back to baking."

"I know you think you love that Mauritanian hick but I don't see him coming around to claim you. He took off as fast as a dog who turned over a hornets' nest."

What I said next surprised the two of us.

"I truly hope you find your rightful place in the world, Peter, but I say to you if it is Catherine you want then you should take Catherine with you wherever it is you feel you must be. Hypatia, however, stays here. Goodbye."

As I turned to go back into the house, Peter shouted after me,

"Whore! Witch! Theophilus said you'd say something like this! I'm going to the desert and hope never to see you again! You're no better than that Harmonia. Just wait. One day you'll be sorry, just like her."

The night swallowed Peter. My skin burned at the mention of Theophilus. Worse than the time Peter knocked me down in the market. What brought those two twisted souls together? And when? More importantly, where was Theophilus now? Would I never be free of that man? And I shuddered to think what Peter meant by comparing me to Harmonia.

Later, Tabat made his appearance. As with Peter, I went down to meet him but unlike with Peter I took him by the hand and led him up to my room. We passed the remainder of the night with sweet embraces and farewell love-making. Tabat left just prior to dawn, first telling me in detail how I might find him if I would learn the equestrian arts sometime in the future.

He took with him my earlier misgivings about Peter and apprehensions concerning Theophilus. Out of mind, however, did not mean they could not be up to some deviltry.

☽ 5 ☾

After news of Agrippina's death reached us, I received a letter from Emelia. Usually she waited until I wrote to her first, then she would respond. This letter however came not too long after her last one. I had set it aside unread during my grief and would have forgotten about it had not the cat snagged it out from under some other things thrown on a shelf. I found him playing with the scroll one evening, batting at it and rolling it around the bedroom.

The motive behind her atypical correspondence was to tell me Orestes' father, Aurel, had left for Rome and Milan. His mother, Monica, was making plans to follow him and her fear was, rather than leave Orestes with his grandfather, she would try to take him across the sea with her.

In fact, this is what happened, as we were to learn shortly after I had read Emelia's letter of some months earlier.

Emelia showed up at the lakeside estate at noon one day shortly after I had read her letter, distraught. In tears, she explained how whenever she tried to see Orestes, Monica would call her the worst names and demand she go away. Her son no longer needed a whore and she should forget she ever brought a son into the world, for it was god's will he now be raised properly as a Christian. Being Emelia, she continued to try to see her son but one day was told by the grandfather that Orestes had gone with his grandmother to join his father in Rome.

Not long after, she received a brusque letter from Aurel saying he no longer would have anything to do with her. Furthermore, she should forget Adeodatus—the new name they had conferred on the boy—and should consider herself lucky to have served a higher purpose. Unless she felt to repent her sins and convert, she was no longer needed.

By this time in her story, her tears were no longer of loss but of seething anger.

"That bitch! It's all her doing! She turned Aurel against me. She has him believing he belongs to this new god. Now she has my son. She will try to do the same to him. I won't let her! His father may be weak—minded but my son has my blood in him. I won't let her get away with this!"

She went on in this way while Theon and I did our best to calm her down, assuring her everything would come out all right in the end.

Later that same day, a message for Theon came from Alexandria. Its content was to announce the Patriarch Theophilus had been coronated as Pope of Alexandria in this year 101 Anno Martyrum. What is more, Theophilus made a personal request for Theon to come see him, prompting him to say,

"Year of Martyrs, indeed. So now they put a pettifogging, smart—mouthed lawyer in as their new bishop? I expected one day this would come about and now it is here. I can't really refuse his request, so it's time we go to Alexandria to find out what's what and discover our fates."

"Emelia, you help Hypatia pack and get ready. Oh, by the way, she is your cousin now, in case she hadn't told you before."

☽ 6 ☾

Compared to Heliopolis, Alexandria is a veritable hive of activity. Streets are wider, thousands more people buzz about, and the markets are more raucous, especially the central agora.

When we first arrived, it seemed to me there were temples, churches, shrines and cult buildings of every description on practically every corner. The priests, priestesses and diviners of each vied to outdo all others in the opulence of sacerdotal vestments, exotic masks and makeup, hypnotic chanting and music-making, and boulevard processions featuring extreme physical practices or sensuous nude exercises and dances.

Soldiers were and still are everywhere present.

After the quietude of Theon's estate, I found myself unprepared for the transition from country life to the excitement and agitation of this metropolis and entrepot.

Even the necropolis through which we passed on the west end of the city teemed with mourners, hawkers, mountebanks, mystics, soothsayers, oracles, homeless children and animals – and more soldiers. It seemed even the dead could find no rest in this place.

Once we passed through the great Gate of the Moon marking the western entrance on the Via Canopus, I could not know I never would leave Alexandria again by land, only now and again by water. At the time, what I thought was but a temporary visit for Theon to conduct some business and meet with Theophilus, the new Bishop of Alexandria, in reality was as if a heavy door was slammed shut to bar further egress. The Gate of the Moon both opened me to a new life and made it impossible to go back to my old life. Whatever I would make of my life from that point on, it would be here.

Theon used to maintain an apartment in the old official section, the Bruchium, close to the site of the old Mouseion and Library. Since losing his first daughter nearly twenty years ago, he moved his city residence to higher ground in the Rhakotis district, close to the Serapeum and the Lageion or Hippodrome. The home was a unit in a more upscale complex, a kind of ditior insula. Given his plans for the Serapeum, he said such proximity suited his purpose well.

Besides, he said he preferred living among the Egyptians and foreign immigrants—Syrians, Libyans, Ethiopians, Arabs, Scythians, Persians—to the snooty Greeks remaining in what was a dying part of the city. For one, he claimed he liked their spicy food better. Emelia slyly contended he liked their spicy women more the older he became and by adopting me it gave him standing, if not celebrity, among them. I punched her in the arm for saying this.

One of the first things Theon did upon our settling in was to send for a notary with whom he had had previous dealings. I had been living as his adopted daughter for some time now, but he said it was necessary to make my status official. The notary would register my name and our relationship with the City's Hall of Records, so if any questions or issues arose in the future my status would be unassailable.

I was still naïve about such subjects as the need for legal circumspection and closure around things like identity, property, ownership. There was so much I took for granted being raised by an officer of the Roman army. Even after all that was taken away, I felt privileged and cared for. How else explain everything I had come through and the gifts, both material and spiritual, put in my path?

The notary turned out to be a middle-aged, epicene Abhiran, who arrived in a closed litter escorted by two muscular footmen; one of whom went in front to clear the way and announce his master's passage, while the second followed closely behind to shoo beggars and urchins away.

The notary stepped out of his palanquin in front of our quarters, signing to the front runner to retrieve a box with an inlaid mosaic design from within the litter. At first sight, I could not tell if this official was man or woman, as the person before us was heavily made up and dressed in flowing robes.

Emelia nudged me with her elbow and gave me a knowing wink when I turned to see what she wanted, as if to say she knew what was what.

Stepping over the threshold of our street-side door, the person was introduced by a footman with an unpronounceable name I cannot remember. Then, with a flourish, the notary removed an embroidered drapery to stand before us in colorful pantaloons with a long tunic coming down below narrow hips.

Around his neck was an official medallion denoting his office, and it was suspended upon a heavy gold chain. He had long black hair, oiled and held back off his dark, smooth-shaven face and hanging behind his shoulders to reveal multiple gold rings piercing both ears. His cheeks were slightly rouged, but a deep blue paint covered his lips—or perhaps his lips had been tattooed. A bright red dot adorned his forehead.

Despite being of small stature, he made a considerable impression. Theon and the notary bowed to each other while putting their respective palms together in front of their chests. They exchanged words in a language incomprehensible to me. The man withdrew a papyrus roll from his box and handed it to Theon for inspection. After reading it, Theon said something affirmative sounding in that strange tongue and returned it to the notary. Next removing a stylus and ink block from the box, the notary had Theon sign the document. Then he motioned for me to come over. The stylus was handed to me, while both men looked expectantly at me. This was the first I understood I would be asked to sign anything, so with shaking hand I affixed my name—Hypatia—below Theon's.

With this, the notary signed and melted wax next to his name. Using a seal, he made an imprint in the cooling wax, blew upon it and when it was sufficiently dry he rerolled the scroll and put everything away in the box.

Theon handed the notary a small bag which jingled lightly, so must have held the payment for his services. Both men respectfully bowed again to one another, with the same palms together gesture as before. The notary wrapped himself again after handing off the box to the servant who had come in with him, then was helped into his litter. After the door was closed, the carriers lifted their load and took off.

Once they were well away and we were in the privacy of our home again Emelia could not control her laughter. Theon raised an eyebrow but indulged her without admonishment as one might an adorable child.

Alexandria always had seemed a remote and mythical place to me, despite my having circled around its troubled walls all my life. Now that we had come, I sensed yet another change to who I am.

Tuya plus Catherine plus Hypatia equaled—what? More of a construction, a fitting together of disparate pieces, but somehow unified. The three names with their attached memories, the sum of their narratives, must define me. But is that all? Am I as straightforward as a geometric proof? Q.E.D.? It's finished?

No. This seemed much too simple a proposition. I remembered the Greek mathematicians have another expression or tool which might provide a more satisfactory alibi for my life, if not more precision. It ran like this:

Quod erat faciendum. 'It had to be done…'

So, Tuya-Catherine-Hypatia becomes not so much a given easily proved and dispensed with. That being so, the Tuya and Catherine components were more or less complete, so I thought. Not so the Hypatia piece. But what shall Hypatia do now in this new place?

As I would learn through The Reader, my medallion, this construction was very much a work in progress. A work however extending much farther back than either Catherine or Tuya, as well as into the future well beyond Hypatia.

Always—then, now, in the future—it has to be done. Q.E.F.

☽ 7 ☾

"Cuz, relax. Have you always been this tense?"

"I feel awkward."

"Awkward? About this? How long have we known each other? Relax."

"I'll try."

"You know, the problem is you think too much. Always working on some business in your head."

Emelia and I were together on the bed we shared, as the apartment had fewer rooms than the lakeside estate. It was like our old days together in the monastery. I was on my abdomen with her at my side, leaning her body over mine. She said she had wanted to give me a good, deep massage to loosen me up like the kind she said she always got at the baths. She suggested that I close my eyes. I did so, trying not to think of anything but just feel her fingers and the heels of her hands dig into my tight muscles.

As long as I can remember, I disliked having anyone touch me intimately, except for my mother. And Emelia, when I finally had a real friend at the monastery. Even though I later enjoyed my time with Tabat I nevertheless had been self-conscious and awkward.

However, the longer Emelia worked on me, I found myself more and more able to let go. A memory came back to me of the time just before meeting Mother Nyla, when the two young woman had bathed and groomed me. With that, I let myself fall into the sheer pleasure of letting someone tend to my physical needs; of not feeling I had to do everything myself. Alighting in this state I was able to let Emelia's hands release the unacknowledged tension between my legs without objection, as well.

Too soon, Emelia broke off. "That wasn't so bad, was it?"

Catching my breath I said, "No. No, not at all. Just a surprise. In fact, I really liked it. After all these years I'm still learning about you."

"Well, who could break through that shell of yours before? Anyway, now you know what you've been missing. I'll introduce you to a few other ways to relax later."

"OK. I guess that will be all right."

"Get serious! I know you can't be so edgy as all that! You told me you and that Mauritanian fellow did a lot more than just hold hands out there in the bushes!"

"OK, I understand what you're saying."

"Good. Getting you to loosen up has made me tired. Right now I just want to sleep. See you in the morning."

With that, Emelia turned over and started snoring almost immediately. I laid awake for a few minutes more, feeling both energized and languid, as well as glad for what seemed like having body and mind reconciled, even if just a little. Snuggling up close to her backside with one arm thrown over her, I kissed her softly on the shoulder. Before falling into a deep sleep myself, her earlier question echoed in my head, leading me far into dreams.

How long have we known each other, really? The question was a summons taking me back to the place where the Council of Elders chamber was located, though to a vast library instead. I climbed marble stairs to a colonnaded entryway leading to a pair of large doors already opened to receive me. Inside I immediately headed to a table upon which a large, heavy codex, a book, lay open. Standing over the book I looked down at the open leaves where, to my surprise, I saw pictures of Emelia and me. Not just hand-drawn or painted pictures but ones with such verisimilitude to our actual features they might have passed for miniature women or *homunculi.* And the pictures moved! As they moved words entered my head, telling what I was seeing.

Page after page I read, if watching moving pictures can be called reading. In the space of this dream I learned more about Emelia and me than I ever might have imagined. We had lived many, many lifetimes together. In each we assumed a different physical guise and a different role in a different geographic place. Male, female, parent, child, friend, antagonist. And lovers. Always discovering ourselves through the other. Always growing but toward what?

There seemed to be no end to us.

☽ 8 ☾

My thoughts always return to that weird requiem. There is no doubt in my mind the event was a turning point for me. Things seemed to quicken in the years after. Some of this resulted from an awareness of how short a single lifetime is in the grander scheme of things; even such a long life as Mother Nyla's. Some of this, too, just had to do with getting older, as it is commonly experienced the older we get the faster time seems to pass.

Much however had to do with letting go of my previous notions of reality, which likely was my way of resisting change. Shutting out certain memories and closing myself off to certain experiences had been a way to get through everything, but it had made time feel like a crawl.

Certain memories began to wriggle back on their own into my consciousness as a result of talking more openly with Theon and Emelia. For instance, on our trip to Alexandria I asked Theon what business Theophilus could possibly have with him and how long it might be before we returned to the lakeside estate. His reply was ambiguous.

"Until I meet with him, now he is Bishop, I can't give a clear answer to either question." After some further thought he put a question of his own to me.

"Hypatia, do you know the difference between animal and human skin?"

"What? Is it their fur?"

"Animals don't have pores. They don't sweat like we do; instead, they pant through their mouths."

This was so absurd to me as to sound comical. Theon did have a sense of humor and enjoyed teasing both Emelia and me. I stifled a laugh, which came out as a snort, but something about the remark seemed significant. It took a while before the image of the book in Theophilus' room at the monastery creeped back up into my mind.

Aside from having to meet with Theophilus, Theon regarded our visit as serendipitous so he might begin working on his plans for the Serapeum. He said according to the old manuscripts the temple had been designed to bring worshippers to a level where they were themselves as oracles, without the need for intermediaries like Pythia, the priestess at Delphi. As such, one could speak directly to Apollo or whatever god oneself. This was accomplished by quickening a devotee's higher consciousness by means of special acoustic chambers used for singing meditations to better connect one's thoughts with one's sense of being.

He went on to say the Library at one time had housed an ancient scroll of the Jews telling of Master Builder Hiram's secrets for building their temple on the mount in Jerusalem. There is conjecture he was not killed by the Levites as history records, but instead had escaped to make his way to other holy sites around the Middle Sea. His record of the meaning of the temple proportions later supposedly was influential in building the Serapeum in Alexandria.

Typical of the Romans, said Theon, they always were more interested in splendor and grandiosity, without understanding the underlying geometric principles and how these related to the human body. So, when the Serapeum was rebuilt upon its Rhakotis acropolis, it no longer inspired the same spiritual development as the original. Thus, it was Theon's aim to restore the archetypal purpose built into the temple. He proposed to do this by refurbishing one or more inner chambers, rather than by undertaking the total reconstruction of the temple. Besides, he noted, neither the local prefect nor the governments of Rome or Constantinople had the money or the interest in such a massive project given military and political threats.

"Uncle, this all sounds really wonderful but you promised to help me get Orestes back."

"And I have not forgotten my promise. Anyway, I thought you liked it here in Alexandria with your cousin Hypatia."

"I do. That doesn't mean I want to sit around here forever. I know you. You'll get so wrapped up in this temple business, you'll forget."

"No, I won't."

"Yes, you will!"

I listened to these harpastum volleys going back and forth to nowhere, except I knew they would escalate to Emelia in angry tears and Theon shutting down. So, I quietly suggested,

"Father, why don't you tell us what progress you have made regarding Orestes. I am aware you have written letters to Rome, Milan and Athens and suspect you may be seeking information about Emelia's son and my godson."

This was news to Emelia and it temporarily ended the back and forth rally between my two favorite people. Theon apologized for not having let his niece in on these inquiries though they were yet inconclusive and pledged to let her know whenever he received replies from his sources. He went on to clarify we needed first to be sure we knew where Orestes was being kept and second to make arrangements for him to live and study in Athens.

"What? Why not bring him here? I want him here with me. With us. I don't want to have to move again, especially across the sea."

"Because, dear Emelia, this will be the first place his father, or more likely his grandmother, will come looking for him. Don't worry. Everything will be taken care of."

With a sigh, Emelia hugged her uncle, then turned to me and said,

"Let's go up to the stables by the hippodrome and see the horses. Maybe there will be some nice looking charioteers we can talk with and if not we can always go shopping. I hear there is a ship come in from someplace around where that notary is from and they may have brought in new fabrics!"

"All right. You talk with the charioteers if you want, but I want a look behind the scenes for how the races are organized and the horses cared for. Unless Theon needs me here."

"Go! Both of you get out of my hair!"

Emelia and I looked at each other and smirked as Theon turned around to go back to his research and drawings.

"Come on, Cuz. I can hear the horses neighing for us already. Then we'll check the tailor shops and if they have any good stuff, we can get you some more fashionable tunics. Why you dress so drably still, I will never know."

☽ 9 ☾

True to his word, Theon eventually let Emelia and me know he had received news that Orestes was likely in Milan, as his father was studying or working with one Ambrose Aurelius, Bishop of Milan. He also had heard from the son of a friend in Athens by the name of Delios Pileidis.

Emelia could hardly contain herself at this news. She began grabbing me by the arm, then throwing herself at her uncle to hug him; finally babbling on about leaving that very day while waving her arms around. Theon urged her to be patient, for we would have to wait for better sailing weather before booking passage from Alexandria to Genoa to go overland from there to Milan. From Milan, providing we were successful, we would make our way to Athens, perhaps via Venice, where we would meet up with Delios for further arrangements.

This calmed Emelia down somewhat but her eyes still sparkled brightly and she had an ear to ear grin on her face as she lifted me off my feet and spun us both around.

Interrupting Emelia's celebration Theon said he wanted us all to visit the cisterns. I had until this time not given a thought to where Alexandria's water came from, so was astonished by what I saw when Theon took us underground.

Not far from our apartment, there was a weathered door that we had passed by scores of times by now on our way to this place or that, never giving it a second look. One reason we paid it no mind was that the door was sealed shut with an iron box—padlock. Not surprisingly, Theon had a key for the device and when he opened the door we found ourselves peering down a darkened, stone stairway. He had brought along a lantern, which he lit just inside the doorway. It was a rusted, iron thing he had rigged with a movable, parabolic reflector to create a strong, focused beam if needed.

Descending the stairway, he warned us to use caution because the stairs were likely slick with condensation. In fact, the place smelled clammy and was quite chilly, making Emelia complain about not having brought a shawl with her. I could not help but agree with her, but I also was listening to Theon explain what this place was as we went deeper and deeper into its chthonian depths.

As we already knew, many canals had been dug off of the Nile from time immemorial, both east and west, to different areas for irrigation, commerce and, it turned out, for potable water in towns and villages. One such canal traversed the whole southern side of Alexandria, between the city and the lake. Especially during the rainy or flood season, grated tunnels were opened to allow canal water to flow copiously down into a vast network of cisterns beneath the city. Over time, the Nile mud would settle to leave clean water for bringing up to the surface, either by water wheels in complexes such as ours or by hand-carried jars elsewhere.

Upon reaching the bottom of the stairway, the passage opened into a huge, vaulted chamber. Theon shined the lantern beam around and up, letting us see the place. It seemed to be made of several tiers of arcades atop one another, like drawings I had seen of the aqueducts that feed into Rome. He explained further that such chambers as this honeycombed all of Alexandria's underground. We could not see how they were all joined because the connecting passages mostly were under water. Each of these connections served as a valve which could be opened or closed to regulate water levels by area.

In my mind, I thought if this is not the very bottom of the world, it had to be a stepping off place to the Underworld below. I fully expected to see Charon pole his ferry boat up to the landing on which we stood. The place smelled of the Nile, as well as of mold and decay. Dripping water plopped from the high ceiling in an irregular dribble. Squeaks and weak cries blended in strange counterpoint to the vault's weeping. Occasionally, a splash was heard across the water.

What other living things were down here with us! My imagination conjured mischievous crawlers and swimmers waiting for our lantern light to go out, leaving them to their accustomed sepulchral darkness.

Theon demolished this chimera with one of his lessons. Being the treasure trove of knowledge that he is, he told how after Caesar had occupied Alexandria's Royal Quarter, he was nearly defeated when his enemies withheld water from the cisterns that served the Quarter. He also said it was his opinion that the reason behind the subsidence of the Bruchium was that the pillared arcades supporting the cistern vaults there had collapsed during one or another earthquake.

Such information did not make Emelia or me feel particularly safe. In fact, now I envisioned Caesar's parched soldiers rising from the depths or another earthquake striking to bury us in rubble and water. We tightened our grip on each other's hand, while glancing back at the dimly lit stairway exit.

"This is, indeed, most interesting, Father, but I feel you have brought us here for more than lessons in history, hydrology and engineering."

"Oh, yes, indeed! Listen to this."

Theon set down the lantern and then started droning in a deep, basso voice. The sounds came back and came back again, reverberating off the walls in a veritable chorus. After this demonstration, he revealed he would conduct his acoustic chamber experiments here in the cistern. He would try out different kinds and positions of sound reflectors and baffles to get just the right level and degree of echo. This would be easier than starting to work on a chamber at the Serapeum due to constant interruptions.

Emelia and I had just begun shouting and clapping to make our own echoes, when the lantern sputtered out.

Thinking back on this later, the lantern's going out to abandon the three of us to the total darkness, I realized yet again how much I had always felt a victim of circumstances beyond my control. This impression had caused me to distrust life, but also to perpetuate a kind of hoax upon myself whereby I put blinders on to sustain my private illusions.

For example, memories and dreams increasingly began coming into my awareness after this. Some of these had to do with my parents during our time together in Heliopolis. Oddly, I realized I never knew their actual names. To me they always had been Papa and Momma. Who were those two people? Come to think of it, if soldiers were not permitted to marry, what did that make my parents? What did that say about me and Tem?

Back then things seemed so perfect, but recalling how my mother sometimes railed against my father about needing more money, along with his increasing absences, and how he in turn would ignore her, I began to see how my sister and I had become tokens in their struggles with each other. Tem becoming Momma's favorite and me being recruited by Papa. I began to see that my father, much as I adored him, was not the unadulterated hero I had made him out to be, nor was my mother always such a wise and patient woman.

Outside of the home, things may have been done to me and to my sister, or perhaps allowed to be done, that we came to believe were natural. None of this was any too clear, as it all just seemed part of life, just happening, and needed to be accepted and not thought about beyond that. Except for Tem and I sharing certain incidents, they accumulated in the secret niches of our young girls' hearts.

There were other things, threatening things, I clearly encountered on the river and among the thick reeds that I assumed happened to everyone and about which I had no say. For like reason, I never spoke of these to family or anyone else. More secrets.

Then there was my life in the monastery in Nitria. In so many ways, I began to see what went on there was a continuation of the Great Horror and how it affected people's behavior. The only difference being that Christianity encouraged people to put on a different set of blinders, to keep secrets, the better to ignore the pain and suffering around themselves; as well as to deny or even justify how much they might cause others to fear.

I began sharing more secrets with Emelia, who reciprocated in kind. Also, I told some things to Theon over the space of weeks, thinking he might have some advice for me. He suggested that just as he had been able to relight the lantern and lead us from out of the cistern underground, there were philosophies and practices that might light a path for me out of my inner darkness and self—willed blindness.

This is when I began to go back to the writings of Pythagoras, Plato and others in earnest, looking for answers to questions which I dared not ask myself before in hopes of bringing light into my own padlocked depths. Also, on occasional night-dream visits to what I now thought of as my personal library I asked for books on such matters. To my delight such readings were more like hearing an oration directly from the author's mouth.

Although these visits took place only in dreams, I knew them to be real, as much by how tired I felt in the mornings after.

☽ 10 ☾

Emelia and I would go to Milan unaccompanied, as Theon felt compelled to remain in Alexandria to work on his project, including getting various municipal and other approvals. He had us take with us a couple of trunks he filled with scrolls from the auxiliary library in the Serapeum, with instructions for leaving them with various persons in both Genoa and Milan. This would almost complete the dispersal and sheltering of the most important texts away from Alexandria, many of which would remain at Theon's *domus* on the lake front and many more scattered throughout the Empire and beyond.

We set sail on a small ship, part of the trading fleet Agrippina once owned, though now in other hands. It had docked in the Great Harbor, inconspicuous among the many other ships from many lands. This also marked the first time I had gotten so close to the Pharos lighthouse. Though it certainly was visible both day and night, especially at night with the great fire at its apex, from where we lived in Rhakotis, up close I was truly amazed at both its immensity and the engineering genius making it impervious to natural assaults from land and sea.

Our crossing was uneventful as far as weather conditions went, but this did not prevent me from getting sea—sick. I remembered my soldier-father's stories about transiting the sea from his Macedonian homeland and how queasy he said he had gotten. He must have passed along this susceptibility to me, which gave Emelia reason to jest about my sickly complexion and bad breath. She fared much better than I did, eating everything in sight and boasting how the sea air increased her appetite.

We had been expected at the port of Genoa, where we were met by General Marcellinus, who was there on some temporary business. He treated us with great courtesy and kindness, helping with our baggage and putting us up in a wing of Casa di Syrus, the late Bishop of Genoa, where he, too, was staying.

It took a few days for me to regain my land legs and otherwise recuperate from the up and down rolling of the sea. Emelia had done her very best to contain her restlessness during this time, but the General was aware of the nature of our mission, so released us from his hospitality earlier than he may have liked. Over breakfast on our fourth day in Genoa, he told us everything was ready for our overland journey to Milan in the north, whenever we wished to begin.

I took this opportunity to ask him about the father of my childhood, but he said he had never had direct command of the Fifth Macedonian and knew of my father strictly from hearsay through the Koinotis. It seemed I would have to be satisfied with the explanation Agrippina had given me. At least it showed he was no deserter, neither from his military duties nor from his family.

The General took both trunks of scrolls off our hands to make our travel easier, with assurances their contents all would go into the right hands.

Milan was very different from Alexandria and like a portent of what was in store for Egypt in the years ahead. It was here that Constantine had issued his famous edict of religious tolerance some seventy years earlier. As such, one could say it was the origin of the expanding circle of Christianity. Basilicas appeared to be under construction everywhere and there were no temples or shrines to any but the new god.

As it turned out, arrangements had been made for us to stay in the private lodgings of an elderly couple that were practically in the shadow of the palace of the Bishop of Milan. This put us in very close proximity to Orestes, Aurel and, of course, Monica. We needed to be most careful how we proceeded from here.

As fate would have it, the day after we ensconced ourselves in our lodgings, Emelia and I decided to reconnoiter the city, the better to plan what could turn out to be a hurried exit. On our return from almost a full day of walking about and talking with friendly shopkeepers, artisans and students, we found ourselves walking behind a young man scuffing along with his head down and giving off intermittent sighs. Emelia stopped, then quickened her pace to catch up with the young man as she cried out,

"Orestes! My son, is that you?"

When he turned to see who was calling him, it nearly broke my heart. On his forehead was a bandage blood had soaked through.

"Mama? What…?"

Mother and son embraced, both of them in tears, as I myself was. After kissing his face, she said,

"What is this. What happened to you. Did you fall down?"

"No. No, I didn't fall."

"Then what? Tell me!"

"Father did this."

"What do you mean? You had an accident?"

Orestes lowered his eyes, then looked up at me.

"Auntie! You came, too!"

Emelia was not about to let go of the bloody bandage subject.

"Orestes. You must tell me what happened. Are you saying your father hit you? Well, did he?"

"Yes, mama. He hit me. I am just now coming from visiting a doctor."

The story was clear. Orestes had overheard a discussion between his father and Bishop Ambrose, in which the latter chided Aurel for bringing his son with him. Aurel protested the boy had come with his grandmother after he already had gone to Rome, and how his mother insisted all three go together to Milan. The Bishop stated he was sure Monica was a good Christian woman, wanting the best for her son and grandson; but Aurel was going to have to decide if he wanted to belong to his family or to Christ. It was at this time that Orestes overheard the Bishop say,

"It would be better if your son was carried off by the plague than to be a burden to your advancement in the Church, for I see a great career ahead for you. But, you must choose."

Later, Orestes and his father got into a disagreement and the boy threw the Bishop's admonition in his father's face. This is when Aurel struck his son. Unfortunately, Aurel wore a heavy ring on the hand he used to discipline his son. This opened a large gash on Orestes' forehead and the need for medical treatment.

"That bastard," Emelia growled under her breath.

We cautioned Orestes to say nothing about meeting up with us or of our presence in Milan, though he said he did not wish to return to his quarters in the Bishop's residence. Soon enough, we assured him, we would be taking him away.

Within a week we were on our way to Venice, just as Theon had suggested. We hired a carriage in another quarter of the city, telling the driver to come by our lodgings early in the morning while it was still dark. This way, we were able to secrete Orestes into the carriage, along with a bag holding a minimal change of clothing. The driver had been paid well to look the other way and, besides, by the time he returned to Milan we three would be long gone by ship to Greece.

On the road between Milan and Venice, we stopped to find further medical attention for the cut on Orestes forehead. It had begun to scab over but his doting mother and aunt wanted to take no chances. For sure, this would leave Orestes scarred in more ways than one.

☽ 11 ☾

Athens in our time is nothing like it must have been at its zenith or perhaps it is just our imaginations painting an overly halcyon picture of those times when great mathematicians and philosophers taught in the Academy and the several stoas in the city proper.

There are men, and a few women, nowadays who traipse through the streets dressed in what they call "philosopher's robes". These persons will quote to you from this or that philosopher, having memorized words from Pythagoras, Protagoras, Epicurus, Plato and other schools. They do this for a few coins, but I found none able to discuss the ideas contained in their quotations. One soon gets tired of listening to them, often reciting their lines like bad actors or not so colorful parrots. The readings in my library visits did nothing to help their case.

It took us several tries to find Delios Pileidis. Every driver we asked assured us that he knew exactly where the man lived, but when they had to stop to ask others for our contact's whereabouts, even though we may not have perfectly understood the dialect they spoke, we quickly got away to find another wagon or carriage. Finally, a well-dressed man by the name of Proclus overheard us arguing with a driver demanding payment for having let us sit in his wagon and travel less than ten passi before stopping for directions. Our new protector sent the cheat on his way, then told us he personally knew our Delios. While he would prefer to take us himself to his friend's domus in the countryside outside of the city, he apologized that he had business keeping him in Athens for the next couple of days. So as not to delay us further, he found us a carriage, gave the driver minute directions, and even paid the driver in advance, warning him not to extort any further fee from our trio.

It was very stupid of me not to have connected the name Delios with another protector from my last days in Heliopolis for, indeed, it turned out to be the very same Delios.

He was now a full grown man, tall and athletic in stature. After leaving Egypt, he had gone to his father's estate with Latona, his sister, where they both remained to this day. The two together managed the estate since their father's demise, he having fallen from a galloping horse seven years previously. Neither Delios nor Latona had married since our first meeting and seemed not to require the assiduities normally associated with taking a mate.

As for how Delios knew Theon, he said his father had been a long-time friend of Theon, both belonging to a certain fraternity or organization. With this disclosure, Delios gave me a slight smile and a nod of his head.

Emelia, Orestes and I were guests at this estate for a little over a month. During this time, arrangements were made for

Orestes to continue his education under various tutors in the intellectual, ethical and physical disciplines. He was delighted by this, especially because of the opportunity to learn equestrian skills, which both his father and grandmother had forbade him to do.

Delios and his family had a long history as horse breeders. Of old, they served the military and the equestrian class but for many decades had found it more lucrative to provide animals for *quadriga* charioteers in the hippodromes, mainly in Greece itself. Their estate had a circus track the race factions could rent to train drivers and horses, but race fans were strictly barred from access. His descriptions of how the integrated businesses supporting the sport of racing added to knowledge I had acquired in Alexandria.

It was at this time I experienced a change in my relationship to my magical library. Where before I could visit only in the deepest of dreams while asleep, which sometimes meant I did not clearly remember what I had read upon awakening, I found I was able to call books to me. The first time this happened was while by myself following one of my discussions with Delios. I was thinking about horse breeding when a large book appeared in my lap as if to answer unformed questions in my mind. The book showed what might be called a genealogy of horses and how the various breeds had descended from extremely ancient animals who were much tinier than the marvelous beasts of today. Once again my sense everything is change got reinforced.

I tried retrieving library materials then on a variety of subjects, things which just popped into my head willy-nilly, without luck. In retrospect, I think the library considered my demands as frivolous and unworthy. I would have to be more judicious.

Meanwhile, Emelia, I could see, was quite taken with Delios. She talked about how she loved visiting the stables at the Alexandria hippodrome and how she seemed to have a special love and affinity for horses. Delios, for his part, seemed happy to take her to his stables, where together they curried and fed his favorite stallions.

Her affinity came as news to me, however I felt as the weeks passed I very likely would be returning to Alexandria alone. Indeed, Delios arranged passage for me to Alexandria when I felt it was time to return. Prior to my departure, we were able to have private conversations concerning Orestes and Emelia.

He assured me he saw it as his duty to look after Orestes' education and finding suitable assignments and appointments for him if he proved himself capable, for so Theon had charged him. As for Emelia, she was welcome to stay as long as she wanted, for he understood her desire to be near her son. I snickered lightly at this, making him blush, at which he admitted there might be other reasons for her staying and he had not thought things had become so obvious. Besides, his sister welcomed the female companionship and it seemed she and Emelia had much in common.

We also talked about Theon, Delios' father and the *Koinotis*. Delios had been initiated into the fraternity during an event similar to the requiem in Egypt, but in Athens with a different group of notable people. Like me, he was unsure of what he was meant to do but since his induction he did feel his life was on a different, almost calculated path.

I told him that is exactly how I felt, like I had gotten onto a different time track. I then showed him my medallion, letting out, too, a little about its connection with the ball lightning, Council of Elders, and a wondrous library. Delios said he had not experienced anything similar, asking if I might elaborate. I begged to be excused from his request because I was not yet sure what such discoveries meant nor where they might lead me.

We agreed we should stay in touch. He was interested in Theon's acoustical project and what ramifications it might have for spiritual awakening and capacitance. For myself, I said it was possible I might wish to learn more about equine culture from him. Also, I wished to be kept informed from his perspective how Emelia and Orestes fared. Both of us wanted any information the other came by regarding the Koinotis.

The voyage home to Alexandria from Athens without Emelia gave me time to meditate. My soul-searching brought up a vivid memory, long suppressed, from my eleventh year. As with the account of myself when I was Tuya, I tried my best to capture this experience in writing according to how I experienced it as a young girl.

☽ 12 ☾

The reed boat on the brown river felt brittle from being too much in sun and water. Rickety. Puny.

Making me more vulnerable somehow. If my family stayed here, I would need a new one made with fresh reeds. And given the way things had been going, I would have to make it myself without Papa's help. But by afternoon tomorrow or the next day at the latest, we should be headed upriver on a larger, wooden cargo ship. Most likely this would bring its own share of troubles.

I did not want to think about it. It was just one more thing to worry about, which is why I decided to take my skiff out by myself one last time. I thought it would help distract me.

Paddling to one of my favorite retreats deep within a maze of papyrus, I settled in to put the awful events of the last several months—Papa's disappearance, Mother Nyla, Tem's agony, our eviction—out of my mind.

Then, the light shifted.

While still early morning, the sky seemingly jumped to a brighter blue like that seen at midday. I could touch the blue almost, for it glowed all around me, while seeming to faintly hum and hiss in a strangely musical way, as well. The amulet against my breast felt warmer, too, as though excited by the change in the atmosphere, the bronze coming alive.

At first, it was like being in two places at once. I was standing in front of the skiff. Or some part of me was, because I was still sitting in it looking at my back, yet connected with myself almost like ropes of muscles, tendons and veins within my physical body were straining to keep me moored, even as this other body pulled away to cast off from its earth—bound corporeal twin.

It is hard to describe. Something which should not be...was.

For a moment, I thought this had to be a dream. Sometimes you see yourself separate like this in dreams, so surely I must have nodded off. It would end when I awakened. No need for me to panic, though panic pressed upon my ribcage.

My standing self looked into the fathomless blue as something like a hawk or a falcon in pursuit of its prey appeared, coming with terrible speed at me. It came on fast but gracefully braked and alighted maybe a dozen steps away. Once it got close, what I had taken to be wings no longer seemed like wings. My thoughts tripped over themselves in a jumble. Standing so close to this thing, dread and wonder overwhelmed me with inner trembling.

My eyes saw—not really a hawk nor a bird, but not a person either. The body, tall. A man's, maybe a woman's, maybe a mix of both. It was hard to tell with all the light on and around and coming off it. The head though was decidedly a hawk's. Dark and hooded eyes. Raptorial beak. Feathers for hair.

The creature was like nothing that walked the world of our time. Though alien, my pounding heart filled with the sense of the being's perfection.

Despite my original panic, I found myself wanting more than anything to be with this being, to be taken up in its arms, to be embraced and loved. To be taken away from what my life had become and what I feared it might yet become. I felt sure I never again would see anything so splendid as this ideal vision. Yet, how could it be only a vision? What vision gives off a scent like from the temples on holy days? Can a mere image tug one's heart and soul with the essence of sandalwood or civet perfume?

The hawk-person—this Shining One—beckoned with its right arm for me to come forward; speaking my name in my mind, yet without speech.

By now, I had forgotten about the girl in the skiff, like she belonged to another world, holding on to and troubled by things which no longer concerned me. Looking at the space between me and the Shining One, there were things like stepping-stones that looked like the blue sky had crystallized to create them from the surrounding cerulean space. The being nodded for me to walk across these even though it looked risky and made my heart beat faster. What if I missed a step or slipped? Before I knew what I was doing though, I found myself skipping, pretty much dancing, with a big smile on my face, over those rocks crossing the stream of an aquamarine sky with perfect balance.

Moment to moment was everything. Time no longer pulled or weighed on me. The reeds of the river elongated, as though trying to follow me where they could not and the streaming waters of the Nile murmured my name in a vain attempt to summon me back.

Though it felt like I moved straight ahead, by glancing down I saw each step really was taking me higher and higher in the sky like I, too, might rise with the wind above the river like a bird.

With the first step, I saw myself now lying in the boat. It was nestled safely in among the reeds by the shore. Five long—legged ibises with their sickle-shaped bills and crooked necks stood guard facing the river. Occasionally one would duck its head into the water to spear a fish. They might be working but breakfast was still breakfast.

On my tiptoes upon the second rock, the riverside marketplace spread out beneath me as a whole in a way I had never envisioned it before. I knew many of its aisles and pathways, sectors and stalls but never had put it all together in my mind. Most vendors already were set up and customers were finding their way to favorite hawkers and knots of friends in the early light. Fires burned and the fragrant smoke and aromas of cooking meats, vegetables, stews, and soups curled and bowed with the morning breeze. Camels were being led into the corral for later inspection and sale. The sounds of their braying complaints reached my ears.

Successive steps gave me ever wider views. I saw the city of my birth, Heliopolis, in the way it must look to the birds soaring over its rooftops and the citizens already moving about with purpose. And then I could see Mare Nostrum! And where the great river joined it! These were things I only believed in before, because those who were older and well-traveled, who knew more of the world than me, had described them to me. Now I knew for a certainty, not just that they existed but the intricacies of their shapes, movements, smells, almost their tastes. I sensed the diverse, teeming life they held.

At the last step, more of an invisible platform, I took and held fiercely to the hand of the Shining One, for the sight below caused me great dizziness. More than just Mare Nostrum met my eyes.

Yes, I saw the great river strung out to the south and even where my family would be going; but to the north there rose up another shore and many islands, as well. This must be the place from where my Papa had come as a young man, boarding a ship with other men and crossing this wide sea to be a soldier; to meet my mother; to have my sister Tem and me; and finally to be lost.

Up to this point, my ears had been filled with sky song since leaving the quayside marketplace behind. Now at the side of the Shining One, a sound like rolling thunder came up from below, growing stronger and louder, and it was as though the whole sea below us trembled. Amazingly, the waters along the edges of the sea pulled away from the beaches and cliffs at their margins. I could see ships which had been close to ports and harbors now resting on flat land previously hidden from living eyes beneath ocean swells. I could see men and women standing near what had been the water's edge, most staring in wonder, some in fear, but some dashing out to the fallen ships.

I knew I was witness to an immense tragedy building. I could see a great power swelling far from the shores, like a Colossus girding for battle; ready to smash whole armies with one blow of its sword arm. Or like a pregnant sea goddess nearing the end of her labor and preparing for one great, final push that would deliver untold destruction and misery upon ships, harbors, cities, people and animals within its reach.

Holding me close in its cool embrace, the Shining One pointed down to where the distended sea's pent-up belly was greatest and made a piercing cry seeming as loud as a thousand ram's horns, trumpets and buccinae all blown at once. Released, the water charged irresistibly toward the coasts from which it had retreated minutes before.

Resuming our stationary position overlooking my homeland, it was as if the being lent me falcon vision and I saw into the great city of Alexandria, a place I had heard much about but never visited. Thus, I witnessed the destruction caused by one tall wave after another crashing over breakwaters into its two harbors, there lifting ships over the seawall into the city itself, dropping them on rooftops, slamming them through doorways, crushing any in their path.

Thousands were drowned or pulverized and many buildings destroyed. I watched in complete disinterest, like the god at my side. In more ways than I could know, this experience spoiled me for any normal life.

My eyes though picked out one individual in particular; a girl my own age, pale-skinned and with light hair. I watched as the first and biggest wave swallowed her, grinding her frail body amidst the rock and rubble before dragging her remains—broken bones, shredded flesh, and blood mixed with salt water—back along with countless others to feed whatever god or demon rules the murky undersea.

I asked myself, 'Why was I meant to see this girl among so many die?'

The being, my protector, knew, I am sure. In my mind, he spoke these words to me: "Know that my Father and I are one. Know that my Eye watches over you."

Though I did not comprehend the words, this scene got stained into my soul like a slave's tattoo, indelible and always present to be contemplated for many years until, hopefully, it faded with age.

☽ 13 ☾

Earthquakes around the Nile region have always been a constant. Usually they are small and one gets so used to them they pass without comment. Whenever something larger but still moderate comes along, it becomes a topic for conversation. Of course, everything ultimately gets compared to the quake and inundation that destroyed parts of Alexandria some years earlier. Visitors, too, make comparison with earthquakes in their countries, often meeting the stories of older Alexandrians with a sense of indulgence before relating their favorite tale of earth-shaking destruction.

Well aware of the effects even these small to moderate earthquakes have on buildings, Theon became increasing concerned over the years since my return from Athens about how the Serapeum would hold up over time and what the consequences might be for his project. As I always had helped him with projects, usually those dealing with some branch of mathematics or astronomy, he took me along on walk-throughs of the Serapeum to find and catalogue any damage done to the structure. I would be the one to record our findings, which he then incorporated first into drawings and then into a scale model of the temple.

Theon pointed out the edifice already was hundreds of years old and despite having been rebuilt, the high ground it sat upon would affect it one way or another, too. If the acropolis was solid rock, strong earthquakes in particular would transmit their energy directly to the stone pillars and arches of the Serapeum; whereas if the mount was less solid, earth movements over time would undermine anything set on top of it.

My father's suspicions were well-founded. We discovered numerous hairline cracks and separations between blocks in the temple's outer foundation; larger ones in both basement floors and upper chamber walls where plaster had been replaced and friezes and crown molding showed signs of crumbling. Exterior architectural sculpture also suffered. Pediment and caryatid features in places seemed dangerously close to disintegration and collapse.

The Serapeum's age showed starkly but the priestly caretakers seemed blithely unconcerned about making meaningful repairs. The majority of the offerings the temple took in went to richer ornamentation, ostentatious ceremony, and feasts instead of to maintenance and repairs.

I was beginning to understand how these things worked. The cults of old had established themselves in people's hearts and minds in part by means of massive buildings to impress upon them how small they were and the need for the priesthood as intercessors for their salvation. Now these cults handed down from ancestral times found themselves competing with the new cult of Christianity, which also had embarked upon its own program of building grander basilicas. In either case, the needs of the religious establishment again were taking precedence over the needs of the people.

An exception to this practice I noted in Bishop Theophilus' construction campaign. Certainly, he had undertaken the building of a few large edifices in Alexandria, the better to house the growing number of Christians on their holy days. As such projects took many years to complete however, he also began putting up smaller, simpler structures to serve as reliquaries. These, he claimed, were stocked with pieces of holy men, such as their Baptist, who had been martyred or died under conditions of self—imposed suffering for their god.

The Bishop evidently had hit upon a brilliant contrivance for attracting those hopeful for cures to ailments and afflictions, as well as those with a morbid curiosity with death and putrification. Reliquaries soon cropped up throughout the city and in the surrounding countryside. Some openly gibed about the seemingly endless supply of body parts and secretions available to the Bishop. For myself, it was becoming clear just how important blood sacrifice is to this cult. My long-standing disquiet about Theophilus also deepened. I told myself I would try to find if my secret library might tell me more about this man.

Theon's worst fear came about just over twenty-five years after the Great Horror.

Another strong earthquake, though not as powerful as the one in 365 A.D., struck the Nile region with enough force to cause undeniable damage inside the temple. Much of the smaller statuary and imagery was sent to the floor, where it became fragments and dust. A few archways collapsed and some pillars leaned out of plumb. The priests temporarily abandoned their houses at the loftier levels, while closing the temple to outsiders. For safety reasons, they said, but really to prevent scavenging for every kind of precious metal and wood.

As Theon knew the temple guardians and custodians well, he and I were still allowed access. In fact, we were hired to conduct an assessment of the damage to and safety of the structure. We accomplished this within a few weeks, with a resulting appraisal reporting the building had for all intents and purposes outlived its usefulness. Theon submitted along with our evaluation an outline plan for construction of a new temple, along with an estimated cost of replacement, which included the salvaging and reuse of undamaged materials.

While the monumental statue of Serapis in the Great Hall was apparently undamaged, Theon suggested the time had come to retire it, to move beyond visual symbols and flights of fancy to more meaningful spiritual education and guidance. Doing so, he argued, would usher in a new age of enlightenment and harmony.

Of course, this plan was called preposterous and our scrolls were burned. Fortunately, advance payment had been made for our study.

Later, Theon admitted to me though he knew this to be an impossible recommendation, he felt the growing strength of the new cult demanded extreme changes. Given the condition of the Serapeum however, he said he could not continue his work for an acoustic chamber there, but now would take it to the cisterns where his work had started.

He compared the Alexandrian cisterns to the catacombs beneath Rome, where early Christians reputedly worshipped in secret for a long time. Perhaps his dream, too, would take several centuries to fruition.

So, now our work—or some of it—was to go underground.

☽ 14 ☾

Bishop Theophilus' face, so different from how I remembered it, was like a farmer's cheese left too long on a platter on the table. Where it was not covered by untidy beard like overgrown mold, the flesh had a mushy, pap-like appearance and the black eyes recalled decomposed cheese fly larvae. He seemed a creature who spent too much time indoors under poor lighting, except perhaps for ominous outings on the darkest of nights.

This was the man who accomplished what the earthquake did not quite finish and what Theon had been unable to do through more straightforward, human motives.

The final destruction of the Serapeum came about as a result of totally serendipitous circumstances, of which the Bishop took full advantage, such that some privately thought he must be a great magician.

From the rooftop terrace of our apartment, we enjoyed a clear view of the Serapeum acropolis. The hippodrome, though nearby, was obscured from view by other buildings; nevertheless, the clamor of the crowd on race days was obtrusive and unavoidable. The shouts and cries from the circus did act as an alarm however, so shops and homes along surrounding streets often were shut up in the expectation of vandalism or worse carried out by one or another or all of the race factions.

Much of the disorder and disruptiveness that Alexandria was renowned for was birthed in the hippodrome. Especially the Blue and Green factions enjoyed nothing better than deadly brawls, often not satisfied unless their mayhem infected other parts of the city like a virulent plague. Thus, it generally was not just faction ruffians who got maimed or murdered, but innocent men, women and children, as well. Those more fortunate to be in their way only were robbed, sometimes being left totally naked as a gang made off with everything they had been wearing.

These sport antagonists almost always were young men, though some mainly adolescent girls joined them. They fashioned their hair in outlandish styles they fancied were Hunnish in nature. Likewise, their clothes, martial devices and decorations, which they wore like uniforms, were barbarian in appearance; as were the tattoos upon faces, arms, legs or other parts of their anatomies.

Faction members always were armed. They concealed short swords, knives, knuckle spikes and maces of all kinds in their clothing to enter the hippodrome, but sported them openly when in the streets, even flaunting them before soldiers.

On one race day, the cheering from the hippodrome rabble was especially resounding and must have carried well beyond the city walls. Later, we learned what had happened. A certain charioteer, who went only by the moniker Son of Mary, fell from his vehicle while rounding a turn. Normally, this would result in serious injury or death for a driver, but definitely signified the end of the race for such a person. Son of Mary though quickly regained his feet and his quadriga. He reentered the race to everyone's surprise and won.

As fate would have it, Bishop Theophilus had accompanied the Prefect to this race and was seated in the Prefect's reserved box with him, shaded by a canopy, as well as by his hooded black robe. As Son of Mary whipped his horses across the finish line, the Bishop stood up and shouted,

"A miracle! In the name of Christ, a miracle!"

Spectators in the vicinity who heard this took his words up as a chant, which before long spread throughout the stadium.

The story gets murky from here due to conflicting accounts, so it is hard to say who said what and directed the aroused crowd towards the Serapeum. Most agree though there were black robed monks mixed in with the mass of race devotees, urging them on. Having surrounded the temple, the crowd soon routed the priests from their citadel and began attacking the building, inside and out. The heavy doors in the front were the first to go. Taking them down loosened stone masonry in the adjoining pylons and lives were lost as blocks and debris crushed skulls below. And so it went, until the mammoth statue of Serapis was torn apart.

Pieces were taken to the theater in the Bruchium district, where they were burned to the delight of the crowd.

At one point, the Bishop got himself hoisted up upon the remains of a wall to declare the victory of Christ over the pagans.

This, Theon later said, was the tipping point.

Scroll #5: "Gate of the Sun"

Setting: ALEXANDRIA

☽ 1 ☾

Rome had broken faith with Theon, so Theon withdrew more and more from Rome.

He said he had been slow—unwilling—to comprehend how thorough were the changes overtaking the Empire during his lifetime. Imperial edicts banned sacrifice, which he never understood the use for in any case, so he said nothing. The reaction against Emperor Julian he considered childish, so he dismissed it. The desecration and wrecking of temples—not only the Serapeum, but the Isis Temple, the Caesareum and the Temple of Kore, along with hundreds of others, all destroyed or converted to other uses—all seeming more the acts of unemployed hoodlums or contentious sacerdotal opportunism, he privately reproved but just stood by.

Theon now said all these had been warning signs.

Not until the outright prohibition against any but the new state religion did he awaken to a clear progression he said he should have stood against earlier. By the time Emperor Theodosius issued his prohibition, he recognized a threat of wider implications, not just to religious tolerance but to the broad freedom of inquiry. In the final analysis, he admitted, Rome had broken faith with itself by allowing dual rulership leading to the ascendancy of Constantinople and subversion by sectarian superstition and fanaticism.

The cisterns thereafter became Theon's new place of refuge and occupation. A place he could continue the pursuit of science as he knew it. A place he could call his own. Theon spent more and more time encapsulated by the sweating walls of the cisterns, even sleeping there. He surfaced for meals, but then began storing food supplies in the underground, competing with the rats for his sustenance.

Shortly after the destruction of the Serapeum and well prior to his self-interment, I helped Theon lay the groundwork for his study of sound, acoustics and music. This meant going back to Pythagoras, or what little was known of his work, for he left no written records. We had to go by what others had said of his teachings and life. To some extent, I also was able to supplement our knowledge base by calling up readings from my magical library. It seemed we were going to have to work at discovery rather than have it handed to us.

A pupil of Plato, Xenocrates, wrote that Pythagoras himself had discovered the relationship of musical pitch with the length of a vibrating harp string. Theon thus took as axiomatic everything has a number and without numbers nothing truly could be known. For him, this was a natural law guiding his experiments. What he sought to accomplish in the cisterns was to develop not only a formula demonstrating the relationship between direct sound and reflected sound, but a kind of sonic geometry from which to build sound rooms for stimulating higher consciousness.

"Hypatia, it should be obvious when we hear our voices come back to us as echoes, there is much distortion in how the sound has been reflected."

"I understand what you're saying. Because you want to build the perfect acoustic chamber, there are good reflections that support this and bad reflections that hinder it, is that right?"

"Exactly right. Now, if we can determine how to either eliminate the bad reflections or get them to harmonize with the good ones, I should be able to construct a working model down here."

"Are you sure? This is such a huge space. Wouldn't it be better to work in something more self-contained and comfortable? It is so damp and cold in here and our feeble light does little to illuminate the whole space."

"Likely that's what this will end up as. A smaller space. I mean, just look at this place. If we're talking about reflections of sound, why should it be any different from reflections of light? There are so many surfaces here going every which way, I think to harmonize all of them, while not impossible, would just take several lifetimes. I may have to build a more concentrated space on one of these landings or even above ground, once I learn more about reverberations down here. It seems a shame to waste such an available resource, don't you think?"

"Father, I just thought of something else, too. When you said it is like light, I recalled how different surfaces absorb light in different amounts. Here we have various kinds of stone works along with water and who knows what else may be lurking in the dark. I'm sure it has to be the same for sound, too. Or so I think."

"Thank you, daughter, for you have just made this even more complicated and confusing!"

Theon and I took a small fishing boat from the north shore of Lake Mareotis to our Draconis Domum, where we were met by Juba who escorted us from lakeshore to house. Once there, we immediately set to our task; combing through the library and scattered piles of scrolls looking for anything to do with Pythagoras, music, sound, light, engineering and things remotely related. These we piled into a wagon, which Juba drove back to the lake, where we picked up another boat by prearrangement for our return to Alexandria.

I could not help thinking as we bumped along the road to connect with our boat that something had changed about our former abode. I could not put my finger on what, but it seemed linked somehow with Juba. His demeanor seemed more formal and aloof than I remembered.

I let this pass though, for Theon and I had much work ahead. We both undertook a writing campaign to contact those who had taken custody of Library materials, asking them to search for relevant treatises. After I catalogued and summarized what we had on hand, Theon went into what he called his sképseis or cogitation stage. I knew better than to interrupt during this important period, which was fine because I was developing a separate idea of my own.

There were some ideas bubbling up in my mind from my review of past works as they might pertain to Theon's endeavor. These ideas had to do with the quadrivium mentioned by Plato; that is, the study of arithmetic, geometry, music, and astronomy as the basis for education. During my visit to Athens, I sadly learned the famous Academy of old was all but defunct. Perhaps it would have a better chance here in Alexandria?

I decided I would enlist the help of my old associate, Synesius, in setting this up. From our correspondence following our initiation, I had become aware of his having received a traditional paideia education as an aristocrat, albeit more of the country gentleman sort. Such training incorporated the quadrivium along with liberal arts, physical culture and equestrianism, but also important social skills needed for being a contributing member of the civil order.

My purpose was to counter-balance the crowd mentality characterized by the race factions and burgeoning religious divisions increasingly swaying rational political discourse and decisions in Alexandria. Helping to shape civic leaders guided by the Golden Mean, I reasoned, would return both wisdom and beauty to our city, making it a beacon for the rest of the world, just as Pharos was for those at sea.

Such an educational foundation would be as critically important to elevating consciousness as Theon's contemplated sound room invention.

In my letter to Synesius, I explained I hoped together we might petition the Prefect to fund our endeavor, for it was not uncommon for government to sponsor philosophers and teachers for the common good. To widen its appeal, our academy would be open to any and all serious students, in the belief anybody and everybody might benefit from proper scientific, moral and civic education.

I also explained it was my feeling this course of action accorded with the precepts, unspoken though they were, of the Koinotis.

☽ 2 ☾

Prefect Flurus deflected our petition for pecuniary support on the grounds such ideas had been tried in the past and proved to be a waste of money. Alexandrians, in his experience, were too fractious to stick with any discipline or curriculum for very long. If, however, we could prove the value of the idea by showing a steady attendance of twenty to thirty pupils, he would be happy to reconsider our petition.

I talked him down to a core of ten to twelve dedicated students.

Although he would not provide us with fiscal backing from the city's coffers, he did give permission for us to utilize public buildings as ludi. An interesting choice of words, yet we took him up on his offer by suggesting that as the Old Library had fallen into disuse and become overrun with the homeless and vagrants, we would be pleased to begin restoring it to some of its former high purpose.

We began by standing at the bottom of the steps going up to the Library's entrance, announcing to passersby that two weeks hence they might attend a lecture on moral philosophy. The following week, we posted papyrus bills in the main agora and in the few days prior to the lecture we paid criers from our own purses to walk the streets, shouting among other criers touting baked goods, sausages, the names of officials running for office, along with bookmakers taking bets on the next races.

While demeaning in a certain sense, it brought home to us what the Prefect had said that there were too many things vying for citizens' attention, not just day by day but hour by hour. Nevertheless, out of the hundreds of thousands of people living in Alexandria, we felt confident we could find ten serious students.

Synesius and I had agreed beforehand we would adhere as much as possible to a Socratic method. Instead of giving a standard oration, we would look more to address the concerns of those who came to listen, the better for people to see philosophy is practical, not a lot of nonsense having little to do with their lives.

For a first attempt, we drew a sizable group of people. As people tend to come and go at such events, I counted perhaps seventy who stayed throughout. It was instructive for us to learn how different groups of people thought about ethics.

About one-third of attendees were what are called representative or common citizens, including tradespeople, warehouse men, city officials, students and one sea captain looking for something different to do while in port. During the course of our open forum those in this group said about ethics that,

"Ain't ethicalness all about doin' what the law says? Leastwise, that's what I thinks and more people ought to pay mind to that, is what I thinks."

A more thoughtful and elegant response from the well-travelled seaman was,

"Well, I certainly agree with what the man says about obeying the law but, as we know, laws vary by both geography and time. So, I would propose that ethics pertain to the standards of behavior of whatever is acceptable by one's society. It is important to fit in, no matter where you find yourself."

Perhaps another third of the crowd consisted of rabbis, teachers and, mostly, Christian ecclesiasts. These latter were dressed in the black robes that had become a common sight everywhere in the city. They held views best summarized by,

"Ethics is what my feelings tell me is right or wrong, but only if my feelings are first disciplined and guided by study of holy scripture." Or,

"Ethics is following God's Laws." And,

"It's all and only about what are the right religious beliefs and teachings of the True Church."

The last third of the audience was a total surprise to us. Some of the more outrageously dressed adherents of the Blue Faction entered as a group. Except for their belching and farting, they contributed little. The most we got them to express any opinion or idea on ethics came from a tattooed young woman.

"I got no idea what you may mean by that word. Do you know?"

This elicited laughter and foot stomping from her companions; groans and disdainful snorts from others. It was noteworthy, however, that all of the faction fellows remained throughout.

Word obviously spread about we two upstart philosophers, Hypatia and Synesius, for subsequent attendance at our talks never again reached those numbers. In large part this is because neither the race factions nor the clergy came as a group again, though we did get individuals from each who were mostly curious.

By the time we reached a stable number of students—fifteen, in fact—Flurus was no longer governor over the Alexandrian Province. A new man, fittingly called by the name Alexander, had worked himself into the position. Thus, we found it necessary to plead our case anew, but this time we had experience, adherents and reputation in our favor.

All for naught.

Present in the Prefect's audience chamber during our petition for support was Bishop Theophilus. He sat in an honored position next to Alexander, the latter often conferring summisse with him or looking to him for a sign.

"Magistra Hypatia, the good Bishop has informed me of your worthy efforts to elevate the quality of our citizenry, describing various of your teachings, etcetera. But can you assure me there is nothing in your teaching that might be construed as paying homage to any of the old pagan gods or slanderous against any other religion or subversive of the authority of the Emperor in Constantinople or any of his appointees?"

"Honored Prefect, I do so assure you."

"Well, that was short and to the point, wasn't it?"

The Prefect and the Bishop put their heads together again. While they huddled, I cast a sidelong glance at Synesius who was standing next to me. He was normally quite relaxed but his posture at this time was rigid. My scalp started to prickle, but I mentally kept telling myself there was nothing wrong. It would be normal for a man of the Bishop's stature to be close to governing officials, the Prefect included. After all, I had answered the Prefect honestly. There was no need to overreact or think our petition would not be given fair consideration.

When the two completed their private discussion, Alexander looked from one to the other of us. The Bishop covered his mouth with his tented hands, elbows resting on the arms of his chair. His eyes gleamed like a jackal's circling its prey.

"Hmmm. Magistra, you are the daughter of one called Theon, are you not?"

"Theon is indeed my father, Honored One. I see you know of him, so you must know what a great and generous and wise man he is…"

"Yes, we know of this Theon. He is the one who spends his days and nights beneath the city, spinning his plots for covering the land with a new kind of pagan temple. This we have heard."

"No, no! It's not like that. There is no plot and there is no desire to raise up a temple to any god. His only aim is the investigation of the science of harmony and music. There has been a misunderstanding…"

"Indeed, there has! You misunderstand us if you think to trick us into funding your father's efforts under the guise of your little academy. Your petition is denied."

With our eyes and cheeks hot, we retreated through the knot of other petitioners, feeling like we had been purposely put on display to discredit us. By the time we reached the outside I was clenching my fists and loudly asking of no one in particular,

"Who does Theophilus think he is? I knew him when he was just a simple camel driver called Jason! What an upstart! Just shows how far you can get with nothing but a clever tongue and a knack for taking advantage of others! Grrr!"

During my growing rage over the insult to my father, Synesius avoided eye contact. Finally, he excused himself and said we should talk later.

☽ 3 ☾

Over the two and a half years or so Synesius and I spent together, aside from our attempts to build up a model academy in Alexandria, we plumbed the greater depths of philosophy in many late night discussions. Those few of our adherents who remained following our public disgrace often joined with us for simple meals, wine and the incidental herbiferous potus. Willy-nilly, our sessions took us into the reality of how rationality and irrationality seem to coexist in the cosmos and the futility of denying one or the other.

I mentioned during one such session having read scrolls by and about Anaxagoras illustrating how those two qualities held equal dignity within the soul and intellect. I did not mention where I had read these, but after explaining a little about his scientific accomplishments, I brought up his respect for life's mysteries and the necessity for the soul to be educated over its long journey.

"How can the journey be so very long when we see the young dying all around us every day," asked one man?

It was Synesius who answered,

"You have perhaps heard of the Orphic mysteries? This information generally is kept very secret, for those who are initiates say you lead more than just this current life in the body you now have."

"So, by a long journey the philosopher means traveling from one life to the next? One body to another? How can this be so? Why don't I remember having lived before?"

"Yes," said I, "That appears to be just what Anaxagoras meant, but not just him. Many others have written about this very phenomenon, including most recently a Christian philosopher of note. His name was Origen and he espoused the idea of reincarnation nearly a century and a half ago."

Synesius added, "As for why we do not remember any lives previous that, too, is a mystery. It has been suggested being carried for nine months in the womb, while our new body takes form, this ordeal wipes out much of the soul's memory. The final shock of being born into this world again works like a mason's chisel to cleave us from former lifetimes."

"What then could possibly be the goal or the end of such a journey taking a man through many lifetimes," asked another?

"Having heard many orations on this subject, including some by our esteemed Bishop here in Alexandria," I offered, " It is clear the goal depends upon who is talking. Besides Origen, there was a more recent Christian theologian by the name of Arius who asserted the Hebrew and Christian scriptures support the idea of the soul's migration. Its purpose is to culminate in God, the All—In—All. This Arian doctrine has caused a great deal of conflict, such that it is widely regarded today as being against the teaching of the Church. The Bishop, as you likely are aware, is adamantly opposed to what he calls a false doctrine and has done all in his power to stamp it out."

Synesius interjected a stern warning here.

"What Hypatia means is that it is heresy. So saying, you can well understand why it would not be wise to talk outside of our small group about such matters. Both for your personal safety and for the sake of the rest of us here. I think this is something the Orphic initiates themselves understood all too well."

Not long after arguing the pros and cons of the case for reincarnation, Synesius begged his leave of me and Theon, saying he felt the need to return to his hometown of Cyrene. Coincidence or not, his decision came on the heels of Theodosius' edict.

About this time, one of Emelia's many letters arrived. She had remained with Delios and Latona at their estate outside of Athens since our joint visit there and for the most part had been happy during her years in Greece. She had only lately heard of the death of Monica however, which actually occurred not very long after my own return to Alexandria. At first, Emelia said she gloated over this but before long she realized how little joy there is in delighting over the death of another. Particularly, in this case, because it was the death of her son's grandmother.

As for Orestes, he continued to prove himself to be every bit as sedulous as his father Aurel, excelling in all of his studies and activities. He had grown into quite the young man; one whom many mothers eyed as a catch for their daughters. Slightly taller than average, he had dark hair, dark eyes, and a most handsome face and muscular body. Only the scar he had received at his father's hand spoiled what would be his perfect looks, but even this projected a certain aura of boldness and self-confidence. According to Emelia, he never seemed to feel self-conscious of it.

True to his word, Delios had arranged for Orestes to do a stint in the military when he was of age, being sure to keep him as part of a local detachment. He quickly moved up from a stable hand to subaltern positions within the equestrian order and from there to that of a decanus with a squad under his command.

When the time seemed right, Delios obtained his discharge, which carried with it Orestes' immediate attachment to certain official personages in the Athens city government, all of whom were men of wealth and standing. Rumor had it Orestes had become so well regarded that the provincial governor was considering him for inclusion on his staff and for even greater things.

With her son's education and career well launched, Emelia declared she was wanting to return to her parents' home in Carthage. Neither parent was doing well and might not last much longer. Her father's old injuries had become quite rheumatoid, making him able to walk with only the greatest of difficulty and with much pain. She said she wanted to sail directly to Alexandria rather than the port of Carthage, so she might visit briefly with me and Theon, for she was unsure how long it might be before she could visit again. I was overjoyed by this news, especially because I thought she might be able to help me talk her uncle, my father, from out of Alexandria's nether region.

☽ 4 ☾

My thoughts and emotions during this period were very perturbed and confounded. I was glad to have Emelia with me, even for a short time, for she was someone I always felt I could trust and confide my secrets in.

"Hypatia, of course you're burned up by what that piece of camel dung did to you. I'm just surprised you haven't already hired someone to knock the camel crap out of him."

"Believe me, such things have crossed my mind, Emelia. There's no question Synesius and I were the victims of foul play, but I can't think of why. The reasons remain very unclear to me."

"Reasons? What difference do those make? How many times over the years have you told me what a deceitful ghoul Theophilus is? Do you think he needs reasons? And even if he had them, it's not like you could use logic to change his mind. No, the man just takes pleasure in hurting people and he seems to have it in for you for some reason, too."

I took this opportunity to tell Emelia about a dream, really something mysterious I saw in a book in my library, concerning Theophilus. The two of us were shown walking along a road side-by-side. We came to a fork in the road and needed to decide which way to take. I could see some distance down each and one way did not bode well for Theophilus. The other was better but he would have to surrender his sense of self-importance and desire for power to take this path. In short, he would have to choose humility.

"Well, at this point, it's not helping any to dwell on the Bishop. I'm just glad you're here. You always have helped to keep me steady and to make the right decision about so many things."

"You'll think this funny, sister, but I feel the same about you. But tell me what else is on your mind. Maybe we'll find something hopeful there to lift your spirits."

"I don't know what might be hopeful about Theon spending more and more time below in the cisterns. It started off as just another one of his scientific projects, which might have been successful or not. In the past however if he was unable to break a problem, he would put it aside and move on to more fertile fields. You know how he is."

"All too well. But what are you saying?"

"Emelia, I'm really worried about him. For all intents and purposes, he lives down there now. The only times I see him are when I take food to him or just go down to check on how he is doing."

"What? Is he using the cistern as his latrine now, too? The city's drinking water? Gods! I always thought he would go off the deep end sooner or later."

"No, he goes in a bucket and carries it up topside, putting it outside the door during the night. He must be paying someone to empty it. But, listen, he looks terrible. He's gotten gaunt and pale and he hasn't bathed properly in I don't know how long."

"You mean, he stinks."

"Yes. You know what a stickler he has always been for cleanliness, so this has me really worried. What should I do, Emelia? Tell me. You've never let me down before."

"Well, Hypatia, I know this much. You said the Prefect used Theon as an excuse to turn down your petition, right? So, I think all of this intrigue has more to do with him than you. Although I'm sure that damn Bishop remembers you from the monastery and was glad to stick it to you, too."

"I guess you are right, but what of it?"

"Don't you get it? They're watching Theon. How else would they know he's in the cistern? It probably means someone is watching you now, too."

Prior to these reversals over my Alexandrian Academy and Theon's state of mind, I had been filled with a modicum of joy and confidence. I had much to think about due to the resurgence of long-suppressed memories. But while talking with Emelia I said I felt maybe I had let myself be lulled into a false felicity and, really, things had been too good to be true. And now, despite myself, my rancor toward Theophilus blossomed like a mouth canker, a constant bedevilment that would not go away.

Emelia theorized I just needed a new direction following the recent setbacks. She said this comedown was completely natural and to be expected but this, too, would pass. She did apologize for not being able to offer anything besides platitudes, but I assured her just her presence and caresses were helping to restore peace to my heart. Nevertheless, I did not wish to keep her longer because of my little problems, for she was needed more by her parents and should make haste to Carthage.

After she left, I threw myself into the management of our household affairs—something Theon normally handled. Since his sinking into the underground, our family financial matters had suffered. I had been putting off delving into these in the hope Theon would return to take care of things. Because certain merchants and provisioners were now calling for payment, this work fell to me.

I knew, of course, that Theon had maintained a ratio, an account, in the form of gold plates with the Serapeum *trapeza*, a deposit bank operated by the temple. I supposed despite the temple building itself having been destroyed, the trapeza must have continued and taken up residence elsewhere in the city. I set out to discover its location and then determine the state of our finances as soon as possible.

What I found was after the fall of the temple, not only had all Serapeum accounts been taken over by the episcopate, but Theon had moved our account. I regarded it as much mine as his, a family asset but unfortunately the trapezítes to whom I spoke claimed they did not know where Theon had moved the account. Perhaps, they suggested, I should try one or another of the argentarii or silver dealers in the area, as they typically took on such business.

This proved to be a useful recommendation. The fourth shop I visited was an elderly Syrian gentleman named Liban, who was both dealer and smithy. Sensing my naiveté in matters of money, he offered to educate me if only I could come back in the evening when business was not so brisk.

I did return and found our conversation most helpful. In the process of describing how the Alexandrian banking system worked, with its myriad money-changers, money lenders, collateralization, risk, interest and such things, he inquired about myself and my father. I told him about how we had come to Alexandria and how we lived, but not about the cisterns; telling him instead that Theon was away on business. At his behest, I also described life at our Draconis Domum, with its large house, slaves, groves, vineyards, papyrus factory, and more.

When I had finished, he was silent for some moments, stroking his beard and staring at me. Finally, he said,

"Kyría, are you absolutely sure your father, Theon, owns the properties of which you speak?"

"Why, yes. Of course! I mean, why would he not be the owner? He lived there. We lived there. For many years, enjoying the fruits of the land and the respect of everyone. What do you mean by such a question?"

"Please, please, take no offense. I ask this in order to help you, for this is a matter of utmost importance for you. Now with your father away—unreachable, as you say—and his account having been moved to you know not where, there are things you need to find out. I speak not only of the location of his account but of what the nature of the account might be. It is imperative, I believe, for you to know exactly what his relationship is to the estate near the banks of Mareotis, too."

"I don't understand why it would be different from what I've said: that he owns it. What else could it be?"

"My dear, in my years working here, I have dealt on occasion with such estates and the people associated with them. It is not unknown for these to be organized along the lines of societatis. Do you understand what that means?"

I knew of one society and that was the Koinotis, but whether it was involved in fiscal matters I could not say. So, I responded to Liban thusly,

"No. It sounds though like this is going to be another part of my education that you have so kindly undertaken."

"Exactly. To be brief, a societas is an organization that may own property, be that land or some other valuable asset, wherein one individual or group puts up the capital, while another trustworthy and capable individual is hired, as it were, to work the property as overseer or manager. Do you see what I am saying?"

"I think so. But my father himself hired an overseer called Juba, so would that not make him the owner?"

"Maybe but not necessarily. On a large estate like you have described, it would be too much for one man, or one woman, to manage. Parceling out that job to others would be part of the job of the society's trustee."

"I am beginning to see the problem here and I thank you for enlightening me. Might you also be able to tell me where or how I might discover the nature of our domum?"

"That all depends on where it was organized. Usually, that would be the city or province where the people who put up the capital live. If they are in Alexandria, you might find some document in the Hall of Records here. You mentioned earlier your father dealt with a certain notary in the city. He might be able to help you."

"I am most grateful to you, sir. Thank you very much."

This new information was not the kind of directional change Emelia had had in mind, I was sure. However, on the positive side, these matters diverted my mind from thoughts of Theophilus, at least temporarily. As I discovered later, not being in my thoughts did not prevent him from further villainy.

☽ 5 ☾

Finding the notary turned out to be a simple matter due to his peacockish notoriety. Rather than have him visit our apartment I walked to his post, where I was made to wait in an anteroom with other clients. As he had been when first we moved to Alexandria, the notary was brisk with the clients ahead of me, speaking to them in as many languages as they had brought with them, so it was not long before I could present my need to him. He recognized me and called me by name.

Once situated in his office, I explained about Theon being away and how I now had responsibility for all our household affairs, including handling our accounts. I also disclosed my discussion with the Syrian silversmith that raised the question of ownership of the Mareotis estate.

As I spoke, the notary did not look at me but seemed preoccupied with his hair; however, because he nodded or made humming interjections from time to time, I assumed he listened. Finally, still looking away, he said,

"As you are Theon's daughter, a fact for which I bear a certain responsibility in your "birthing,' as it were, so we might even say I am as an uncle to you, I believe it would not betray my duty to client confidentiality to reveal, let us say, some most pertinent information for your benefit.

"On the day when I officiated over your adoption by your esteemed father, we completed another matter, as well. Of course, you were unaware because your father had instructed me to speak in a foreign tongue unknown to you. The matter of which I speak pertains to the question you bring me regarding Theon's estate. An estate, as your silversmith surmised, that is actually not Theon's."

The notary confirmed the estate was owned by a societas. What is more, he told me the governors of the organization were from the military leadership in Nicopolis, the provincial army garrison just to the east of Alexandria. The purpose of the societas, among other things, had been to provision the military in the Fayum or delta region with oil, grain, wine, papyrus and other items. I knew the military were recipients of much produced by the estate, but assumed they made payment to an account under Theon's care. Additionally, the notary said the terms of Theon's contract stated if he were to leave the estate, he must appoint an interim replacement, pending approval by the governors. Thus, along with my adoption, he had transferred his commission to Juba.

Stunned as I felt to hear this, another matter came into my mind at the mention of the military.

"Kyrie, I suspect you know from Theon that the father of my conception had been in the army and that he disappeared without a trace. The centurion in command of his legion told my mother his pension would be held in trust for my sister and me. I remember him saying so very clearly. Would you know how I might apply for this?"

"Yes, I do know something about it. Unfortunately, any claim you make very likely will go unsatisfied. You would need to prove your identity and your relationship to the man who was your father. I can tell you they would need to have your mother attest to these facts and it is my understanding you would have difficulty finding her and obtaining this."

My face dropped as the notary spoke, as much from the realization I probably never would see my mother again, as that the last connection with my original father also was lost to me.

"My advice to you is to forget the pension. Your efforts would be better spent elsewhere."

Looking directly at me finally, the notary said,

"Now you know all that I know. I'm sorry I have no information about the account for which you seek. I can tell you from hints your father dropped, he had set aside a considerable part of his earnings as estate director. I also believe the military settled him with a pension, just as they do soldiers who put in their twenty-five years of service. If you would know more, I advise you first to pay a visit to this Juba to find out what he knows.

"Oh, and one last thing, if I may. Get your father out of those damned cisterns before it is too late."

I left the notary's office in a daze. I was not sure if I was more affected by Theon's not sharing such critical business information with me, or by the fact my second father, like my first, had been affiliated with the Roman army, which always acted in its own interests first.

I felt my whole life had been built on lies. Lies of the army. Lies of the Church. Even lies from family and friends. My life was going in circles and once again I had no control over anything.

Unannounced, I arrived by boat at the western shore of the lake. This time by myself. I found Juba without difficulty. He had firmly ensconced himself into the house, taking over his former master's room and moving his family and concubine into others. While he was surprised to see me, he understood my concerns, assuring me he would do his best to answer all my questions.

Juba invited me in to the room adjoining the kitchen for dates and a sweetened drink of some kind. I noticed the large tom cat sleeping on a cushion in a corner of the room. He half-opened his eyes at my entry, then went back to sleep. At least some things had not changed, though he looked much older and like he had seen many battles in his day. I sent a consoling thought to him, for hadn't we all seen as much?

After relating my visit to the notary, Juba said there was one thing I needed to know from what the notary had told me. Since the transfer of the operational directorship, the ownership of the societas had changed hands. It seemed the Levantine and African bishops had pressured Constantinople to take over such estates, assuring the Emperor the Church would minister to the physical needs of soldiers as well as to their spiritual needs. As a result, the assets of the Nicopolis societas were endowed to the Church and its governorship had been transferred to Nitria.

I stayed the night at the estate, Juba's wives having made a place for me. My mind was in a ferment the whole time, as well as on my return to Alexandria's southside docks the next day. Should I confront Theon with what I now knew? Should I travel to my old home in Nitria on my own to inquire about Theon's pension and insure continued payment? I decided to delay the latter course because the trip would take me away from Theon for too long. The notary was right. I needed to get him above ground before doing anything else.

☽ 6 ☾

As I turned down our street toward the apartment complex, I saw two faction members standing outside our door. Getting closer, I recognized by their shirts one from the Blue Faction and the other from the Green.

Odd, I thought, they appear to be working together peaceably rather than insulting one another and brawling. Spotting me, they both trotted my way, speaking rapidly so all I could understand was something had happened to Theon in my absence.

What I had dreaded since his descent into the cistern had occurred. The evening of the day I departed for the estate, he was found unconscious, half in and half out of the door to that cavern. The discovery had been made by a Blue, who went for help but ran into a group of Greens who immediately circled and blocked him. After explaining his discovery, the Greens sent a scout to verify the story and, once substantiated, all went together to Theon's aid.

In trying to move him, it was found he had broken a leg, as well as having sustained multiple contusions on his face and other parts of his body. A stretcher was obtained to move him up to his room, where he had been undressed, his wounds tended to, and finally put to bed.

Both factions took turns caring for Theon, waiting for my return. He had regained consciousness, only to hazily stammer something about being attacked while at his work below ground. Somehow, he then managed to crawl back up the stairs and open the door. After that, he had blacked out. Because he was in much pain due to the leg injury, someone had procured a mild henbane mixture, which also was making him somewhat delirious. At least, they assured me, the fracture was not of the open type, else he likely would have bled to death. Boasting, one told me he had suffered worse as a result of free-for-alls in the hippodrome and this is why they knew how to take care of such things.

The fellow's limp, his scars, and encrusted discharge from one half-closed eye did not do much for my confidence, but I expressed my gratitude for their charity. They demurred, yet did not hesitate to point out how other citizens had seen Theon's body hanging out into the street but none of them stopped to investigate. What really got my attention was when one of them asked,

"Do people like them have not ethics? They think they are better people and only say bad things of us! No heart. They have no heart."

I knew Theon was over sixty years of age at this time, which worried me because I also knew from medical texts the older one gets the more dangerous an accident—or in this case, an assault— can be. Theon's incident was especially severe and there was no telling how long he would take to heal, if he ever healed at all. I would have to find a surgeon who now could check his leg to assess the extent of damage, what my father's prospects might be, and tell me how best to treat him.

For the first time in many years, the prospect of being on my own loomed large once again. I had passed my fortieth year and despite my broad education under Theon's tutelage coupled with my own thirst for knowledge, it seemed I still remained ignorant about so many things in this world.

It is said Helen of Troy eased Priam's wounded warriors by casting "a drug into the wine of which they drank to lull all pain." The doctor said she most likely had administered an opiate tincture received from an Egyptian queen. Once reserved for elites, it was now available to any who could afford it. This he gave to Theon for his pain.

Though I had sent for the doctor soon after finding Theon in bed where the Blues and Greens had lain him, it had been nearly a week since his trouble and the leg was still inflamed. Before trying to reset the femur, the doctor prescribed fomentations of hot, salty water to reduce the burning and tenderness, while continuing with the opium medication.

The doctor said because the break had not cut through muscle and skin, and because it was in the middle of the femur and not close to either the hip or knee joint, Theon had a much better prognosis for recovery with minimum complications. His age though was a factor to consider. Until the inflammation subsided, a wooden splint was applied to the whole leg to keep it immobilized and prevent any further damage, as well as to minimize pain.

Night pain was the worst and after several sleepless nights for him and for me, I increased the amount of medication given so both of us might find rest.

When he was not sleeping, Theon wanted company and became much more communicative than before, to the point of being absolutely chatty. Obviously the influence of his medication, I took advantage of this new volubility to inquire about our fiscal condition. Where did he move the account formerly with the temple? Was he aware the societas now was controlled by the Christian monastery in Nitria? Had his pension been affected by this move and how had he arranged to receive the proceeds from the pension?

I was shocked to learn he had taken physical possession of the gold plate bullion from the temple, without then securing it with another trapeza or a procurator. I was doubly shocked when he admitted he had hidden at least one talent of the plate in our living quarters beneath the floorboards under a heavy chest at the foot of my own bed. He babbled on about how no one would suspect me to be hoarding and hiding such a valuable cache.

If this was more than drug-driven blather, it meant he could disclose this not only to his daughter but to any visitor. A talent's worth of any material would be too heavy for me to move easily, which meant I would have to find someone trustworthy to assist me.

First, I needed to know what he meant when he said "at least one talent" was in our home. Where was the remainder and how much was it?

Theon giggled no matter how hard I pressed him for this information. So, I dropped it temporarily to focus on matters closer to hand. I thought I could get Liban to set up an account accessible to both Theon and myself, at least until he was in better condition to resume his responsibilities.

And that is what I did. Because Liban did not regularly deal in gold but only silver, he said he would exchange the metals, the easier for him to track changing market values. Of course, there would be transaction fees but he would waive his, taking but a small management fee for handling the account. He explained further, so I would understand, he would not keep our physical assets himself, for he only stored enough silver on his premises for making cups, plates, jewelry and other ornamentations. Instead, he would maintain the paper account, which I was free to inspect at any time, and arrange for merchant credits as needed.

Theon brushed aside my questions about his pension, saying it bored him and anyway the topic was unimportant. I was unwilling to let this go, so wrote to the monastery to determine the pension's status. Also, I wanted proceeds to go directly into our family account with Liban, something he already had agreed to take on along with the other family business.

It took a few weeks, but I received an official correspondence bearing the Abbot's seal saying all was in good order and the pension would be administered as I had directed. The Abbot also wished me well and prayed my father would make a speedy recovery. While nursing Theon through the worst of his rehabilitation was difficult, I felt I had gotten our situation under control and was quite pleased with myself. My father, like my father before him, would not be with me always; thus, it was imperative for me to learn all I could about modern money management. Necessity often is the best teacher.

☽ 7 ☾

Theon eventually had his leg bone reset, a painful process involving the tying of straps on both sides of the break; then several people pulling contrary-wise. For a time afterwards, he was fitted with a different, slightly more flexible kind of splint consisting of several wrappings of linen cloth; the inner layer dipped in wine and oil, the better to draw out inflammation and promote rapid healing, and the outer ones stiffened with resin. His leg never did return to its full strength though, despite long periods of massage and baths with oil, salt and nitre.

This unfortunate affliction affected us in several ways, some badly and others that could be construed as beneficial.

While the broken leg was the most obvious injury Theon sustained, his doctor conjectured the beating he had suffered had substantially bruised the hip joint on the same side. He explained how such incidents can result in a progressive deterioration of the joint, a kind of post-traumatic arthritis. Theon found he needed a staff to get around comfortably, once he was up on his feet again. For this he commandeered my old staff, long unused, given to me by Amma Talis for martial training.

This meant over time the pain from the arthritis increased, too, with the result he demanded a steady supply of the pain—killer his doctor had prescribed during the initial rest and rehabilitation period. I never thought to withhold the medication from him, but it was clear he was becoming more and more enslaved by it. He never again mentioned his acoustic experiments or wanting to return to the cistern. This was just as well because it was clear someone was either trying to stop his work or appropriate it for themselves. It was just as clear a great many people, if not the whole of Alexandria, knew of his work in the cistern and such notoriety likely had made him someone's target.

Theon now seemed completely content with allowing me to keep charge of our finances. From time to time I brought up the matter of the additional savings he had stored up and hidden, but each time he either brushed the question aside or ignored it. I began to think there was no additional storehouse, that it was just something from his delirium; besides, our account with Liban was more than enough to take care of our needs, especially with the pension supplement.

For his part, Theon spent his days eating and drinking with friends at one or another taberna or food stall, sometimes also keeping the company of young people of the factions, who enjoyed his stories. We installed a garden on our rooftop terrace which he became fond of working.

My contact with Liban and the pecuniary world opened new avenues for me. He had no children to whom he might pass on his business and none of the young men he had taken on as apprentices over the years had stayed on.

"Kyria, I have noted that you are very quick. You pick things up about this trade in a short time that others take months to understand, if ever. Watching how you took over your father's responsibilities—well, nothing short of amazing, I think."

"Thank you, Liban, but as you know necessity often can be a spur to learning."

"True, but you have an intelligence that is rare. Just so. And I have something for you to consider."

With this, he pressed his palms down on his table, looked up, exhaled, then looked at me. At first I was confused because he began talking about the many obstacles one meets with in his line of work and how competitive it is. Finally, he paused, lifted his palms from the table and opened them. I waited for what it was he wanted me to consider, until he said,

"So? What do you think?"

"Oh! Forgive me. You are asking me if I want to—what? Join you in your business?"

"Yes. I would be very happy to apprentice you and be your mentor. Of course, only if you are so inclined. I am sure you would do extremely well."

It had never seriously occurred to me to work at anything outside of the universe of books and philosophy. Even running the papyrus operations at the estate was just an adjunct to this. However I had been finding satisfaction and pride in how I was managing our family's money. Before I could speak however, Liban said there was one thing I needed to know before deciding.

"Hypatia, like you, I am of the Association of Illumination. What I am about to tell you is something you must vow to keep to yourself."

"What? Really? Why have I not seen you or known of you before Theon's troubles?"

"Because not even Theon knows what I am telling you. Theon, your father, belongs to what may be called the science and philosophy branch of the koinotis. I belong to the fiscal and economics branch. These two are kept very separate. We bankers know of them, but they know little to nothing about us. As you will learn, we have good reasons."

"But I don't understand why you are telling all this to me. Why now?"

"We know what Theon's condition is. While we really did not expect his sound experiment to be successful, we hoped for a breakthrough anyway in the hope of rediscovering what might be an ancient technology. There is no way now that he is able to complete his work. Nor do you have the skills or the inclination to pick up where he left off, though I am sure you would apply yourself diligently if asked. Besides, you have proven yourself an adept student in many ways and in many other fields. There are those who believe you would serve better by working with finances."

"Do you mean with the finances of the Association?"

"No. Once you are trained and established, you will be working with princes and bishops across the full range of their interests. In this way, the Association always will know what they are up to but also you will be in a position to influence their plans both directly and by means of certain esoteric practices to which you in time shall be made privy.

"You also will be working with others like your father. Scientists. Engineers. People who are gifted inventors and thinkers. They, too, as you are well aware, require money to carry on their work. So, what do you say? Do you accept my offer?"

I agreed to work with Liban. By accepting his offer, I also was agreeing to not say anything of this to anyone. Not to Theon. Not to Delios or Synesius. Not to Emelia.

Liban disclosed my ultimate goal would be to become a procurator, in the sense of taking charge of the private affairs of others. A step towards this first would be to build a reputation as a trustworthy feneratrix, a money lender and bullion broker. He pointed out while there were few other women in this field, it was not impossible to be successful. Intelligence was not enough in itself however. I would have to learn to be tougher.

And so, I applied myself diligently to learning the skills necessary, gradually building up a small clientele under Liban's shop.

I also continued giving one or two lectures or seminars in philosophy at different places in the city, largely because of my positive experience with the youth of the race factions. Generally crude and ill-educated, these young people evinced a readier grasp of the heart of philosophical matters than their more urbane contemporaries, who often were merely pretentious. They proved the goal Synesius and I had set towards improving civil society had been well founded, just misdirected. Additionally, through them I obtained introductions to the faction directors at the Hippodrome, who managed extremely large sums of money to finance shows in the circus.

I never again sought official support for my teaching activity. Because Liban encouraged me to continue the lectures as a way for people to become acquainted with me and ultimately help my enterprise to become better established, I also was glad knowing I never would have to resort to the kind of metaphysical hawking I had encountered in Athens. All things considered, this new direction gave me a sense of stability I had not realized I longed for in this world, which is not always what it seems with upheavals both material and spiritual.

Things soon settled into their new direction with relative ease. Then, about six months into my apprenticeship, I received a letter from Emelia. Both her parents had died and she decided to sell their estate rather than stay on. There were several bidders, including from Primianus, Bishop of Carthage. His was not truly a bid however, as he urged Emelia to pass the property to the Church, in exchange for which she could receive lifetime care in the House of Virgins adjacent to the rectory.

Apparently, he was willing to overlook her status as a husbandless mother, but Emelia was familiar with the kind of life the residents of such a house endured, so declined. She wrote of how shocked the Bishop seemed at where she instructed him to put his offer.

Once her affairs in Carthage were settled, she said she would like to come live with me and Theon. I had told her about her uncle's accident and how his recuperation had gone, as well as his general physical and mental condition since then, including his continued use of one or another analgesic. She suggested with the two of us to watch after him, I would get some relief and have less to worry about.

I longed for her to join me, imagining her hands softly upon my skin, but until it happened did not allow myself to dwell overmuch upon such thoughts.

☽ 8 ☾

The first rains came early in December, heavier than usual after an extremely dry summer and fall. Theon continued much the same, while we still awaited Emelia's coming, as unforeseen snags had held up her plans. There was a rhythm to life in the city I conformed with, adopting it as my own. Things were harder than before Theon's mishap, but we were getting by and I was more or less optimistic about our future.

As if to signal how ill-founded was my complacency, thunder from a storm off the coast rolled concussively over Alexandria one night. Lightning flared brighter than Pharos, offering no solace to any caught on the open sea. Through the loud thunder, a pounding at my door came to my ears. Then a voice.

"Hypatia! Hypatia! Open up! Let me in! Please!"

"Who is it? Who are you and why do you hammer at my door so?"

"You know me! I am a friend. Please, let me in."

Picking up a knife, I went to the door and put my hand against the wood. It was cold. Rain flushed garbage, offal and more down the street, reconstituting what the summer's heat had condensed to a more exanimate state, now waking into renewed putridity that seeped into the house. I undid the latch with my left hand, gripped the knife harder with my right, then stepped back as I pulled the door open.

A black robed figure stumbled forward into the anteroom. I hunched down, knife at the ready, feeling like cold fingers had gripped my heart. I tried to focus my thoughts, while dragging the palm of my free hand down my tunic to dry it. Regaining its balance, the figure straightened as it turned to me. Jerking both arms up, the figure tossed back the hood of the robe.

"Peter!"

"Yes, it's me. I need your help, Hypatia."

"What's wrong? Where've you been?"

"It's been terrible. But I need to eat and rest. Tell me though, how are you? And Theon, is he well?"

"Close the door and take that awful black thing off. You're soaked. Let me find something warm of my father's for you. Sit by the hearth while I do so and find something for you to eat."

Peter was so exhausted we did little talking that night, however his parting words to me following his dismissal from the estate still rang in my ears. Though I had noted he no longer called me Catherine, I kept a knife hidden on my person just in case. In the days that followed however, he did not seem such a threat and we caught each other up on our lives.

After leaving Mareotis, Peter said he traveled about, crossing North Africa through Mauretania to the Pillars of Hercules and even going over to Cordoba. Though already exposed to the Christian religion, he met many holy men, as he called them, who convinced him he should try to follow in their footsteps. With this decision, he backtracked to the Nitrian community in Egypt where we two had ended up after the long ago catastrophe. Once there, he began more thoughtful studies as a catechumen. Eventually, he had gotten baptized in the Church, but held off on making a decision toward ordination into the priesthood. Instead, he took on what he called Levitical duties, including those of being a Reader as part of church services.

When I asked what had been holding him back from the priesthood, he admitted he still harbored reservations. These concerned not only his continuing perplexity about his life's purpose, including whether there might be hope still for the two of us together but also the conspicuous captivation of the Church leadership by things of this world, which seemed at cross-purposes to the advice of the holy men with whom he had met on his travels. He said it was almost as if there were two different religions under the single banner of Christianity.

As best as I can recall, Peter's words ran like so:

"Recently, a long-simmering argument between the Nitrian hermitages and the Bishop of Alexandria came to a boil. On the surface, the disagreement had to do with the teachings of Origen. As you would expect, Theophilus condemned these as heretical; but really I'm pretty certain it all had to do with money. There was enough evidence of bribery and misappropriation of funds on both sides, to be sure. Emotions got so heated that some adversaries came to physical blows with one another.

"After this, Theophilus called a synod of the region's bishops to meet in Nitria. He contrived to have Origen's followers denounced, but then these barricaded themselves in the church and so had to be driven out forcibly.

"The Bishop thereafter had them indicted on some trumped up charges. He got five or so monks of no standing whatsoever to testify and bring the indictment. This he took to the Prefect in order to have an arrest warrant issued. To insure the warrant was enforced, he came to Nitria himself with a military escort. But that's not all. He also brought a cadre of armed, black-robed monks, such as seem to be everywhere. These men set about burning cells and books and I know for a fact they killed any monk who would not speak out against Origen and toe the line the Bishop had set.

"As for me, I barely escaped with my life. Perhaps mistaking me for another Peter who was Archpresbyter of the monastery, one of the Black Monks came at me during the night. Only by overpowering him did I get away, disguised as one of them, as you saw when first I came."

Rumors and hearsay about what had happened in Nitria circulated in Alexandria; some favorable to Theophilus, many not so favorable, while some disapproved both sides. What soon became clear however was by destroying the monastic community there, all its assets were declared the property of the Bishop of Alexandria. These included societatis estates with their revenues, trapeza accounts, inventories of precious offerings made to the Church, rare books and much else.

To many, these occurrences seemed to be the usual quarrels between different camps within a large and growing institution with no significant consequences for those outside the controversy. I felt otherwise, for I began to see the opportunities Liban had talked of. Nevertheless, I did not think I should put too much trust in Peter's account of what had happened. I would wait to see how this played out. Ramifications were not long in coming.

In the aftermath of confiscating Nitria's wealth, Theophilus declared henceforth any pensions owed by a societas would be held in perpetual trust by his bishopric. Should a pensioner find him or herself destitute, such person might channel a petition through the Prefect's office to the Bishop for assistance. If the petition was deemed meritorious, food and shelter would be provided through a charity house, but only after the person surrendered any remaining wealth in their possession.

In effect, Theon's pension was stolen. I had no doubt Theophilus was taking much pleasure in backstabbing Theon, me and who knows how many others, priding himself in his cleverness all the while. Theon and I would have to live hereafter on what remained of his savings and whatever I could earn in my new capacity as a budding procurator. I now had great incentive to take up my secret new role in the Association.

☽ 9 ☾

Spies were everywhere. They might be anybody. Friends. Neighbors. Merchants. Colleagues. Some, like official couriers of the magistrates, were obvious. Others, not so much, for they were hidden in the folds of everyday life. Of these invisible ones, some enlisted as spies, remunerated or coerced. Most, I believed, had no idea the extent to which they were used and manipulated.

I came to such conclusions after thinking about how Theon's excursions to the underground chamber were so widely known, particularly to the authorities and to the Bishop. Not to mention the Koinotis. The rich and powerful clearly thought his activities extremely important but also perfidious and a danger, if not today then tomorrow, to Empire and Church.

Following this thread, it also seemed even more apparent to me it had been the work of a spy, or multiple spies, who had brought about the destruction of Agrippina. How else account for the capture of one who took such precaution to safeguard her followers and friends? Surely, she had been betrayed by someone on the inside.

Spies might be anybody. I included Peter as a possibility. I even had to ask myself if I had been an unwitting spy. Had I talked too freely? Trusted overly much? Who have I hurt, helped to destroy, without knowing how I may have contributed? I must be more careful in the future.

Peter stayed with us but for a few days, during which time he laid low to evade roving detachments of Black Monks who may have been rounding up Nitrian escapees thought to be apostates. Most of this time he spent with Theon, chatting and helping him about the house. I left the two of them alone, for I was much too busy just to sit around nor did I wish to spend much time with Peter. It was good for my father to have someone he knew other than myself for company, as it gave me time to arrange a letter of credit for a small amount; enough to get Peter away from my house and back to Mauretania if he chose to go that far.

Following Peter's departure, I felt once again I could relax a little, not be always on my guard. I just hoped Theon had not babbled on about anything important and I always listened for any hint from Peter to this effect. Another reason for relief was during Peter's stay I had found various objects, like roughly made charms or fetishes, hidden around the house; objects I believed placed by Peter to influence me to regard him favorably through what to me seemed naive sorcery.

On the other hand, Peter's visit and his mention of having passed through the Mauretania region resurrected thoughts and feelings about Tabat. I remembered Tabat's parting invitation, as well as the thrill of his calloused hands. I had been too long without human touch by man or woman, making me heartsore and prey to fanciful longings only relieved somewhat by self-stimulation.

Not long after Peter's departure, two more unexpected guests came by.

The first was Synesius. Since leaving Alexandria for his home in Cyrene, he had resumed his previously comfortable life and become a leading aristocrat in his community, giving himself mainly over to hunting and literature. However, he got himself into some awkward political situation, so decided it wise to take a brief vacation, during which he visited Antioch and Athens. In the latter city, he sharply criticized the School of Athens, such as it was, for their obdurate opposition to Christians. As he had expressed to me often enough, it hardly mattered what religion one chose as long as one could be true to his philosophical principles.

News of this reached his home and he became a kind of local hero among Christians, who soon pressed him into being a representative of Cyrene at the Court in Constantinople. Synesius always took his civic duties seriously, having made a special trip to the Emperor's city to appeal for financial aid to offset military expenses made in the defense of his region. On his return, he made this stopover in Alexandria, during which time we discussed many things.

Among these were his further thoughts on the distinction to be made between philosophy and religion, the latter being more symbolic than anything, though not in the popular mind. I had to agree with him the writing was on the wall concerning Christianity versus other religions. Also, I told him I hoped more people like him would be in positions of authority to help bring greater balance and tolerance. Particularly after my studies into Orphism, Egyptian arcana, and so forth, it seemed to me the mystic heart of Christianity hardly differed from any other spiritual way.

Remembrance of my ascension at Heliopolis had confirmed this for me, but I chose not to share this with Synesius. There was something in his manner that seemed off. At one point I openly wondered why a man such as he remained unmarried, to which he became evasive and apologetic. There was something he was not telling me.

The second visitor was the Bishop of Alexandria, but not coming in any official capacity. On the face of it, he came to deliver a book to Theon. As always with this man, his motives undoubtedly had been carefully thought out.

"Ah. It is Hypatia now, isn't it?"

"Yes. As I'm sure you know, after Theon adopted me I changed my name."

"Yes, yes. From Catherine. I remember. Well, you have changed your name one more time than I then."

"Perhaps. But if we count the fact everyone just calls you Bishop, I would think that makes us even."

"You always were the clever one, you were. Too bad our collaboration did not continue when we were together at the monastery, don't you think? The Church always has need of those with quick minds."

"It was never clear to me it was my quick mind the Church was interested in. As a woman, it seemed to me men who were less than quick generally were more favored, perhaps due more to their conformity than to their ability. Not to mention how some of the collaborations you formed did not seem always to work out very well for your collaborators. It makes me wonder, too, if your arrogation of Theon's well-earned pension was somehow tied to a thwarting of some design of yours."

"Well, certain abilities have been more prized than others, I should say. And as the Apostle told us: everyone to their proper place. But enough of this banter, for I have brought a gift for your adoptive father, for Theon. It is a book he will find of special interest, I'm sure. I hope you see my being here and bringing a small token of friendship shows in no way has there ever been hostility between your father and me. Nor between you and I. Is he available for receiving a visitor?"

"I must tell you he's napping at present. Certainly, you may leave your special book with me and I'll ensure he receives it. We have some familiarity with your taste in reading materials, so you may count upon my father giving special attention to your kind gift."

"I see. But let me tell you something about this book and its author for you to pass on to your adoptive father, of course. In fact, you both have some knowledge of the author. His name is Aurelius Augustinus Hipponensis. You doubtless know him by the name Aurel, the name his former concubine found so endearing. What was her name again? Oh, I think it was something like Floria? No? Then, Emelia? Just so."

"Theophilus. What are you up to? Or should I ask Jason?"

"Back to my old name, are we?"

"Tell me, do you go by other names that I should know?"

"No, no, you shouldn't think like that. Look, I just knew you two would be interested in this book, so I had a copy made especially for you. For Theon, but you are free to read it, as well, for I remember you are an avid reader. It is titled "Confessions" and gives the true account of this man's struggles with his faith and how he finally is led to embrace the One True God and His Son, Jesus Christ."

"I have heard many such stories. What makes this man's so different?"

"Oh, I think you will find the personal details to be quite touching. Well, I'll be on my way now. I do hope your adoptive father continues to improve after his unfortunate accident in the sewers. I mean, the cisterns. I realize it has been several years, but sometimes these things just go according to their own pace. Oh, one last thing, that young Synesius dropped by my simple parsonage on his way to Constantinople. We had a delightful conversation. Very challenging, I must say. You should come by yourself, as I daresay your thoughts likely are very similar to, if not derivative of his. We might have a very enjoyable conversation, don't you think?"

Theophilus held out the book for me. I looked at it skeptically but not seeing any stipple or off-color to the cover, I accepted it. Nevertheless, after he departed I made my way to the public baths.

☽ 10 ☾

A time came when Liban told me he felt he was no longer able to carry on business in Alexandria. I suspected he may have been reassigned, so to speak, by the Association, but said nothing. His plan was to retire back to Syria, where perhaps some family yet survived. Fortunately, we had long ago put our heads together in preparation for such a day. When he was satisfied the transition would go smoothly, all clients informed and willing to continue doing business with me, by then a journeywoman procurator and broker, he took his leave and set sail for Tyre.

His parting advice to me was a reminder about the Church being more and more involved in a vast array of financial affairs, including banking, trade, investment, trusts, as well as subsidizing sovereigns, aristocrats, and the like. He also advised whatever feelings I might harbor about the Church's practices in general or any particular member of their clergy, I would do well to keep those to myself and never openly take sides. There was enough disunion and rivalry, he advised, between different parts of this growing religious empire for clever persons to maneuver to advantage.

Liban also commended me for having gained the trust and the business of both Green and Blue factions with the Circus. Given their growing political importance, working with their directorates put me in a special position to gain advance information about the highest levels of government and men of rank.

I listened attentively to Liban's advice, particularly about always trying to take the long view and to be patient as events unfolded. Liban had been kind, helpful and trustworthy, in every way deserving of my respect. As he spoke about Church and Empire, my mind turned to thoughts of what the future might hold and what exactly I was meant to do in my new role with the Koinotis.

Emelia never did come back to Alexandria and, for reasons I did not understand, we had lost touch with each other. I would have asked Peter to look in on her should he go through Carthage, but I did not feel right about putting my friend in his path. Maybe she had decided to go to Athens, if not to see her son, who may have been transferred elsewhere by now anyway, then to spend time with Delios, for it did seem to me her feelings for Orestes' father finally had gone cold over the years.

After reading that man's so-called "confessions," I wondered why Emelia had stayed loyal to him for as long as she had. For anyone who knew this Augustine, even second-hand as I did, it was clear he was both fabulist and promoter. Most outrageous to me was his claim his son had died.

I complained to Theon about such fabrications but despite his having taken a cursory look at the book, he did not spend any time really studying it nor did he feel inclined to discuss it. On top of this, he did not seem particularly upset that his niece, Emelia, was persona evanuit. Disappeared. This was not so remarkable perhaps, because with each passing year he slipped more and more into his own world. He was happy enough in the beginning, but took diminishing interest in things beyond the four walls of our apartment or the terrace garden.

His doctor said Theon undoubtedly had injured his brain when he had fallen down the cistern steps. This had become the story everyone now believed. It was no different than those told of pugilists who take strong blows to the skull. This, combined with advancing age, was moving him to a simpler kind of life and was told I ought to regard it as something my father earned after so many years of hard work.

He also warned I likely would have to devote more time to caring for my father in the years ahead, because often such cases lost part or all of their ability to do things for themselves.

And so it was.

Theon's once brilliant mind which stretched so easily over so many diverse subjects became increasingly lackluster and inelastic. I remembered with sadness the days and nights his energy and ideas drove others to look at the world anew from fresh perspectives. There were his many friends in every quarter of the Empire and well beyond it. There were his many mathematical, astronomical and scientific papers and accomplishments, many of which I assisted him with as part of my own tutelage.

He always saw his experiments and works as next to nothing compared with those of his predecessors in both the near and ancient past. As he told me, his greatest achievement was in the preservation of these antecedent works making up the canon of philosophy, literature, physics, oration and more by spreading them throughout the civilized world.

His vision for the Library was as a kind of distributed system of knowledge open to any and all who thirsted for knowledge and he felt his premonitions about the dangers of over-centralization were being born out. Of course, such statements belonged to earlier, more lucid times for him.

Along with his mental decline was his creeping physical decrepitude. He complained he was always cold, even in the middle of the summer, so kept himself wrapped in robes and blankets. Though his broken leg had healed in its fashion, the rheumatism in his hips and knees became so severe he often was unable to rise from his bed in the morning; resorting to pharmakha for relief from pain. After a time, he remained in bed, never getting up, not even for the most basic of physical needs.

Theon's sensitivity to cold came about the same time I began experiencing night sweats and hot flushes. On top of these, I found myself getting irritable over things which previously I had hardly noticed.

So, the doctor was right. The burden of Theon's care did become more onerous, but not solely due to his condition. I did recall my mother long ago prescribing Lion's Tail, Lycian Sage, Chamomile and other herbs for women's changes, so sought out a female chemist. I also took to sleeping on our rooftop many nights to escape the retained heat of the day inside.

Eventually, I had to hire caretakers to minister to Theon's cleanliness and nutrition. As he had become much beloved by many of the faction members who were no longer so young and who needed work, I found several willing persons to tend to him for modest remuneration, often being content with meals and a place to sleep in our overcrowded city.

This course helped restore a modicum of my sanity.

One day, while taking a break from meetings with clients and prospects, having sent my assistants out to bring in late *usurae* and rents, it occurred to me again Theon may have cached some part of his savings in the cistern during his work in Alexandria's basement. I promised myself this time I would look into my hunch as soon as this month's accounts were settled.

☽ 11 ☾

The pandemonium surging from out of the hippodrome was its usual discordant medley of hurrahs, horns, drums and crowd delirium on the afternoon of my descent. I had chosen a race day, counting on the streets being empty, with no one to see me. What with carrying an armload of torches, a covered clay ember pot, a sack with food and water I also could use to carry out anything I might find, I am sure I would have raised suspicions.

The lock on the door to the cistern stairwell was the same as I remembered, but looked to have been broken. In any case, it would have been easily opened for I used much more sophisticated devices in my business.

Stepping onto the topmost landing, closing the door behind me, I was grateful for the cool, moist air coming up from the water. Small noises reached my ears, which I attributed to rats scurrying away after hearing my entry. Having been down on several occasions to check on Theon, I was no longer so unnerved by the place as I had been on my first descent.

I put down my bundle to open the ember pot so as to ignite one of the torches. Once lighted, I picked everything up again except for the pot and carefully made my way down the stairs.

It had been a very long time since I had ventured into this place. My bladder was signaling with some urgency now I was there and I hoped Theon's latrine bucket remained. My fingers and toes tingled in anticipation of what I might discover of Theon's. Admittedly, I thought it unlikely he would have cached anything here, but it was worth a look. Besides, it now occurred to me he may have built something or left something pertaining to his acoustical studies. I do not know what I would do with it if he did, but my pulse quickened as did my desire to investigate.

To my surprise, at the farthest place from the stairway on the bottom landing, the flickering torch light showed the outlines of a modest, plain structure. I was sure this had not been there on my last visit, so it either was something of Theon's doing or had been thrown up by one or more street people. I rejected the latter idea as I got closer for it seemed too well constructed.

Before reaching the small building, light from the torch showed a number of floating objects on the water to my right. I held the flame closer to one and saw it was a candle resting upon something like a very small boat. About a dozen of these bobbed up against the edge of the landing. I wondered if Theon had used these to provide greater illumination to see by or if he had been trying to create a certain atmosphere for his sound experiments.

When next to the building, I judged it as approximately ten cubits to a side. It looked to be a perfect cube, reinforcing my thought that Theon was responsible for it coming into being. The material of the outer wall was brick and I assumed there must be a wood frame of some kind, especially for the roof.

Other than the fact it sat where it was, in a dark reservoir beneath the city, there was nothing extraordinary about it.

I found a handle on the water side of the building, which I gently tugged with no result; so I braced my stance and pulled harder, though with just one hand while still holding a torch with the other. This had the effect of opening a door, but not enough for me to get a clear view of the inside. By wedging a leg inside and pushing my back against the wall and shoulder against the door, I was able to swing the door to where it opened at a right angle to the building. Turning and standing in the open doorway, I extended the torch inside.

What I saw was an unexpected marvel, making me suck in a quick breath.

My first sensation was as if I'd shrunk and been transported to the inside of a bee hive. The walls looked like a honeycomb, with projections covering all four walls and the ceiling. I did not know how Theon had gotten the ones overhead to stay in place, but I immediately understood the concept of the place.

Mentally comparing the outer dimensions of the structure with the inner dimensions, it was obvious he had utilized a lot of insulation; at least a cubit's worth of padding in some places to neutralize echoing. Touching one of the side wall projections, I guessed it might have been terracotta or plaster. The spaces between them were deep, probably to dampen or collect stray sounds.

On the rear wall of the structure however a polished metallic bowl of a parabolic nature had been mounted, facing the doorway. It threw back a distorted, deformed image of myself in the doorway. The reflected light from the torch was particularly concentrated and much too bright to look at.

The floor was flat but carpeted, also helping to soften the sounds. I assumed the room would be vastly superior to the echo chamber outside of this special room. In one corner I saw, too, there were some old scrolls and a few papers scattered about. The loose papers appeared to be covered with mathematical formulae, geometric figures, astrological symbols, and Theon's eccentric doodles. He also had left a hardbound codex of some sort.

Forgetting about the possibility of money being stashed in this place, I gathered as many of the documents to take back with me as I could in one arm, including the codex, as I still held the torch in my other arm. Standing up, I turned and went out the door, which I tried to close with the heel of my foot. Just then I heard a shuffling sound behind me but before I could turn to look, something struck me on the back of the head. Hard.

☽ 12 ☾

"Wake up now. Wake up!"

My cheeks were stinging from someone—a man, judging from the voice—slapping my face, telling me to wake up. Opening my eyes, all I could see was a dreadful silhouette kneeling over me. My back was freezing and all my skin had turned to gooseflesh. I realized I was lying on the cold, hard floor of the cistern made all the colder due to my bladder having let go sometime earlier. Troubling as this was, it suddenly struck me my clothes had disappeared. Another slap to my face made me flinch, more from humiliation than the blow. I wanted to cover my body but my head was throbbing so painfully I reached up to hold it with both hands instead.

The man's voice reverberated harshly through the crypt-like space.

"Ah, that's better. I need for you to be awake for what comes next. For your lesson."

"What? Who…? Peter, is that you? What are you doing?"

Flickering lights off to one side of me caught my attention. Turning my head with difficulty, I saw a small armada of candles afloat on the cistern waters. Each candle burned inside a cylinder of reddish glass set upon its own little raft. This gave a hellish aspect to the water, as though it was smoldering bitumen and the weak flames the souls of the damned cast adrift for eternity.

"I knew it was just a matter of time before you came down here again. So, I wanted to give you a worthy welcome, a torchlight procession, if you will. Do you like it?"

"Peter? What's going on?"

"Peter Panifex? That pipsqueak? How could you think he would be capable of anything close to this? Or what I have in store for you."

"Theophilus! Is that you? Gods, what are you doing? Where are my clothes?

"Your lesson, Hypatia-Catherine. You remember, don't you? The lesson you skipped out on back when you were my catechumen. We were about to consummate our sacramental bond when you got cold feet. Remember? I was so very disappointed in you."

"What are you talking about? Why did you hit me? I was just leaving. Can't we talk about this lesson outside?"

"But I don't really blame you entirely, you know. I realize it was the influence of that desert woman, or should I say desert women? There were several, weren't there? Always meddling in things they knew nothing about. Well, that all got taken care of in time, didn't it? But, to answer your questions, I need you to be in this place for your lesson and, no, there is nothing left to talk about. The time for talking is over, so that we can complete your training to make you pure in the eyes of God."

"Where are my clothes? Why are you doing this? You are supposed to be a righteous man. An example to others. I demand you let me go!"

"Soon enough, my dear. You will be released soon enough. You know, I had big plans for you. For us. The night you rode away—yes, I saw you go on that camel—I was so angry I cried. I prayed and prayed after that for guidance, until finally God answered me. And do you know what He told me? He said the day would come when we would be reunited. And look, here we are! I knew when you went to live with Theon and I knew when you came to Alexandria. Of course, I also knew everything that Theon was doing down here. You can't deny our God works in mysterious ways."

He said this last jeeringly, while pinching and shaking one of my nipples roughly.

"Keep your filthy hands off me! You're mad. We never had any bond, sacramental or otherwise."

Laughing, he said, "Oh, but we did. We do. And I was about to prove it to you by taking you out to my special church. You know the one I mean because you were there once. But now I've decided this will be my new special church here in the city. Don't you think it's much more convenient? And now you're the first to join, to heed the call, to my Basilica of the Sacred Well of Alexandria. What do you think of the name? Do you like it? Or do you think the Basilica of St. Catherine the Martyr sounds better?"

Theophilus spoke calmly but there was a menacing edge to everything he said. Even in the reddish, crepuscular light given by the votive candles, I could tell his jaundiced eyes were crawling over and probing my body.

He went on talking about his secret Dragon Sanctuary in the desert, telling me how he had discovered the stony remnant of a dragon from an age gone by and how it had clearly been a sign for the work he already had begun. This work he saw as helping to purify people of their sins; sins that clung so tightly to them that baptism by water alone would not be enough to cleanse them. This is why he had been called to prepare them to stand clarified, as it were, before The One Who Made Them.

He said while he worked with the former Bishops of Alexandria, he learned I was staying with Theon at a place my father called his Draconis Domum. Certainly not a coincidence. This is when he began taking an interest in Theon and everything he did. He told me, too, the only way Theon eventually had been able to carry on his underground experiments so long was due to the support of the bishopric. He said he had an interest, of course, in their outcome for their possible implications in designing future basilicas.

Everything I now saw in the cistern, he told me, belonged to the Church, to him. The cubical structure with its unique sound properties, the drawings, the mathematics, even what he called the Satanic astrological conjurations. All these had been bought and paid for by the religion Theon and his sham secret society, the Koinotis, had worked so fruitlessly to overthrow.

I should not have been surprised to hear Theophilus bring up the Koinotis, given his apparent knowledge of not only my every move, but Theon's and everyone associated with him. My thoughts raced to Emelia, Peter, Synesius. Would they come to harm? And what about Liban? How much did Theophilus really know of him? What had this deranged man done to these and other people over the years? What might he be doing even now?

As if reading my thoughts, he laughed bitterly and said,

"Don't act so surprised I know so much about your goings on. People are not who you have assumed them to be. Take that smart young aristocrat friend of yours, Synesius, whom I'm sure you had sluttish designs upon. Did he happen to mention to you he got married here in Alexandria after he returned from Constantinople? I doubt he did but you should know it was to a lovely Christian woman. You may wonder how I know this, so let me tell you. I was the priest who officiated at his wedding ceremony. We'd discussed his conversion and the need for him to marry in Constantinople when we both were there on business. He belongs to us now and likely will be made a bishop himself one day in that backwater of his called Cyrene.

"Well, that's enough catching you up with gossip and small talk. Let's get on with your final lesson."

During all of this talk from Theophilus, as paralyzed with fear as I was, I managed to slowly get myself into a sitting position, then to kneeling, so I could better cover my nakedness. I noticed the codex I had carried out of Theon's cubicle lay next to me and on top of it was my medallion, so I picked them up. Hugging the heavy book close to my body for protection I grasped the medallion in my fist such that its hard edge protruded between two fingers.

When Theophilus stopped talking, he came so close to me the reek of his unwashed body made my gorge rise and my head pound even more. I turned my face away but he grabbed me by the hair and forced me to look into his twisted visage. He then produced a small, curve-bladed knife from the folds of his robe. Brandishing this close to my eyes, he explained it was to be the tool of my absolution. I should know then its name was Absolutio, because we were going to get on extremely familiar terms with each other.

With his voice turning more vicious with each word, Theophilus recited,

"'For the soul of the flesh is in the blood and I have assigned it for you upon the altar to provide atonement for your soul, for it is the blood that atones for the soul.' See, if you had stayed to study under me, you stupid mongrel, you would know this from Leviticus 17:11. But, it is too late for that now."

The next prayer he attacked with greater vehemence, "'O Lord my God, I now, at this moment, readily and willingly accept at Your hands whatever kind of death it may please You to send to this sinner beneath me, with all its pains, penalties and sorrows. Amen.'"

So saying, Theophilus drew the blade of the knife expertly across my forehead just below the hairline. He pressed the sharp edge just enough to part the skin without cutting into bone, causing blood to flood into my eyes and down my cheeks. All of my muscles jumped and with a gasp I cried out in anguish. Unfazed, he deftly used the razor edge of the blade to pull the skin and hair away from my scalp with a wet tearing sound to expose bare bone.

Having penetrated me, he gave a great whoop as his instrument opened me further. With this the image I had seen in my library of the two of us at that decisive fork in the road appeared in my mind. I realized somehow we had arrived at this time by prearrangement but that the final outcome was yet undecided.

His victory yell became a kind of acoustic projectile that shot through the open door of my father's sonic chamber. There it was gathered, amplified and transformed by the rear parabolic mirror to be instantaneously fired back as a deeply resonant and forceful tone into this frightful abattoir.

The returning sound—which was as much felt as heard—pulsed through me, quickening both my body and my medallion. A bright blue light surged out from the disk to create a halo around my fist. Sonorous vibrations thrummed back and forth off the cistern walls. The combination of pulsating sounds and palpable light from the medallion dazed Theophilus, momentarily stopping his progress. Then another man's voice rang out.

"Theophilus! Theophilus, stop! What the hell are you doing!"

Distracted further from his knife work and turning to see who shouted at him, I knew my last chance to save myself from the fiend was before me.

Dropping the codex I grabbed his knife arm with one hand and launched my incandescent fist up between the scrawny legs beneath his robe. Theophilus let out a long, rasping groan while falling to his side on the landing. I heard his blade clatter to the stone floor but surprisingly his left hand remained tangled in my hair, twisting my head around and dragging me down with him. Both of us cursed loudly. Half-blinded by the blood in my own eyes, I managed to jab a finger in one of the Bishop's eyes, making him let me free. As I rolled away from him, he screamed and grabbed one of my ankles despite his pain when I tried to rise, making me sprawl forward. As I fell, one hand landed on the dropped codex. I picked it up and scrambled to my feet just as he struggled to his knees, gasping for air and hampered by the length of the monkish robe.

With both hands, I lifted the thick book over my head, crying,

"No! No! No you don't! You stinking son of a bitch!"

With each shout, I brought the book down upon his head and shoulders harder and harder until a hand restrained me and a man's voice said,

"Hypatia! Enough."

☽ 13 ☾

Some months later, Synesius and I warmed ourselves on my rooftop terrace, each relaxing on divans brought up just for such occasions. My scalp had healed after a fashion, though I always would have a hideous scar across my forehead and my hair in front never quite came back as it had been. If Emelia was here, I'm sure she would say that is what scarves and shawls really are for.

The breeze coming off the sea was strong and cool, but the walls around the terrace protected us and also kept the sun's heat from blowing away. Synesius had just returned from Constantinople where he had reported on Theophilus.

"Plato's cave. Surely you remember the story."

"Yes, of course I do, Synesius. And I believe I see the analogy you are drawing here."

"Magistra, you are older than me and wiser in many ways. All I mean to do is to draw your attention to something I think you understand quite well. Please forgive my audacity if it seems I suggest otherwise."

"Not at all. I owe you a great debt of gratitude. If you had not shown up when you did, I would be dead now. Only a blind person would have ventured into that cistern alone the way I did, so clearly I was like the prisoner in the parable you mention; seeing only what I wanted to see, had been entrained all my life to see, despite my years of study in philosophy. Despite spiritual visions given to me. I still was chasing shadows on the wall, illusions."

"I'm sure it's not as bad as all that—"

"Yes, I'm afraid it is. And you're like the freed prisoner, are you not? The one who's seen the light of reality but returns to the cave to free his fellow prisoners. It was only in those final moments when he was distracted that I recognized my utter foolishness. I knew I had but one chance to free myself."

"Understandable. I heard him tell you how he had officiated at my marriage, which temporarily halted me from interrupting; but once he drew his blade and said he had given it the reprehensible name of Absolutio, I suddenly remembered all of your suspicions from years earlier which you'd told me about. Then there was that uncanny sound that halted Theophilus. When I saw him begin to recover his senses, I knew if I didn't do something, not only might you be lost, but so would I…and so would he."

"Synesius, you've always been so very generous. I don't know if I can be as forgiving as you. At least not yet. I must say I have no regrets whatsoever about causing him harm. By the way, you mention hearing the amplified sound from Theon's chamber, so I ask if you also saw the remarkable blue radiance filling the cistern?"

"I did not see what you describe. You have mentioned something similar at other times pertaining, I think, to your medallion. I do not doubt your senses but suspect this light is something meant only for you. Anyway, you were perfectly justified in dealing severely with Theophilus. We now know he had been quite busy over the years in his persecution of others. It seems likely to have had far less to do with helping to formulate the true doctrine of the Church than with darker reasons of his own. We can only imagine. However, I can assure you his influence going forward will not be so great."

"Do you think they will demote him or possibly even excommunicate him?"

"Oh, I very much doubt that. It's the way of most large organizations. As long as he didn't directly hurt the interests of those above him or incite a great deal of public furor, he'll be left alone but without his former influence. Fortunately for him, the truly horrible misdeeds he may or may not have done in his past were committed in secrecy, so there's no certain evidence for an indictment. Who knows? He may ultimately be thought of as one of the truly holy, for there's yet time for him to make amends, I would think."

"I imagine, as well, as a result of the forceful blows I gave to his head, his barristerial mind may never be as deft in argument as before. It's lucky for me Theon had left such a heavy book in his experimental room."

"Yes, not to mention the room itself with its sound collecting mirror! But who would believe the irony of it all, that it was a hardbound folio of 'The Republic' by Plato that demolished your malefactor!"

And so it was. Books always have figured importantly in my life. This one literally saved my life with help, I think, from another special book from my library. It was Augustine Aurelius' book, however, his purported confessions, that ultimately convinced me to complete my own personal account of these times. That and the encouragement of a well-timed stranger to write a memory book so others might have some small insight into who we were that lived in the great city of Alexandria. All this during a disjointed time between two great ages, Aries and Pisces, when it seems the whole world was in upheaval.

While my story goes on past this writing I will end it with one more tale, plus an incident. After that, unlike Augustine, I may never write another word but just continue with my work here in Alexandria or elsewhere, trying to be what help to others I am capable of. I understand now it is not enough for the *Koinotis* to meet in secret and bemoan the direction of events over which we have no control. This sets us apart from the changes going on and makes others suspicious of our motives. We need to work with cooperation and good will with others when possible.

I can be a financial intermediary, like Liban taught me, for money seems to be at the heart of human affairs. My ties with the racing factions in Alexandria and elsewhere have strengthened and, while I am not indispensable to them, they know me to be honest, fair-minded and reliable. Through them I have been able to extend my connections to include horse breeders on both sides of Mare Nostrum. I think my fathers would be proud of me.

I am particular these days about whom I trust, including even other members of the Koinotis. For instance, though Synesius explained why he had come down to the cistern—for which I am eternally thankful—questions remain unanswered in this regard. Better to heed Liban's advice about disclosure of the veiled branch of our Association of Illumination.

The last story to be told here is the story of the death of Theon—by the luck of Sors, my father, my mentor, my lot. It begins with a dream, as all true beginnings do.

While basking beneath the rays of Aten in midday on our open, rooftop terrace, I enjoy a kind of silence never heard in Alexandria or, I dare say, any place where humans live in such dense habitation. It is the kind of silence with only the wind filling the sails of clouds overhead; with the distant beat of the salt sea upon the shore; with the deep singing waters of the Nile impregnating the Two Lands.

In this tranquility, there comes an uneven bumping sound, like ungainly footsteps ascending the stairway from the bottom compartments. The source of these footfalls becomes clear as a young bull camel emerges from the portal on to the terrace. The camel is completely white with aqueous, dark brown eyes. We recognize each other immediately. He is the great-grandson of Mother Nyla's fabulous animal, a knowing soul descended from royalty of its kind. He has arrived without manmade accouterments such as bridle, saddle, blankets or any ornamentation whatsoever, for he is not one to be tamed or used for human purposes.

We speak directly to each other's mind.

"Have you come far?"

"Not nearly so far as you, Magistra."

"What business brings you here to this city, to this street, to this rooftop?"

"I have come to fulfill the promise of my mothers before me."

"And what promise is this?"

"Your gift remains as yet not fully realized. Now would be a good time for you to explore its many uses."

"I see. But first, do you have a name by which I may call you?"

"Yes but it is much too long for you to use when you have real need for me. So you will find that I shall answer to the name 'Journey' whenever you sincerely call."

The white camel now comes nearer and with his soft, whiskery muzzle he warmly nudges the medallion hanging around my neck, indicating that I should remove it and lay it upon the ground. This I do and then take a step back. Like another camel from legend, Journey stamps a fore hoof upon the medallion and that which has been most of the time just a lackluster ornament since I first received it long ago suddenly assumes a spherical shape, about the same size as an ostrich egg, though in color it is a translucent blue hue.

Within the jewel-like sphere, there is much movement and a shifting of things for which I have no description. Though I never properly saw into the stones Mother Nyla and Agrippina used for seeing, my sense now is what I see inside this globe must be similar. Perhaps, I think to myself, one day my living library will allow me to read and interpret what looks like just so much commotion to the unschooled eye.

Journey stamps his foot again but not upon the medallion-globe this time. The impact of this sends a quiver through the bluish orb, causing it to expand such that it first envelopes both myself and my visitor, then continues until it seems the whole apartment building is swallowed into its insides, where it feels everything is connected to everything else in a gossamer web.

I feel my heart expand in concert with the orb, knowing this to be the harmony sought by so many before me through so many means. A fine, golden thread in this web network begins to vibrate gently and with love. I follow its spiral line with my knowing heart, finding it comes from Theon's room below. I look to Journey, who signs I should leave to answer this call.

In retrospect, I am not able to say when dream turned to not-dream, or whether I ever knew the difference in the first place. What I do know is from the terrace I go downstairs and enter Theon's room. He lies still on his bed, but there is someone else in the room standing next to him. The hooded figure's back is to me. For a moment I think it is the Bishop come again, but then I realize this person is much too tall to be him.

We three figures live and breathe within the blue light of the sphere. We are connected, I see now, by normally invisible filaments; some are straight, others twist into elaborate filigrees and designs we have made to entwine each other, the better to hold ourselves in place. Threads spread out from each of us in an infinite number of directions to connect with other people, places, things and times.

Times. Yes, other times; times holding past and future lives, each with more people, places and things connecting.

The tall person by the bed, aware of my presence, turns to look at me.

"Agrippina!"

"Yes, my sister, it is me. Theon has called for me to help him return."

"Return? What do you—? You mean he is dying?"

No sooner do I utter these words than Theon reaches up to grasp Agrippina's hand, yet his body remains perfectly still upon the bed, both arms at his side.

"As you see, your father is ready to pass over. More than ready to leave this body behind to join me."

In an instant, Theon stands beside Agrippina, both somehow much younger in appearance, looking like they must have in their middle twenties or so. They are smiling and their eyes glint with joy at this reunion.

Agrippina reaches out her other hand to me, saying:

"Hypatia, you may come part way with us, as far as the Gate of the Sun at the city's edge, but then you will have to go back. There is much for you to see, much yet to learn. As you have guessed, too, the Koinotis is now in your hands.

"Fear not. You have many friends and helpers, and much yet to do before you come home again. So, take my hand, sister."

I take her hand. And Theon's. We three walk to the eastern Gate of the Sun.

☽ 14 ☾

Once beyond the Gate, Agrippina and Theon disappear. For a brief moment, I feel all the love in my life has gone with them. A cold wind from the sea enwraps my body as tears well up in my eyes. From deep in my heart a mournful wail escapes my throat and I sway side to side. It is not long before this song of lament turns to one of praise and then joy. The wind, now but a breeze teases my hair and dries my cheeks. From far above comes the high-pitched cry of a falcon but the only god to be seen is the one who is in everything.

Where the blue of the sky meets the blue of the sea, I am.

From behind me, a voice at once familiar and foreign.

"Hypatia!"

The End

ACKNOWLEDGEMENTS

> *I have prefaced these volumes with the names of my authorities. I have done so because it is, in my opinion, a pleasant thing and one that shows an honorable modesty, to own up to those who were the means of one's achievements…*
>
> —Pliny, *Natural History,* Preface

This story has its basis in the scholarship of many others whom I feel I must acknowledge by listing some of my sources.

I am most indebted to Maria Dzielska (*Hypatia of Alexandria*), who planted the idea the "literary legend of Hypatia" might be different from the real Hypatia, especially that she likely was born much earlier than supposed, i.e., before the oft-ignored Great Tsunami of 365 A.D. that killed an estimated 5,000 people in Alexandria. In addition, I delved into many books and papers in support of the legend; things one might glean solely on Wikipedia without having to buy a putative scholarly book. Such study ultimately led to my own comprehensive forensic analysis (*The Case of Hypatia of Alexandria*) presented at the 2018 Hawaii International Conference on Arts & Humanities.

To better understand Late Antiquity, I relied, among others, upon Anthony De Cosson (*MAREOTIS, Being A Short Account Of The History And Ancient Monuments Of The North-Western Desert Of Egypt And Of Lake Mareotis*); Patrick F. Houlihan (*The Birds of Ancient Egypt*); Hugh Elton (*The Roman Empire in Late Antiquity: A Political and Military History*); Fik Meijer (*Chariot Racing in the Roman Empire*); John, Bishop of Nikiu (*Chronicles, 84.87-103*]; St. Augustine of Hippo (*Confessions*); Synesius, Bishop of Cyrene

(*Letters*); Clément Flaux, *et al* (*Environmental changes in the Maryut lagoon etc. – Journal of Archeological Science, 2012*); E.M. Forster (*Pharos and Pharillon*); Richard Alston (*Soldier and Society in Roman Egypt: A Social History*); Darin Hayton (*An Introduction to the Astrolabe*).

Finally, as much as I may disparage the "literary legend" found in Wikipedia, I have relied on this source of free information for many other things and believe we should support it.

One special character deserves to be singled out. Theophilus of Alexandria, elected to the bishopric in 385 A.D. and later sanctified by his Church, is regarded by the faithful as a beacon of early Catholicism. Scholars give him mixed reviews, e.g., Norman Russell (*Theophilus of Alexandria*). I have made him into a villain and for this I relied upon David Owen (*Profiling: The Psychology of Catching Killers*) and Val McDermid (*Forensics: What Bugs, Burns, Prints, DNA, and More Tell Us About Crime*). This decision, like everything else in the novel—all its potential errors, misinterpretations and sheer liberties with the facts—are solely the responsibility of the author.

Lukman Clark, Riverside, 2024

Coming Soon!

Other Books By The Author

- The Book of Adam & Other Poems
- Egyptian Elegies
- Hypatia: In Her Own Words
- The Alexandria Scrolls
- Etsuko

Screenplays

- There Goes The Son [Pilot]
- The Virtual Ring [Short]
- By The Sea, There By The Sea, By The Beautiful Sea [Short]

Lukman Clark also has written many short stories and hundreds of poems.

Awards

- Readers Choice – 5 Stars
- Firebird Award - Magical Realism
- Firebird Award - Visionary Fiction
- Literary Titan Silver Book Award
- Outstanding Creator Award - Historical Fiction

About the Author

Award-winning author Lukman Clark lives with his wife and two cats in Riverside, California. He works as a fulltime writer and gardener in his own backyard.

He is a veteran of the U.S. Navy from the Vietnam Era.

Lukman has earned a Bachelor of Arts with majors in Communications and English Lit from UCSB/UCSD followed by a Master of Business Administration in International Marketing from UCLA. From there he went on to executive positions in banking, finance and investment, petroleum equipment manufacture, art museum management. Then there were farmers markets management along with nonprofit strategy & fundraising consulting.

www.ingramcontent.com/pod-product-compliance
Lightning Source LLC
Chambersburg PA
CBHW070822020826
48982CB00014B/271

* 9 7 8 0 9 7 8 8 7 5 2 4 4 *